A Love
That Blooms

By Holly Whitworth

This one is for everyone who has a dream of becoming something. Never give up. Keep dreaming.

Chapter One

Claire

My best friend, the one I love more than anyone, is getting married at the end of this summer. I am so excited for her, but something deep inside me just wishes I could have what she has and feel how she feels for someone. I would like to think that I have been in love before, but it was always mostly just lust. I want that love that you can feel deep inside your bones, the kind of love that makes you smile when you catch just one look from the person you love. I, unfortunately, have never felt that way before.

"Claire… hello? Are you listening to me, or are you in another world"?

I am in another world.

"Earth to Claire…Hello"?

Right, Emma's talking.

"Sorry! I was just thinking. Oh, never mind; it's nothing. What did you say again"?

She does not need to know I have had love on my mind since watching a romance movie last night. I still do not understand why I keep watching them, all they do is makes me cry, and then I go to bed and dream about prince charming knocking on my apartment door to come to save me. I hate to admit it, but I have officially hit rock bottom regarding love.

"Are you going to help with the order for Reid Anderson? Remember him; he occasionally orders a bouquet to take to his grandmother at the retirement home."

Of course, I remember Reid Anderson; he is easy on the eyes. He is what most women would describe as tall, dark, and handsome, with his dark hair, skin, and eyes, and he dresses as if he came from the gym, but I am pretty sure he is a firefighter. He is very muscular, which usually is not my type, but Reid is an exception. I would rub his muscles any day of the week.

"I'll do it, and I'll make sure to give him good service when he gets here" I wink at Emma.

Since Emma's fiancé, Baker, and his brother Ryan Hayes bought us this new fancy flower shop right next door to their Real Estate company, we have been nonstop with new customers. The guys have helped get our names out there, and now the flower shop we wanted as little girls is more than we could have ever dreamed. I did not see something like this happening the night we met them at The Bar a year ago, but now Emma has met the love of her life, and I have made a new friend in Ryan.

Emma leaves the office while I sit in the office chair, staring at the computer screen. I need to find a repair person to fix my sink at the new apartment I just moved into not long ago. Since moving into my new place, which is closer to the new flower shop, I have had nothing but problems with everything. I type plumber into a google search and write down a couple of names and numbers on post-it notes to take to the front counter so I can make calls before I head out of the shop today. Once finished, I take my post-it, walk out of the office, and stick the note to the front counter computer.

"Let me guess, something else is wrong at the apartment, or those are your new potential dates," Emma asks as she glances over at the note.

"Unless I want a date with a plumber…There's a leak in my faucet, and the constant drip noise is driving me nuts." I say as I walk over to my workstation so I can start working on the bouquet for Reid Anderson.

"Are not plumbers normally older bald guys who cannot keep their pants up, and their cracks are always hanging out? Isn't there someone else you could ask to fix it"?

"Gross…. I should ask someone else."

"Did you ask Ryan, isn't he the one who has been helping you with everything nowadays"?

I take hydrangeas and peonies out of the bucket to place them on my workspace, "Well, he's busy with Lena tonight; I don't want to bother him."

Ryan has been at my beck and call since he helped me track down my ex-James, who robbed the old flower shop and tried to kill Emma. Thankfully, Ryan was willing to help me then, and we got him taken away for a long time. So, now Ryan is always down when I ask him to help me out with something. He never complains, and sometimes he offers anyways since he knows I am all on my own.

"Lena… She is a bikini model from California. I feel like I cannot keep up with all the women Ryan has been with these days."

"She is the second bikini model in six months. Stacey was the first one. There were others, but he was not with them long enough for me to remember their names."

I lay out brown paper and start stacking the flowers in the order I want them. Reid has been coming in for a couple of months now, and I know his charge; he always wants something small with light pink and purple flowers. After putting the bouquet together, I roll it up in the brown paper and wrap twine tightly around the outside to make sure it stays together. Once done, I take it to the stainless-steel cooler at the back wall of the shop and set it inside until he comes to pick up his order.

"So, what are you and Baker's plans for this weekend?" I ask Emma as she is working on the computer at the front counter.

"He wants to stay out at his parents this weekend, so after I leave here tonight, we will be heading that way. I will be back Sunday night, but you know you can call me if you need anything."

"Thanks, but I do not think I will need anything. My life is not thrilling. I will just watch Netflix and order takeout." I say with a frown because my life has not been exciting in months.

I tried dating apps, and after six dates with six different guys, I knew it was not for me. I thought it would work out, but I never heard back from any guys after the first dates. Then I went through the phase where I thought I was the problem. Emma straightened that out quickly, telling me there was nothing wrong with me and that the guys were crazy for not going on a second date with me. What would I do without my best friend, Emma? So, since I gave up the dating apps, I have been staying in on the weekends, and sometimes I will go out to the Hamptons with Emma and Baker to stay with his parents on the beach, but I always feel bad for being the third wheel. I prefer to stay in these days and hope that one day, mister right will show up at my front door.

I hear the front door open, and when I look up, I see Reid Anderson. He is wearing black gym shorts, a dark green dry-fit shirt, and a black baseball cap backward. My lady bits start tingling. This man is a smoke show.

"Hey ladies, how are you doing this evening"?

"Great! Claire finished your order not long ago. She can go grab it for you" she nudges my arm, and for a reason, I do not move.

He looks over at me, and we lock eyes for a minute. What was I supposed to be doing?

Emma nudges my arm again, oh yes, the bouquet, "let me go get that."

I walk to the cooler at the back wall, which is a little walk, but I take my time anyways because I know my face is red; I am so embarrassed. I open the cooler, take out the bouquet, and then take the same time to get back to the front counter as I did, walking to the cooler. I set down the bouquet on the counter when I reach the front. "Here you go."

"So, Claire, Emma here said that you have a faucet leak in your apartment. I can fix that for you if you would like me to," he leans over on the counter.

"You do not have to do that. I have a list of plumbers to call later that I can have come to fix it for me."

"It's no problem; I would like to help you out since you are always generous enough to make me the best bouquets."

If my face was red before, it is now the color of a lobster.

"Well, thank you."

"Give me your number, and I can come by tonight after you get off. I will not be long at the retirement home" he gives me a big grin.

I give him my number, tell him where my apartment building is, and let him know I should be there around six o'clock. He picks up the bouquet and walks towards the shop's front door. When he pushes open the door, he turns back to me, "I'll see you later, Claire."

"See you then, Reid."

Once he is officially out of sight, I turn to Emma, slapping her on the arm. "Why did you do that"?

"Owe... You should be thanking me for that. If I did not tell Reid about it, you would have had to call Carl, an old man with plumber's crack," Emma says as she grabs her arm in the spot; I smacked her. "Also, this is your chance to get a date with him. I do not think he is seeing anyone."

"Look, he can come to fix my sink, and that is it. You know my record lately has not been good with men, and I do not want to make things awkward when he comes here to pick up flowers" I wave my hand in the air.

"Whatever you say... Now listen, I need to pack for the weekend so I can head out, but you will let me know what happens at your place tonight, right"? Emma starts taking off to the back of the shop, and I do not answer her. "Claire... right"?

"Fine, I will give you all the details. Like what wrench is used to fix the sink and how long it takes Reid to fix it, there will be no other details to fill you in on. Now bye, Emma, have a great weekend," I wave to her as she walks into the back office.

This is simply great. My place is a mess, and I have exactly two hours until a hot firefighter with his hat on backward shows up to fix my leaky faucet. This is not how I wanted my weekend to start. I lean over the counter, placing my elbow on the counter. I rest my chin in the palm of my hand, taping my nails on the counter with my other hand. I watch everyone else around the room work at their workstations on the rest of the orders for the day. I enjoy this new place because we have six employees besides Emma and me. I need to get out of here as soon as possible, to make not only myself look presentable but my apartment, the apartment no one comes to visit, and the same place that I wanted to just lounge in my sweatpants all weekend. I watch everyone for another minute or two before I decide.

"I'm out of here; I'll see you all, you lovely people, on Monday morning" as I take off out the front door.

I set off down the sidewalk to my building right around the corner. I keep replaying the conversation with Reid in my head the whole time I walk. I should thank Emma for getting someone else to fix my problem, but she did not have to get him.

Once around the corner, I make my way through the double front doors of the building. This place is much better than the last apartment building I used to live. I push the button to open the elevator, and once inside, I press the button to close the doors. I never want to take the elevator with a stranger. The elevator stops at my floor; I walk out and walk down the hallway to my apartment, number 222. I have a thing with numbers being the same, so I knew this place was for me right when I saw what number it was. Weird, I know.

I unlock my door, and the place looks worse than I thought when I walked inside. I have unfolded laundry piled up on my table, plates, and cups all over the kitchen island, blankets on the couch, and dirty clothes on the floor. What can I say? I know I am a messy person. I try, but whenever you live alone and never expect company, you do not care how your place looks. I could leave it like this and tell Reid what kind of person I am, but that would be so disappointing to Emma, so I should pick up this mess and show him who I am not.

A Love That Blooms

       I start picking up everything that is a mess, beginning with the ridiculous mound of laundry I have on the kitchen table. I throw it all in a basket and then open the hall closet door and set the basket in there. It is not like he is going to open the closet. I put away all the dishes in the dishwasher, then folded the blankets on the couch. Once I finish that, I pick up the dirty clothes on the way to my bedroom and throw them on my closet floor. My bedroom does not matter; I will not be bringing him in here tonight. I walk into my bathroom and look at myself in the mirror. My long red hair is down, so after I brush it, I leave it that way. I touch up what little makeup I am wearing and then strip out of my work clothes, throwing them on the floor. I walk into my closet, grab another Bloom shirt, and then slip into black leggings. I did not want to look desperate, so I toned down my look.

       Since I left early, it did not take me too long to pick up. I decide to relax on the couch while I wait for Reid to show up. I clicked on the TV and left it on the channel it was already on. I lay down, resting my head on my favorite pink pillow.

       My style for my apartment is random; I love color, so whenever I find something to my taste, I buy it and place it wherever I think it should go. I have a dark green velvet couch with deep pink pillows. My coffee table is metal with a rectangular wood top. My kitchen table matched my coffee table with modern wood chairs. My walls have pictures of the beach and places I have traveled. I have plants throughout my apartment, and they keep me busy with their watering schedule. I only got them because they gave me something to do at home.

       My phone pings, and when I open it, Reid says he will be on his way soon. It feels so odd getting a text from him. He has just been a customer that I have admired from time to time. I usually let Emma do all the talking when he comes in; I do not want to embarrass myself, exactly like I did today. I relax, looking up at the ceiling and telling myself to stay calm and not let him make me nervous. I have been unsuccessful when it comes to men lately, and even though this is not a date or anything, I do not want to ruin my chance at getting to know him.

I get up from the couch when I hear a knock on my door. You got this, do not blow this, Claire.

I open the door, and there he is, mister smoke show wearing what he had on earlier today but carrying a tool bag. "Hey Reid, come in."

"Claire…thank you," he says as he nods while walking in.

"Again, thank you for coming by. You did not have to do this" I close the door, then follow behind him to the kitchen.

"It's not a problem; I don't mind coming by to help you" he turns to smile at me.

He starts looking at the sink to figure out what could be wrong with it, so I sit at the kitchen island and watch because I cannot think of anything better than watching a smoking hot guy fix something.

"So, Claire, did you have any plans tonight," he asks while looking under the kitchen sink.

"Sadly, I have none. I would hang out here all night, watching a movie."

He does not say anything but continues inspecting my faucet's problem. He gets up under the sink and takes a tool from his bag. It looks like he is tightening the head of the faucet and then running the water for a second before turning it off. The drippy faucet instantly stopped dripping; it's fixed. Now I feel like a complete idiot; I could have set that myself.

"Looks like it's fixed; it just needed to be tightened," he says as he turns to me and leans up against the counter with his arms crossed.

"Wow, I am so sorry you had to come over for that. I feel terrible."

"Claire…" I love the way he says my name. "As I said, it's no problem" he turns to start putting his tools back in his bag and then zips the bag up.

"Well, thank you so much. I guess you can get back to whatever you had tonight" I get up from my chair so I can walk Reid to the door.

"You need someone to help you watch a movie? I do not have any plans for the night."

I give him a big smile, remembering I told Emma nothing would be happening tonight. "I would like that."

So, Reid stayed at my apartment for a couple of hours, and it turned into a beautiful time. We watched a movie, more like talked than observed, and ordered pizza. I did a decent job telling him about myself and trying to get to know him, and the best part of the evening was when he left, he asked me if he could take me out the following evening.

And just like that, I got what I considered a second date. Finally.

"You got this, Claire," I say to myself as I look in the mirror. I just finished putting on a dress I had from the back of my closet. It is a long, short sleeve V-neck blue floral wrap dress, and I slipped on a pair of flat sandals. I left my hair down, curling it into wavy curls, and just put on a touch of makeup with lip gloss. I have no idea what he has planned for us tonight, but he texts me today to tell me he will be here around seven to pick me up.

I did not tell anyone about what I was doing tonight. Everyone took off for the Hamptons for the weekend but me, so I will not be running into anyone tonight. I told Emma that Reid had just fixed my sink and nothing else. I did not want to get her hopes up if tonight turned into a disaster, so I promised to tell her about tonight if things ended well.

I hear a knock at the door; Reid is here. I leave my bedroom and walk down the hall to the front door. I open the door, "Hey."

"Claire… You look great," Reid says, wearing a pair of black shorts, a blue polo shirt, slide-on shoes, and his hair fixed.

I blush, "Thank you, you do not look so bad yourself. Come in while I grab my purse."

He walks in behind me, closing the door.

I walk to the kitchen table to grab my small purse with a long strap and place it over my shoulder. "So, what are we doing tonight"?

He is standing by the door with his hands in his pockets. "I was thinking we could get something to eat and then maybe take a walk through the park."

I smile at him, "That sounds perfect. I am ready to go."

We walk out the door together and then exit the elevator. I will make this one exception when riding in the elevator with a stranger.

Once outside, he says, "I thought we could walk tonight. The weather is perfect, and everywhere we go is not too far from here. Is that all right with you"?

"Yes, I walk almost everywhere, so that will be fine."

Before we take off down the sidewalk, he unexpectedly grabs my hand and holds it while we walk. Things are off to a good start tonight.

"So, what does Claire like to do for some fun"? He asks me.

"Well, if I am not at the flower shop, or my apartment watching movies, I normally go to the Hamptons with Emma. Her fiancé Baker Hayes's parents live there, and most weekends, we go to the beach or swim in their pool; recently, we started beach volleyball tournaments with everyone getting in on the fun. I normally get stuck with Ryan on a team, and we have won every tournament. I can be a competitive person when it comes to winning something."

"That sounds like fun. Who is Ryan"?

"Ryan is Baker's brother. We have become friends since his brother is marrying Emma. And they own the flower shop. I am surprised you do not know of them, considering they are all over New York with their realty company," I answer as we continue down the sidewalk, he is still holding my hand.

"Yea. I do not think I have ever heard of them. I keep to myself when I am not at the fire station. I am not from here. I moved here about a year ago when they put my grandmother in the retirement home. I was at a point in my life where change would be good for me, so I moved here from Hilton Head, South Carolina."

"I am not from here either. Emma and I came here from Florida five years ago to dream of opening a flower shop in a big city. We grew up together and acted like sisters since Emma was an only child. I do love it here, though, and it is nice to go to Hamptons occasionally because, during the summer, it reminds me of being home."

"I have not been to the beach since I left. I imagine it would be fun to have a place like that to go to whenever you want to remember where you are from."

We come up to the park, and I stop walking. "You know, I am not sure what you had planned for dinner, but I know there is a food stand in the park that sells the most amazing hot dogs. I am not sure if you had one, but I can promise you that it will be the best thing you will eat here in New York City."

He gives me a concerned look like he is thinking about it. "I think I have heard about these, but you know I have yet to try one. I did not have a plan on where to eat, so I will follow your lead" he holds his hand for me to walk into the park. Still holding hands, I lead us to the food stand.

This night has gone smooth so far; our conversation is effortless, and his holding my hand has been lovely. I cannot remember the last time I had a night like tonight. All the dates I went on while on the dating app were at a restaurant. They always left after dinner.

We reach the stand, and both stop when we get to the line. This stand can get busy during the summer months in the park. They only serve a hot dog, and you tell them what toppings you want. I always get mustard, but I am interested in what topping Reid will pick for his. I think you could judge a person for what toppings they put on their hot dog.

"So, Reid, what has been your favorite thing about New York City so far"? I ask while we wait.

"I would say this right here" I smile at him, and he squeezes my hand, then continues, "I have not done anything fun and exciting since I moved here. I spend time together with the guys sometimes at the station, even when I am off. They are the only friends I have made here. I have not seen the big deal about the city just yet, and that is because I have not explored it."

"Well, I will make sure we do explore sometime. I have not done fun things here, but I do know where all the decent food is," I say as we take another step forward in the line. "But all the parks are the best, and the people. I have met incredible people while working at the flower shop. What did you do back home before coming here"?

"I was a firefighter there too, but I was just starting as one. I have learned more here than I would've there, so that is one good thing about this place."

It is now our turn to order; Reid points to me to call first, "hot dog, just mustard, please."

"I'll have the same," he tells the man before taking out his wallet to pay.

Same toppings as me, nice.

He hands the man the money and tells him to keep the change—another win.

The sweet older man makes up our hot dogs and then hands them to us. "Thank you," we both say at the same time.

When we walk away, Reid points to an empty bench. "Want to sit here"?

"Sure," I say, then take a big bite out of my hot dog, and he does the same.

He smiles big once it goes down, "Wow, Claire, I am impressed. This is unbelievably good."

"See, I told you..." I tap his arm with my hand. "I'll have to show you all the best food places around the city."

"I look forward to that."

We eat and then stroll around the park before leaving to return to my apartment building. We have been gone a couple of hours, but it feels longer. While on our way back, he holds my hand again, and this is a feeling I like.

"I wish I could stay out longer tonight, but I need to be at the station early in the morning. Tomorrow, I work a twenty-four-hour shift, so it may be a couple more days before I can see you again" Reid nudges my arm with his elbow.

"That's okay, and I will be able to see you sometime after work this week."

When we reach my apartment building, he will walk me up to my door but instead, he stops right out front. He turns to look at me. "Thanks for coming out with me tonight, Claire. It was good getting to know you."

"Thank you for inviting me" I grin

"I'll talk to you later, okay," he says, and I nod.

Just when he is going to kiss me, he starts walking away. "Bye, Claire"

I wave as he is walking. "Bye, Reid"

So, it did not end with a kiss, and I am okay with that. Tonight was just what I needed. I feel like I am finally back in the game of dating. Hopefully, this goes well with Reid, but it feels good to feel wanted again. I feel like I am one step closer to being able to have a date for Emma's wedding, and I would like to think it would be Reid.

A Love That Blooms

Chapter Two

Claire

Over the weekend, I did not tell anyone about my date with Reid, and now that it's Monday, I have plans to let Emma know about it. I have not kept any secrets from her since the time I did not tell her about who broke into the Flower shop. I will never hurt her like that again.

I did not hear from Reid yesterday while working at the fire station. He only texts me a couple of times about maybe getting together again later this week. I stayed inside my apartment all day cleaning so I would not have to worry about it again if he came over this Friday night. I must ensure I do a better job keeping it clean throughout the week.

I walk into Blooms, our flower shop, and lock the front door behind me. I am always the first person here every day. I like to be the one to open the shop for the day and make sure it is clean from the night before. Emma is always the one to come in after me, and I figured that would be the perfect time to tell her about my date with Reid before everyone else shows up. I check stations, then turn on the front computer when I hear the front door open. I look to see Emma, Baker, and Ryan following behind her.

"Good morning, Claire," Emma says.

Ryan is carrying two coffees in his hand, placing one down in front of me. "I brought you a coffee."

"Well, thank you, Ryan, that is so very kind of you" I leave the coffee on the front counter while ensuring the computer is set up for the day.

"Why didn't you ask me to come to fix your sink for you? Emma said you had a problem, but someone else was supposed to come to fix it for you. You always call me," he says with a concerned look, staring at me until I look at him.

"I knew you had plans with Lena, and I did not want to bother you. Emma got someone to come to fix it. It was not that big of a deal and needed tightening. He fixed it in like 5 minutes" I finally look at Ryan, and he seems upset with me.

"Claire, call me next time. I was not busy, and you know I will always be available for anything you need. Who was the guy anyway"?

I look around the shop, and Baker and Emma are in the office because I have not seen them since they came through the door. I do not want to tell Ryan about the date, but I guess I can at least tell him who fixed it.

"Reid Anderson," I say and then check the shop, ensuring it is suitable for opening.

"Reid Anderson? Who is that guy, and how did you meet him"? he asks while following me around.

"Ryan... What does it matter? He is just a customer that Emma asked if he could fix for me so I would not have to call someone. Why are we still talking about this"? I stop and turn around to him.

"Because Emma mentioned it was a good-looking guy…" he frowns

"And?" I throw my hands up. I am starting to get annoyed with him questioning me.

"Did he ask you out"?

He cannot be serious right now.

"I am not talking about this... Don't you need to be at work"?

I walk towards the back office to check on Emma and Baker, and hopefully, it will shut Ryan up with his fifty questions. I do not need to tell him anything about what is going on with Reid, and he does not need to know. The office door is open, and they kiss each other goodbye when I enter the door frame.

"Do you not get enough of that at home… Baker, your brother is trying to get into my business this morning. I would like it if you would take him back with you."

"He's been worried about you all weekend since he seems to be upset you didn't call him," Baker says, walking out of the office.

I take a seat in one of the chairs, shaking my head. "It was not a big deal. It was an easy fix."

"How did that go, Claire? You never text me about it. Did he ask you out on a date"?

I blush, and every single one is staring at me to answer.

I cannot hold in my smile, "Maybe."

I look over at Ryan, and he does not look happy. I just do not get it.

"Claire… really," Emma says, taking a seat at the desk.

"We went out Saturday night and had a fun time. He wants to get together sometime this week."

I might as well spill the details since Ryan seems so interested, and I was going to tell Emma anyway.

"We are going to head over to the office. We will see you two later," Baker says

Emma nods, and after the guys walk away, I wait for the front door to shut before asking Emma what Ryan's deal is.

"He just had a bad weekend. Lena was giving him a tough time about who knows what this weekend. They hardly spoke, and when he heard me talking to Baker about you, he even got madder that you did not call him. I did not ask questions, so I do not know what his real deal is"

I sit there for a minute, watching her go through the orders on the computer.

I do not understand Ryan sometimes. He has been a big part of my life since we met at the bar. Baker always had him helping me by driving me home, watching after me after the accident at the old shop, he helped me find my ex, James. We worked together to get him in jail for all that he did to Emma and me, and then he made sure I had a great time at the gala last summer by being my date, and then he's been there to help me with anything else since then. Ryan will invite me to lunch or dinner when he knows I am alone and insists we be on the same team for the volleyball tournaments at his parent's. He also does not talk to me about his dating life, and I do not speak to him about mine, so I do not understand why he feels like he needs to know who Reid is and if we went out. We are just friends, and he was never like this when I was dating on the dating app.

"I'll go turn the open sign on up front" I get up from my seat and start walking to the front.

I just have this bothering feeling now.

My phone goes off in my pocket, and after I turn on the open sign in the front window, I pull it out.

Ryan-Sorry about this morning. I had no right to ask you about this guy.

Me- Thank you, Ryan; it is okay

Even though this morning was unusual with him, I want him to know it is all right, so there is no weirdness going on with the two of us.

I grab the coffee Ryan got me, and I head to my station so I can get right to work on today's orders and take my mind off things. I take vases from the shelf and line them up on my workstation. I look at the flower orders on the paper I had printed out and then figure out which flowers I need. Once I gather all the ones I need from the flower buckets, I finish putting them together, doing three orders at once. I like my mind to work overtime, so I tend to do more than one order at the same time. It is just something that works for me. When I finish one, I slide it to the side, spend the next, and then the last. It does not take me long, and Emma is standing at the front counter taking orders on the phone. We like to work just for the first hour of the workday and then have the other employees come in later so they can close it for us. A different schedule than we had a year ago, but I love this way so much better. Emma and I needed a break from running a shop all by ourselves.

After taking all the arrangements to the cooler, so they will be ready for the delivery drivers, I meet up with Emma at the front of the shop; she is still on the phone. I take a sip of my coffee, then place it on the counter. That is when I noticed the order written on the side of the cup, a Large iced vanilla latte, extra ice, and an extra pump of vanilla. Ryan knows how I like my coffee. He has always been great at remembering unimportant things.

"Hey, I know you do not mind, but I must leave before lunch today. Baker and I have wedding stuff we need to do."

"How fun… I love that Baker wants to be involved in the wedding planning."

"You know him. This day has to be perfect," she says, rolling her eyes.

Emma loves Baker so much that she would elope today. She does not need to have a big expensive wedding with hundreds of wedding guests and with all the fancy things. She is straightforward and would be just as happy without all the extras at her wedding.

"I think today will be an easy day if you want to go ahead and get out of here. You already did the shipment order this morning, and it is time for the other employees working today to come in."

"You sure," she says as she is already getting ready to leave.

"Of course, I will be just fine by myself for a second"

She walks to the back office, grabs what she needs, and then goes to the front door. She uses her back to open the door, "Thanks, Claire. Also, don't forget about our monthly dinner with the guys tonight."

Right, the monthly dinner where we talk about business.

It looks like I will get to see Ryan again today.

"Oh yes, I did not forget… Where is it tonight"?

"Our apartment"

"I'll be there," I wave to her as the front door closes.

When we have meetings at their apartment, that means it's essential business. We usually have them at a restaurant, where we talk about how the shop is doing and then things we should change. I want to know what Baker and Ryan have up their sleeve for tonight. In the last meeting we had there, they wanted us to hire more people, and well, now I do not think we have room or budget for more help.

Tonight should be interesting.

Since I let Emma leave early today, I decided to stay until closing since I did not have anything else to do today besides our meeting tonight. I did not want to mess up my spotless apartment by staying home until the meeting. Once I got off, I took a cab to Baker and Emma's apartment.

When the cab pulls up out front, I get out. I do not even reach the building's front doors when Ryan comes behind me.

"I went to your apartment to pick you up like I always do, but you weren't there," Ryan says while he opens the front door for me.

"Sorry, I decided to stay at the shop until the meeting" I walk into the door, and he follows.

I forgot that Ryan and I always ride to our monthly meetings together.

Ryan stays quiet throughout the elevator ride, and we walk down the hallway to their apartment door. When we get there, Ryan knocks, and I stay back until they answer the door.

"Come in," I hear Emma's voice through the door. Ryan opens the door and lets me go in first.

When we walk in, I immediately notice there is no dinner, nothing waiting for us at the dining room table. Baker and Emma are sitting on the couch like they have been waiting for us to arrive.

"Hey, you two have a seat. We want to talk to you about something."

Ryan and I look at each other while sitting across the couch.

"This is not a normal business meeting tonight," Baker says, looking at us and then at Emma.

"What kind of meeting is this then"? Ask Ryan.

"Today Emma and I did wedding planning, and after talking and thinking through stuff… We have both decided that we think the two of you should be the ones to make sure all the final additions for the wedding finish."

"Do what now? I don't understand"? I say, confused.

Ryan relaxes back, resting his arm behind me on the back of the couch.

"We want the two of you to stay in the Hamptons next week and ensure everything with the wedding is the way we want. You will stay at our parent's guest house, and we have a daily schedule."

I blink and throw my hands out, "Excuse me, but I thought you liked planning the wedding together. Why do you want us to be the ones to finish the planning for you? Also, the guest house only has one bed; how do you expect us" I wave my hands between Ryan and me, "To sleep there. Can't he sleep at your parents' house"?

"Well, our parents are hosting some of their friends next week, and the only thing available is the guest house," Baker says

"Since you are the maid of honor and best man, we know you would be the best person to get the job done. The two of you work so well together. Baker and I want to enjoy the wedding, and we do not want to worry about any more planning. I will have a folder full of everything we envision for the wedding, so it will be out there for you."

I look over to Ryan, "Do you have anything to say"?

"I do not have a problem with any of this. I know us," Ryan places his hand on my thigh and looks me in the eyes "are the best people to do this for them, right Claire? We are both grown adults who can share a bed for a week and ensure that Baker and Emma have the best wedding."

I felt warm when he touched my thigh, and it remained after he moved his hand.

I roll my eyes, "Fine, and we can share the guest house… Also, Emma, I would love to be the one to help the two of you plan this special day, so I will make sure it is what you want it to be"

"We can't thank you guys enough for doing this for us," Emma says with a big grin.

"Well, do not thank us just yet. You can save the thank you for the big day when it turns out to be the most amazing wedding for the two of you." Ryan says.

I do not understand, and he cannot think next week will be fun. On the other hand, I am incredibly excited about being able to take a week off from the shop to stay at the beach and plan my best friend in the entire world's wedding but having to share the week and process with him is not something I am looking forward to.

My phone sounds with a text, and I get up to walk away when I see it is from Reid. He wants to know if we can meet for dinner before he needs to go in for his next shift. Since there is no food for this business meeting, I tell him to meet me at the sandwich shop in thirty minutes.

"I am sorry to run, but I need to go somewhere. Is our meeting here over"?

"Of course, you can go. I will see you tomorrow. Thanks for agreeing to next week," Emma says, getting up from the couch. She makes her way over to me and hugs me.

I hug her back, "Anything for you."

Ryan gets up from the couch, "I can give you a ride."

"Thanks, Ryan, but I will just take a cab" I open the front door and turn back. Ryan looks upset that I am leaving.

"I'll see you guys later" I walk out, shutting the door behind me.

I do not even reach the elevator when Ryan catches up to me.

"Where are you going"? He sounds out of breath

I click the elevator button, "I'm meeting someone for dinner."

We walk into the elevator together. Ryan stands across from me, looking down.

"Where are you going"? I ask him.

"I guess home."

We both stand there in silence until the elevator door opens, and I walk out before him.

"Claire…."

I turn my head back to him.

29

"Yeah"

"I can't wait till next week."

"Me either, Ryan," I say, opening the front door of the building and walking out.

It might have sounded like a terrible idea, but maybe a week with Ryan is just what our friendship needs.

When I leave the cab at The Sandwich Shop, Reid is already waiting for me. He is leaning against the brick wall outside, his arms crossed across his chest. Reid is wearing a shirt and gym shorts, with his hat on backward again. You can tell he is not from here.

"Hey, there you are," he says as I get out of the cab.

"Sorry, there was traffic."

He takes my hand, and then we walk inside.

"So, what's good here"? He asks, looking over the menu while we wait in line to order.

"I always get the Italian sandwich with everything on it."

"That will work for me too."

When it is finally our turn, he orders for the both of us and then pays. Then we sit at a booth at the front of the restaurant. Emma and I used to get this place all the time while working at the older flower shop we opened since it is just a few doors down. That flower shop is still open, Baker owns it, and we let Liv and Lexi run the shop, with Emma and me stopping in occasionally to check on things.

"Did you just get off work"? Reid asks after we take a seat.

I looked down at my shirt and forgot I was still wearing my Blooms shirt, with jeans and tennis shoes.

"I closed the shop at six but had to go to Emma's after work. She wanted to talk about something, and then I just came here. When do you need to be at the station?"

"Midnight. It will be a long night."

"How do your hours work with being a firefighter"? I am interested in how this would work for us if we were to be in a real relationship.

"Sometimes I work 24 hours a day, and sometimes I work 12-hour shifts for three to four days straight. It depends on the week or if I pick up a shift for someone else. Tonight, I start my 12-hour shifts for three days. Starting at midnight every night."

"Wow, I do not know how you do it. I could not imagine being up all night and then sleeping during the day to do it all over again the next day."

"It is a hard adjustment. There are days where I want a normal hour job with a normal schedule, but I love what I do, and I like the thrill of not having a normal job."

The server comes to our table and sets down both our sandwiches. We both eat, talking about our jobs and life between bites. When I finish, I push my plate to the side and rest my arms on the table. He ends shortly after me, and after moving his plate to the side, he rests his arms on the table just like me and smiles.

"What"? I smile back.

"I am just thinking about what kind of food you will introduce me to this weekend. I am free on Sunday, and we should do something."

I frown, "I wish I could, but on Sunday, I need to leave for the Hamptons. Earlier, when I went to Emma's house, she and Baker asked if Ryan and I would go to their next week to finalize all the plans for their wedding. So, I will be gone all next week."

"You know, that is a real shame considering my schedule next week isn't that busy." He frowns

"I promise we can hit up all the best food places when I get back."

"And we can go out on another date"?

"Yes, a date" I smile at him.

We get up from the booth to leave. When we get out the door, I feel that Reid will kiss me goodbye this time. He walks up to me, we are face to face, and he puts his hands directly on my arms. He is just looking at me like he wants to kiss me, but instead, he says, "Thanks for meeting me for dinner," and then lets go of my arms.

I nod.

Before walking away, he says, "Let me know when you get back. Have fun in the Hamptons."

Once again, wave goodbye. "See you later."

I just do not get it; he is not ready to kiss me, or there is a reason he has not, or I am just expecting too much too soon. After he walks away, I throw my hands up and then hail a cab, where I will again go home alone.

Chapter Three

Ryan

When I heard there was a chance that Claire was going on a date with a new guy, I did not want to believe it. So, the first thing I wanted to do when I got back from my parents over the weekend was to find out who it was and if it was true. I did not mean to ask Claire so many questions that not only resulted in making her mad at me, but it hurt to know the truth. I have had a thing for Claire since she asked me for help tracking down an ex. All those nights with her, just us spending time together, grew into a friendship I did not see coming. The crush started when she started working next door to me, and I would see her every day. The thing is, Claire does not know about this because I do not want to chance to lose her as a friend. So, I have seen other women hoping this crush on Claire will go away, but it does not. When I am with someone else, I always think about her.

I know my chances of being with her are slim because she only sees me as a friend who can be there for her when she needs something. She depends on me, and I cannot let her down by telling her that there might be something between us besides a friendship. I have never been friends with a woman and have a thing for her simultaneously, so navigating these feelings has been challenging.

So, when Baker and Emma asked us to go to the Hamptons for a week to help them with their wedding, I knew this would be the best week of my life. Claire and I, just us, and no interruptions. So, you would think this would be the week I finally tell her how I have been feeling, but it is not. I do not want to let her know until I know she feels the same way back. I want to use this week to get to know Claire better and to grow whatever this is and will be between us, hopefully.

I set up with Claire last night that I would be the one driving us there and that I would pick her up this afternoon when she finished packing. In Claire's fashion, she did not tell me she finished packing until almost two o'clock. I guess she slept in and did not do her laundry till this morning. I know Claire can be a mess. I have seen her place.

I pull up outside of her apartment building and wait out front for her to come out. After she texted me that she would be down in a minute, I decided to connect my road trip playlist to the car while I waited for her. She comes out the doors, dragging a massive rolling suitcase behind her. She is wearing shorts, an oversized old band tee tucked into the front of her shorts and carrying a folder. I get out of my jeep and meet her around the back.

"Did you bring all your closet, plus your favorite blanket and stuffed animal, in this bag"?

"Ha. Ha. No, I wanted to ensure I had the right outfits for Emma's schedule, so I packed extra clothes."

I open the trunk and throw her bag into the back while she gets into the car. After I shut the door, I get in the driver's seat. Claire is already comfortable in her seat, looking over the folder Emma gave her when we drove off.

"So, we are scheduled to take dancing lessons together on Friday."

"Uh, do what now… Why exactly do we have to take dancing lessons? We are supposed to be planning their wedding, not ours," I say, keeping my eyes on the road, but I can feel Claire's eyes looking at me.

"It says here that we are to take the lessons for our dance that we will have at the wedding and that we are not allowed to tell them no, we are not doing it because they are making us, so there's that"

I check for traffic and then turn. "Nice. I hate dancing"

"Well… I think it will be fun," she says as she continues to study the folder.

I do not want to dance at the wedding, but having my dance with Claire, I think I can at least enjoy that.

We continue our drive by, not talking much, Claire seems to be reading every detail of what is in the folder, and I am not sure what we should talk about, so I stay quiet, but the silence is killing me. I think every minute with her this week I should not take for granted because I do not know when we will be able to do something like this again, if ever. If she sees this new guy, he could be the one for her, and I may never get that chance.

"Anything else in there that I should know about"? I say, breaking the silence.

"No," she says as she tosses the folder into the back seat and then gets comfortable again, looking out the window. I wouldn't say I liked that she gave me a short answer, so I tried to make conversation again.

"I can change the music if you want me to. Just tell me what you want to listen to, and I can change it for you" I just had a mix of all types of music playing.

It got her attention. She turns to me and holds out her hand. "Just give me your phone, and I can find something."

I hand my phone over to her, and she instantly starts searching for something to listen to. I know Claire likes music, but I have never been able to get her to share her favorite type of music.

It does not take her long to find something, and I instantly hear a song play that I do not think I have ever heard before, and it is the eighties.

"What is this"?

"It's a song that makes me happy...just like heaven by The Cure."

"So, I take its eighties music makes you happy"?

"Well, it is just what I listened to growing up. My mother was big on eighties music, so sometimes I listen to this song when I want to be happy. I picture one day having a moment where I can imagine this song playing in the background. A magical moment whether it be a kiss or just a feeling. A moment like, in a movie."

I am already learning something new about Claire on this trip, and we are just starting this little trip.

"So, one day imagine... let us say a kiss, and moment that you are happiest. You instantly will imagine this song playing in the background."

"Exactly," she says excitedly.

I nod and keep driving. "So, can you tell me what your favorite movie is?

"You are going to think this is silly... My favorite movie is The Breakfast Club, and my mother got my name from it."

"Seriously, I love The Breakfast Club."

"Really... I do not know any people who have ever seen it."

"I see it, now... You have red hair, so your mother thought Claire was the perfect name for you because Molly Ringwald was big in the eighties and had red hair."

"Yes!" she says like I just solved a challenging math problem.

This Claire is the one I like most, where she talks effortlessly with me and tells me anything. When things are finally going well for me, her phone goes off. She takes it out of her back pocket, and whoever it was, she spends a minute texting them back. When she is finished, she puts her phone in her cup holder, and I take it as a sign. Whoever it is will message her back, so put it there so she can respond again. We are once again silent, and just like it thought, the phone goes off again, but this time she reads it, and then without responding, she places it back in her back pocket.

She picked up my phone again. Once another song finished playing that she picked, she turned the playlist I had playing back on and then went back to looking out the window. Then we are right back to where we started, but I do not want it to be this way.

"I played football in high school. So, if we were in the movie The Breakfast Club, you would be Claire the beauty, and I would be Andrew the jock. We would end up together in the end. You can picture us in a movie, and you could have your happy ending moment."

She turns to me unamused, "She ends up with the rebel, Ryan. Not the jock. I thought you had seen the movie. Also, Andrew was a wrestler, not a football player; we were just friends. There would be no happy ending moment" She goes back to looking out the window.

Excellent job, Ryan, and there is my moment just to keep my mouth shut for the rest of the drive. I should have at least done my work before trying to impress her. I have seen the movie hundreds of times, but I forgot the ending, which gives me the idea that we should watch it together sometime.

So, we stay silent the rest of the drive, and I know things are not off to a good start for us. I understand how Claire is acting because of all the questions I asked her the other day. She is being short with me, so I do not ask more about this guy, even though I desperately want to know about him and their relationship. I know that is who she was talking to in the car.

We pull up outside my parent's guest house, which is located to the side of their house towards the back. There are cars parked outside their home, proving that they are hosting friends for the week, as Baker said. So, even if she tried to kick me out of the guest house with her, she could not and hopefully will not.

After I get out of the jeep, I go to the back to grab her bag before she can so I can take it in for her. And I accomplish the mission when I get her bag, and she is nowhere in sight. I have both of our bags in hand, looking around for her when I see the front door open at the guest house. She must have already gone in. So, I roll both of our bags to the door.

The guest house is small. When you walk in, you are in the living room with a small couch, and there is a small kitchen off the living room with a table and two chairs. There is one bathroom that is just off the one bedroom, which has a king-size bed. I can see Claire from the bedroom doorway, lying across the bed. My parents have the guest house decorated identically to their home. I take our bags into the bedroom and drop them by the closet door.

"Are you ready to share a bed this week"? I ask her

She rolls over on the bed and then sits up. "You think you can sleep on the couch"?

"The couch is tiny. I am not sleeping on it. We will be fine sharing a bed for a week. I do not even move in my sleep. You will not even know I am there. Remember, we are just friends so that nothing will happen."

"You're right. Nothing is going to happen." Claire gets up from the bed and walks out of the room.

"Where are you going"?

"There's nothing on the schedule until tomorrow. I'm going to take a walk on the beach."

She walks out the door before I can even offer to go with her, and since we rode in the car together the last couple of hours, I decided not to go after her and let her have time to herself.

I walk to the window to watch her walk down to the beach. She takes her phone out of her pocket and makes a call to talk to someone on the phone. She smiled, and I did not know who she was talking to, but her face lit up when they answered. I watch her pace back and forth in the sand while talking on the phone. If today indicated how this week would go, it would be a long week.

Since I have not talked to Lena in days, I do not even bother telling her where I am this week, and I am not telling her who I am with when I talk to her. What is happening with us is not serious and never has been. She has been more of a headache than anything, but I have not broken things off with her yet because I do not want to be lonely. If Claire is seeing this new guy, then the last thing I want is not to be seeing someone and just lying around alone thinking about Claire with someone else.

I have only been dating for a year because Claire was on the dating app. She was going out at least once a month with a different guy. I did not want her to think I was single since she was dating, so I started dating too. It has not been going well for either of us, but this new guy came out of nowhere. All I know about him is his name, which you can guess I searched on. I found out he is a firefighter in the city but is not from here, which is something they have in common, which scares me. She can confide in him for something she cannot with me.

Still watching Claire from the window, she hangs up the phone and puts it in her back pocket before taking off to the water. I watch the breeze blow her long red hair. She takes off her sandals, holding them while she walks through the water. She looks so carefree, and I wish I had just a little bit of her attitude, grit, and generosity. She is one of the most outstanding people I know. She always puts others before herself and does not let things get to her. Seeing her upset when she first started dating and not one single guy calling her back broke me, and I never want to see her that way again. I was there for her then, but only in a friendly manner.

I asked my parents to load the guest house with groceries so we did not have to go out every night this week, and it gave me a chance to show Claire that I have excellent cooking skills. I walk away from the window to see what food the kitchen contains so I can start something for dinner. After a thorough search, I find fresh shrimp and stuff to make a homemade alfredo. I know Claire is not meticulous regarding food unless it is a banana. She has a texture issue with it and does not like the taste.

I check on Claire through the window again, and she is still spending time by the water, so I start on dinner, hoping she will be impressed. I start by boiling the water for the pasta, and then once I throw the pasta in, I start on the sauce. When everything is ready, Claire comes walking through the door.

"What are you making? It smells so good in here"?

"Shrimp Alfredo, I hope you are hungry," I say, turning to look at her.

"I am starving. Thank you for making dinner. We could have just gone into town" Claire takes a seat at the table.

"I had mom and dad stock the fridge so we could stay here every night," I say as I pull two plates out of the cabinet and start plating our food.

I pick up the plates and set them at the table—one in front of her and the other where I will be. Then I take two bottles of water out of the fridge for us and join her at the table.

"Ryan, I knew you cooked, but this is amazing," she says as she takes her second bite.

"I'll ensure you are well fed by the end of the week," I smirk.

We finished our dinner, hardly speaking because Claire had just devoured her plate the whole time. I pick up our mess and start cleaning up the kitchen. I need to prove to Claire that I am different than I was when she met me, and I hope by the end of the week, she can see what a good man I can be. While washing the pans and setting them aside, Claire takes a towel out and starts drying them to help me. I do not know what to talk about, so I wait for her to mention anything.

"Tomorrow, we need to go to the local flower shop to pick the flowers out for them to order them. We should not be there long, considering I already know the flowers."

"Why is she having them do the flowers? Why can't Blooms do them"?

"They are not doing them. Just order flowers for us, so we do not have to drive for three hours with flowers in the van. The Blooms team will be the ones putting them together on the actual wedding day. It just saves us a trip and time that day."

"I guess that makes sense," I say, drying my hands off with a towel.

"Then when we finish there. We need to go to an old man's wood shop to give him the plans for the arch that Baker wants to be built."

"Old man Dan"?

"That would be the guy."

"Oh Claire, you are going to love Dan. He is the kindest older man. He has done woodworking for over 50 years and tells stories of his wife. She passed away a couple of years ago, but he talks about her like she is still here."

Claires smiles and then starts heading to the bedroom. "I'm going to get ready for bed."

I nod and then watch her as she walks into the room.

I am ready for bed too, but I will wait for her to finish before I make my way into the bedroom. So, I lay across the couch and pulled out my phone to check if there were any emails I needed to respond to before tomorrow. I am away from work this week, but I know I still have stuff I need to work on. I brought my laptop with me in case I got a chance to work.

Claire does not take long with whatever she is doing. She pokes her head out of the door to say goodnight. She is wearing glasses that I think look adorable on her.

"Goodnight, Claire"

I go into the room to get ready for bed when I finish. It's dark, so I cannot see anything, and I have no idea if Claire is awake or asleep already. I strip down to nothing but my boxer briefs and slide into the bed. I feel something in the middle, and I immediately think there is no way she was sleeping in the middle of the bed when she wanted me to sleep on the couch. I take a chance on it and reach my hand out to touch her. When my hand meets her, I only then realize it is a pillow. I sit up and turn on the lamp on my nightstand, which startles Claire.

"You can't be serious, Claire. We don't need pillows in between us."

She says, "Oh my gosh, Ryan, you're naked."

I lift the sheets to show her that I am not naked. "See... not naked. Now I am going to throw these pillows on the floor. You are being ridiculous."

"Fine, but if you touch me in my sleep tonight, I'm putting the pillows back tomorrow night."

"That's fine, but I can promise I won't be touching you in your sleep" I pick up the pillows stuffed under the covers and throw them on the floor. I turn off the lamp and then lie back down in the bed.

Tonight is just night one, and she does not want to sleep in the same bed as me. I have more to prove and a long way to go to get Claire to realize I am not who she thinks I am.

Chapter Four

Claire

This trip has been one to remember; we are only on day two. The best thing that has happened so far has been the dinner Ryan cooked for me last night. I did not know he was such a fantastic cook, and I look forward to the rest of the meals he cooks for us this week. When we got into town yesterday, I could not wait to get out of the car from all the awkwardness between us. He has been weird lately when it comes to our friendship. I walked down to the beach, where I called Emma to tell her we had made it here. She went over a couple more things with me on the phone before I spent time just taking in the beach.

I did not want to share a bed with Ryan last night. I did not want to make things more awkward between us, so when I woke up this morning to Ryan on his side of the bed and my leg over his while lying in the middle, I mortified myself. I removed my leg from his quickly and got up from the bed before he woke up. I hope he did not catch it in the middle of the night.

This morning while we got ready, I tried to pretend I did not wake up touching him, and he did not act like anything was different. He did have coffee waiting for me, and he made a breakfast sandwich, and I liked the gesture. I know he is trying to make amends to make up for how he acted towards me the other day.

While on the way to the local flower shop, I figured now was a suitable time to finally break the silence we had had going the last couple of days.

"How is Pamela doing"?

He lets out a small laugh, shaking his head. "Her name is not Pamela."

"I know it is not her real name, but she sure does look like the woman who used to run the beach, in a red swimsuit, her twins bouncing, with a life preserver," I smile.

"I would not know how Lena is doing. I have not talked to her since last weekend," he says, not even looking sad about it.

"Did you two have a falling out"? I ask, waiting because I want to know.

"If I tell you, will you tell me about this new guy"? he asked me, and I was hoping he would not bring him up, but since Ryan and I are friends, he should know.

"Deal, I will tell you about him, but you must answer me first."

"Lena is trying to use me; honestly, she is not worth my time anymore. Last weekend while at my parent's, Lena was trying to get me to pay for her things and trips. I would not budge on letting her have her way, so she left my parents. That was the last time I talked to her. She wants to be serious, and I do not want to be," he says with eyes on the road, turning into the flower shop, and I look at it as my way out to tell him about Reid.

He parks the car and grabs my hand when I touch the handle. "Woah there, Claire, you said you would tell me about this new guy"?

I roll my eyes and turn back to him. "Right. So, Reid is a firefighter in the city. He is from South Carolina and is here because he keeps an eye on his grandmother in a retirement home. He is a customer who picks up a bouquet to take to her now and then. We went out twice and had a fun time. Anything else you want to know"?

He nods, "I want to know if it is serious between the two of you."

I grab Ryan's hand, "We have only been out twice. I would not call that serious. I have not even talked to him since we left town."

Ryan gets a look of relief on his face, and this is the first time I know Ryan is genuinely watching over me, he cares, and it warms my heart to have him there for me.

When we finally get out of the Jeep and inside. A younger girl is working the front counter and says hello when we walk in. I stay back and let Ryan manage all the talking, and he is a better people person than I am.

Ryan walks up to her, "Yes, we need to order flowers. I believe my mother, Catherine, stopped to tell you about it."

"Is this for the Hayes wedding in September"?

"Yes, it sure is."

"We have been waiting for someone to call. We will not be able to order the flowers that week of the wedding. We have the wedding of the shop owner getting married that weekend, and we do not have the room or time to order the flowers," the lady says in a serious tone.

A Love That Blooms

I can tell Ryan is about to get angry, "So you are telling me that there is no way you can order all the flowers? We just need you to store them here for one day. We are almost three hours away and do not have time to bring flowers from the city. Is this the only flower shop here in the Hamptons"?

"Yes, sir, there is no way, and yes, we are the only flower shop. Sorry, but you will have to think of another plan."

Ryan shakes his head, "Well, thank you for nothing, have a wonderful day."

He grabs my wrist, and we go back outside and into the car.

"Ryan, what are we going to do? We needed them to order the flowers. We will be extremely busy with work, at least two days before the wedding. We are talking arrangements for every table, flowers on the arch, and your mother wanted the patio draped with flowers on string lights. I cannot simply give up my maid of honor duties to bring thousands of flowers here. We are not off to a good start with what we are supposed to be doing here." I am panicking.

"Claire, I can promise you, you will not have to do anything. We have many people working at the shop who can do all the work. I will if I need to bring the flowers here the day or two days before the wedding. It will be all right. I will figure something out."

I feel like Ryan folded quickly on that lady inside the shop. The Ryan I used to know took charge, and he would have made the lady order the flowers after he put up extra cash. This Ryan is more likable, and well, he is making me panic right now. Emma and Baker sent us here for a job, and so far, we are failing. Next up on the list is Dan, and he better be all right with the plans for the arch.

Ryan pulls up outside, a tiny white house with a shophouse built to the side. The house is old, and two wooden rocking chairs are on the front porch. Not what I pictured when Ryan was telling me about Dan's house. He said when they moved here, they would come over to visit Dan and his wife, and she would bake homemade cookies while Dan told them stories of his life.

"This is it…I know you are going to love Dan."

We get out of the jeep instead of going to the front door. Ryan leads the way for us to the shophouse. "Come on. I am sure he is in the shop" he reaches out for my hand, and I take him so he can lead me through the tall grass. I have the plans for the arch in my other hand.

We come to the shop, and I see Dan inside, sitting on a wooden stool and working on what looks like a small box. I drop my hand from Ryan's when we walk in. "Hello, Dan"

The older man in glasses, wearing a white shirt and denim overalls, turns towards us on his stool. "Well, if it is not one of the Hayes boys. How are you doing"?

Ryan holds his hand out, and Dan shakes it. "Dan, this is Claire. We are here to bring you the plans for the arch for Baker's wedding."

"You are one pretty lady. Ryan is lucky" he holds his hand out, and I shake it.

"Thank you, but." Ryan interrupts me, "How have you been, Dan"?

I look over to Ryan, who smiles at me in return.

"I have been good. I am so old now that I do not make massive things anymore. I have been making these small wooden boxes instead. You can use these boxes to store important, meaningful stuff. I can carve anything you want on the top."

"So, Dan, you do not think you can make an arch"? I hand Ryan the plan so he can show them to him. He unrolls them and then puts them in front of Dan.

"Yea, I cannot make that. I am just too old to stand for a long time. Last year I got a bad knee, and since Susie cannot take care of me anymore, I have a tough time getting around."

Ryan runs his hand down his face, and this wedding planning is not for the faint of heart. We have had the worst luck so far. We look at each other like we are going to do.

"Dan, what if I come to help you make this? I will do all the work, and you observe."

"I think I can manage that. Remember when I used to try to show you how to woodwork, and you would just watch me and never do the work."

Ryan laughs, "Yes, Dan."

"Well, here is your chance to finally do the work," Dan smiles, bringing a smile to my face.

Ryan picks up the plans and rolls them back up.

"Ryan, your pretty lady here reminds me of my Susie. She is sweet and looks at you like you are her world. My Susie was my world, and she still is. We used to drink tea and rock on the front porch. I would hold her hand while she would stare at me with a big smile."

I do not have the heart to tell him that Ryan and I are just friends, "That is a charming story, Dan. I wish I could have met your Susie."

Dan opens one of his wood boxes on his work desk and pulls out a picture of a lady wearing a dress, an apron tied around

49

her waist, and her red hair back in a ponytail. Dan holds the printout for me to take. "This is Susie, and she is still with me every day."

I take the picture and bring it closer to my face. Susie is beautiful, and I know Dan was the one who took the picture. You can tell from the look on Susie's face in the photo. I bet they have one of the greatest love stories. Ryan is watching me while I look at the picture, and I catch a glimpse of him smiling at me.

"Dan, you were a blessed man. Susie was lucky to have you in her life" I hand the photo back to him.

"Thank you so much for your time, Dan. Claire and I need to get going, but I will be in touch on coming to make that arch."

"It was nice to meet you, Claire. You two take care."

"You too, Dan," I say, and we start walking out of the shop.

Ryan takes my hand unexpectedly and again helps me through the tall grass.

After we get in the car, "So, where to now"? Ryan asks me.

"Um… let me check the folder" I take the folder out from the backseat and open it up. I looked over the schedule and saw that we have nothing else to do today.

"That was it for today. It looks like we are free for the rest of the day."

"Thank goodness. Our luck today has not been good."

"You know, there is a wedding planner out there that will do a better job at this"

"Claire, they want us to do this and trust us. We will work together to ensure they have the best day of their lives, even if that means we must do the work ourselves. We make a wonderful team," he smiles at me.

Ryan starts backing up, and we pull out of Dan's driveway.

"So, what do you want to do," I ask him

He looks over at me, grinning, "How about lunch"?

He stops at a local sandwich shop and runs inside while I stay in the car, which he asked me to do. I am not sure what he has planned. When he comes out, he is carrying a big brown bag, so I have no idea what Ryan just picked up for lunch, but it smells so good when he gets in the car. I decided not to ask questions and just to follow along with what he wanted to do. When we return to the guest house, I go to the door, but he stops me. "Stay out here, I am going to grab a blanket, and then we can walk down to the beach."

Once we get down to the beach, he lays out the blanket while I hold the food bag. When he gets it situated, we take everything out of the bag. He bought sandwiches, salad, and sides.

"You did not have to do this."

"I know I did not, but I wanted to. I miss spending time with you. I know we will be together all week, but that differs from the time we spent together."

We both start eating, and when I get a chance, I ask him, "What exactly happened to us? We used to do everything together."

"Dating… We both started dating, so we have not been able to hang out much. If you had to ask me, though, I would pick hanging out with you over dating."

I blush, "Ryan, how are we supposed to find our forever if we just hang out together all the time."

He shakes his head and looks out at the ocean before saying, "Don't you think if we both stopped looking, maybe one day our soulmate, or in your case, the happy ending, will just show up."

"I have thought about that… I used not to care, but since Baker and Emma fell for each other, I see how happy she is and how in love they are. I cannot help but want the same thing for myself. I have been putting pressure on myself to find myself forever. I will spend my weekends watching romance movies alone, and I cry while watching every one of them."

He frowns, "You really should not do that to yourself, Claire, that kind of pressure is not good for someone like you. I know you do not want to but stop thinking about your "happy ending" and just try to spend every day doing the things that you love doing. Like Claire, I know. When you stop looking, your forever will come"

I smile at him and then get back to eating.

Ryan could not be more right. I do not need to put pressure on myself anymore. I need to go back to the Claire I was before. I needed a date to Emma's wedding, dating app Claire, and maybe I should take things slow with Reid. This time with Ryan is like old times with us, and it made me realize how I miss him. He knows me better than anyone besides Emma, and I should take his advice because this Claire has not been happy.

Chapter Five

Ryan

As I sit here and watch Claire asleep on the couch, I reminisce on the last couple of days. After what we thought was terrible luck trying to order flowers on Monday, Dan turned us down for making an arch. We had better luck yesterday when we went to an event planning a place to rent the chairs, tables, tablecloths, and all the other stuff Emma had on our list. Claire took over while we were there, and it was fun watching her light up when talking to them about everything to make their day just what they wanted. Hours later, we returned to the guest house, where Claire declared it Taco Tuesday, so we ate the tacos I made while watching a movie on my laptop. Claire chose an action comedy, and we spent the rest of the night laughing.

Today we had an open schedule, so since my parents were out of their house for the day doing who knows what with their friends, Claire and I snuck into their backyard and went swimming in their pool. Hours later, we returned to the guest house, and I knew Claire was tired from not sleeping well the last couple of nights, so we watched another movie on the couch, her feet on my lap while laying her head on the armrest. It did not take her long before she was out. I spread a blanket over her and then closed out the movie so I could work on emails while Claire napped. She should sleep for a while, considering she has been tossing in the night, and I know it is because she is worried that she will get too close to me while sharing a bed. I will not forget waking in the middle of the night to her leg across mine, I could have just moved it for her, but I liked the feeling of it being there.

I am completely through with my emails when I see Claire's phone light up on the coffee table. I know I should not be evading her privacy, but I cannot help but wonder who it is that messaged her. I look over at her, she is out, and then I look back at her phone. She has not been on her phone since we first arrived, and I still wonder who she was talking to that day. I should not look, but I cannot help myself. I sit up and lean over to tap the screen. It says a new message from Reid. My stomach sinks. This trip is just getting good, and I do not want someone like him to interfere with my plans to prove to Claire that I can be the man she needs. I pick up her phone and open the message. I choose not to go through all their messages but instead just open the thread and close it, so she will not even know he sent her a message and then put the phone back down. It was wrong, I know, but I just wanted her to myself and no distractions besides what we were here to do.

I make dinner while she finishes her nap, and guilt runs through me as I realize she will return to him and figure out she missed his message.

"Hey, thanks for letting me nap," she says, coming up behind me in the kitchen.

I look at her, "It is no problem."

A Love That Blooms

She hops up on the kitchen counter to sit and watches me with her arms crossed.

"We have cake tasting tomorrow, and they want us to pick the cake."

"Us?" I say, surprised.

"That is what the instructions say. We pick the flavor and the look. I know it will be fun for both of us," Claire smiles.

"It will be. I am not sure we have ever had to decide on something big together" I continue making dinner.

"What if we do not like the same flavors"?

"I am not worried about it, you have good taste, so I would just let you pick" I reach into the cabinet behind her to grab our plates, and she leans forward, our faces close together. I hold the plates, closing the cabinet, but I do not move. I stay there.

"That is sweet, Ryan," she says, and I place my hand on her leg, "Anything for you, Claire."

I walk away and start plating our food.

"Well, technically, you would not be doing it for me. You would be doing it for Emma and Baker."

I laugh, "Want to run into town for ice cream after this"?

"I would love that," she says, jumping down off the counter so we can eat.

Once again, Claire ate one of my meals in record time, and she asked if I would take the top off the Jeep before we ran into town for ice cream. So, I work on that while she gets ready. She insisted that she needed to look nice, and I think just for a second that she might be treating this as a date. I consider any time with her a date. I get the final piece off the top of the Jeep. Then Claire comes walking out the door. She wears a navy short-sleeved sundress paired with sandals, and her long red hair is down in soft curls.

I cannot hold back, "Wow… you look incredible, Claire."

She blushes, "Thank you, Ryan."

"What exactly is the special occasion"? I ask, just to see what she says.

"You are taking me for ice cream, and I felt like dressing for the occasion" she taps my arm. "So let us get going."

She did not say this is a date, but I will take her answer as that is what she wants it to be, so that is what it will be. Tonight is my chance, and I will show her just what I wish to, her.

When we get to the place, it is an older metal ice cream parlor that has been around here for years, but they have the best ice cream. Claire acts as if she has never seen this place before, "This has to be the cutest place I have ever seen."

"This will also be the best ice cream you have ever had, promise."

We get out together, and I let her take the lead after I hold the door open for her. She looks around the place before walking up to the counter to look over the menu.

"I want to try I all, but I will just get one scoop of the rocky road on a cone. What about you"?

I look at the menu, "I think I will get the same thing as you."

She does not know it, but it is what I always order. We tell the lady what we want, and then she tells me our total is $5.55. I take out my wallet but notice Claire looking at me with a smile. I hand the lady money and ask her to keep the change. The inside tables are full. So Claire and I walk back outside and sit on the bench by the door.

"Thank you for taking me out for ice cream. I enjoy the wedding planning stuff, and you cook every night, but it is nice to get out for something else."

"You are welcome" I rest my arm over the back of the bench behind her and sit back.

We eat our ice cream in silence, watching people go in and out of the parlor and couples enjoying sundaes together. I do not want to waste time with her in silence, so I try to think of a good question to ask her.

"Tell me something about you that I may not already know"?

She thinks about it and then says, "I have this weird thing with numbers all being the same. Like my apartment is 222, and when the lady told you the total for the ice cream, I see numbers lining up as a sign for something."

"They call that angel numbers like someone is watching over you. The numbers have the meaning."

"Right, and 555 means a welcoming change, transition, but it could mean anything," she says just before finishing her ice cream.

I think about what she just said, and this sign could mean a change in our friendship, which could mean it would be a sign for her that she should welcome the change in us.

"So, what do you take from the sign"?

She leans back on the bench into my arm, and anyone walking by would instantly think we are a couple. So, I take that as my answer when she does not say anything but instead asks me a question. "Tell me something I do not know about you"?

"This will not be surprising to you considering my history, but I have never been in love with someone. I have had strong connections with a couple of women, but I have never been in love or feel like I want to be with someone forever."

She laughs, "Sorry…" she places her hand on my thigh. "I am not saying this to be rude, but I am not surprised. When I first met you, you came across as someone who would not settle down for anyone. I know that you have seen many women, but I think in the last year, I have seen a change in you. You are closer to finding someone you can love and be with forever."

So, she noticed the change but did not know that the difference was because of her. I used to only think of money and finding women. I wanted things just a year ago that I think are ridiculous when I look back now. I wanted to be so rich that I could vacation anywhere in the world and pick up any woman I wanted. When Baker turned down that deal last summer, it was the best thing to happen to me. Since becoming close with Claire, I realized I do not need those things to be happy when the happiness is right in front of me. All the nights helping Claire move into her new apartment, seeing her laugh at the way I helped her decorate, and fix her constantly running toilet, and those things brought me more joy than any vacation or night out with a woman ever brought me. Just seeing her work hard at the shop, constantly giving to others, and never complaining are more moments that make me want to be with her and only her.

"You want to do something fun"?

"What did you have in mind"?

"It is a surprise" I get up and hold my hand out for her to take, and she takes it.

We get in the car to head to the outskirts of town. She is just watching out the window, her hair flowing in the wind. I turn on a road that then takes us down to the beach. Here is a place I have not been to in years. I stopped the jeep went we got up to the sand.

"Have you ever taken a ride along the beach"?

She looked at me, surprised, "You mean we are fixing to drive this jeep in the sand"?

I laugh, "Yes, I am going to drive along the water."

She gets the biggest grin, "Can I stand in the seat while you drive"?

"You can, but please hold on and be careful. I do not want anything to happen to you."

I slowly drive onto the beach, and she squeals with excitement. When I get close to the water, she stands in her seat. I go a little bit faster, but enough that I want to be cautious with her standing. The sun is setting on the beach, and I could not have picked a better time for us to come down here. This part of the beach is away from home; there are never people, so it is just us. I look up at her, her hair flowing behind her, arms out, and she has her eyes closed. She is just taking in this moment. I drive down and then turn around to go back in our direction. She is still standing and taking it all in until we get to the end of the beach.

She sits back in her seat, and I stop the jeep to where we are watching the sunset, "Ryan… that was the best surprise of my life."

I laugh, "There is no way that was the best. It may be high up on the list but not the best."

She looks at me seriously, shaking her head. "No, it was the best, and thank you."

I take her hand in mine nervously, and she does not hesitate. "Claire… there is something I want to tell."

She looks at me, and before I can say anything, we hear a buzzing noise in the car. Claire looks all over and then picks up my phone from the cup holder, "Pamela is calling you."

I thump my head back on my headrest and run my hand down my face. Of all the times the headache wanted to call me, it needed to be when I was about to confess my feelings to Claire. I took the phone from Claire and ignored her phone call. She ruined my perfect moment, and I am sure all she needs is money, which I am not about to give her. I need to break things off with her so she does not have the chance to ruin anything else.

Instead of asking what I would tell her, Claire asks, "You want to head back to the guest house"?

"Yea, it is getting dark. We should get going."

I am in all sorts of emotions right now, angry that Lena called, unhappy I did not tell Claire how I was feeling, and glad because I just happened to be part of one of the best surprises in her life.

When we return to the guest house, Claire gets out and immediately takes off for the door. I want to take my mind off what just happened, so I stay outside to put the top back on the jeep. I have a slight feeling she may know what I was going to say, and she will try to avoid any chance for me to tell her.

I walk inside to find the place dark but only the lamp lit. Claire is already in bed, and that is when I realize my intuition is correct, and I know I am back to square one. Today just was not the day to tell her.

"Ryan, try this one" Claire slide one of the cake sample plates over to me.

"This looks like it is going to be sweet" I use the fork to get a bite of what looks like sprinkled cake and vanilla icing. I put the taste in my mouth. It is sweet, and I make a gross face.

Claire laughs, "Yea. I did not think you would like that one."

She uses her fork to get a bite of what looks to be just white cake and vanilla icing.

"Oh my… It is the one," Claire moans like it is the best cake she has ever tasted.

I used my fork to taste the cake she had eaten. "That is the one."

The baker comes over to the table, "How is the tasting going"?

Claire looks at me and then turns to the lady. "We would like this one" she points to the plate at the cake we both decided we liked.

"The is the wedding cake. It is an almond cake, with an almond buttercream icing."

"Okay. We want that flavor and the cake to be just a simple white three-tiered cake," the lady writes the order down while Claire gives her the instructions and the date we need the cake.

Claire and I looked at cakes in books for an hour before we both decided to order an all-white cake, and Claire added flowers to the cake once it arrived so it would match everything else at the wedding.

We have been so into wedding planning today that I have put what happened last night in the back of my mind. When I went in last night for bed, Claire was already asleep, so I did not get another chance to talk to her before bed. I am taking what happened last night as a sign that it is not the time to tell her anything. We both have other things going on in our lives, and I should not throw my feelings for her into the mix. I need to break things off with Lena and see where her relationship goes with Reid before I tell her anything. I could not sleep, knowing that if she disagreed with my feelings, it could be the end of our friendship, and I was not ready to risk that. I let a nice night out with her get to my head. It could have ruined any chance with her if I had told her. So, from now on, I need just to let our friendship be just that, a friendship.

"All right, you are all set for your wedding day. Thank you for coming in and ordering with us. Good Luck with the rest of the wedding planning."

Claire laughs, "Thank you so much, but we are not the ones getting married. We are planning this for our friends."

"Well, that is so sweet. We thought you two looked so good together and assumed it was you."

Claire smiles, looks at me, then back to the lady. "We are just the maid of honor and best man."

"Thank you, ladies, for your time today, have a great rest of the day" I walk to the door and hold it open for Claire.

"Thank you," she says as she walks out.

"Where to now"? I ask after we get into the car.

"Let me check the folder. I was only thinking about cake, so I forgot what comes next." She gets the folder out from between her seat and the middle console.

She looks over the schedule and then closes the folder. "There is nothing else for today. We just have the dance class together tomorrow. So, we are good to go home tomorrow night."

The thought of this trip ending tomorrow is not a good feeling. That will happen as I do not want to return to the way things were before this trip. She will return to dating Reid, and I

A Love That Blooms

know I need to end things with Lena officially. Our friendship will then be the same, and we will both do the same routines that we always do.

Chapter Six

Claire

Today is the last day of this beautiful week, and I will finish the trip doing the one thing I hate doing, dancing. I still do not understand why Emma and Baker signed us up for a dance class or if we had a dance at their wedding. Yesterday after ordering the cake, Ryan and I spent the day at the beach. I walked along the shoreline while he sat in the back of the jeep with something on his mind. He has been different since the other night when he took me on one of the most exhilarating rides on the beach. He had something to tell me before his call from Lena, and I felt once he took my hand that it had something to do with how he felt about me. I wanted to know what he was going to say, but then thinking about the phone ringing, it was a sign that I was not supposed to know.

He again made me the most fantastic dinner, and then we finished watching another movie on his laptop the night. When it came time for bed, he went to bed before me and was asleep before I got into bed. So, when I woke up this morning, it was no surprise that we had already been up, and he left me some breakfast with coffee on the kitchen table, along with a note that said he was at his parent's and would be back. I got ready alone, and it made me realize that getting ready with him was a nice feeling.

"You ready"? I hear Ryan say from the front door.

I look out from the bathroom, "Yes, just one more minute."

I spray perfume on myself and then take one final look in the mirror. Since it is dance class, I wear a long sundress with sleeves and sandals. When I come around the corner, I see that Ryan looks good, wearing khaki dress pants and a white button-up. He has his blonde hair fixed and has grown a little scruff this week, which is a good change for him.

"Ready now," I say, walking into the living room.

He watches me walk into the living room with a smile on his face and then turns to open the door for me. I always notice the unimportant things he does for me, opening the door and letting me walk in first. He may not see that I notice these things, but I appreciate them.

We park out front of the dance studio, and I start sweating and wipe my hands onto my dress. Ryan looks over to me, "Claire, you can do this. We danced at the gala together last summer, and we can do this."

"That was different. No one there told us we were dancing badly. I do not want to mess this up for Emma and Baker."

Ryan lets out a laugh. "You will do an amazing job. I know from experience."

We get inside, and the instructor, Jane, takes us to a room towards the back of the studio. We walk into a room filled with windows on one side, mirrors on the other, and hardwood floors.

"Claire and Ryan, it is nice to meet you. Now let us start this dance lesson. I will ask you to stand face to face with each other."

Ryan and I walk up to each other, face each other, and then I let out a nervous laugh, which makes Ryan smile.

"Now, breath in and out," she asks, so we both do it in unison.

"Good. Now Ryan, take both of Claire's hands" Ryan takes both of my hands in his, and his hands are so soft. I noticed the last few days he has excellent hands, and mine fit in them.

"This is for you two to get comfortable with each other. Now stay like this for a minute, and we will move on," Jane says.

We stand there, holding hands, and I want to laugh, but Ryan smiles, so I smile back.

"You are comfortable with each other already. So, Ryan, I would like you to hold up one of your connecting hands and put your other hand on Claire's hip. Claire, I want you to put your hand on Ryan's shoulder, and now you will take small steps. Start forward, then side, and then back. Do it over and over until you get into a rhythm."

We do what Jane asks, and she watches us with a straight-faced look. I do not know if we are doing it right, but she does not stop us, so we keep going.

"Good, Good, you two know what you are doing. Just continue"

I watch Ryan's face; he is enjoying this, and I feel like we make an excellent team regarding tasks. We always have been able to work together very well.

"Alright, now I want you to get closer together. Claire rests your head on Ryan, and I want you to put your arm around Claire and bring her closer to you."

Here it comes. I do not think I have ever danced this close to anyone.

We once again do what she said, and Ryan seems comfortable, and I try to relax so I can enjoy this learning experience.

Ryan whispers in my ear, "You are doing great."

I look up at him and smile before mouthing, "thank you."

Jane is off to the side with her serious face just watching us, so we continue for another few minutes until she tells us to stop.

We quit dancing and separated ourselves from each other, and the feeling of him letting go of me left me with a weird feeling.

"You are doing a wonderful job so far. I would like you to return to the basic dance position we started with, but this time I would like you to try to spin Claire around with one hand, and when you have that down, try to dip her back."

Jane comes over to us, helping us back to the primary position, and then when she has us the way she wants us, she steps back and watches us with her arms crossed. We start slow, doing the same thing we started out doing, and then Ryan holds me and spins me, and I cannot help but smile. He has me close before spinning me out again when I return to him.

"You are naturals. My job here is done," Jane says, clapping.

Before we stop, Ryan holds me close again, spins me out, and then takes me in his arms, dipping me back. Our faces are almost touching, and he stares at me, grinning instead of picking me up. Here would be the perfect moment for a kiss with him, but we cannot do that here, and I am not sure if we ever can. I clear my throat, "I think we are good here."

Ryan finally pulls me up, "Right, sorry."

"Wow, you two are phenomenal. I do not think I have ever seen a perfect pair with chemistry like the two of you," Jane says, walking over to us. "You two will do a fantastic job at the wedding."

"Thank you," I say.

"Well, you are good to go. Thank you for coming in today," Jane says, holding her hand out to shake Ryan's hand and mine.

"Thank you for teaching us today," Ryan says before taking my hand for us to leave.

"See, that was not so bad, was it"? Ryan asks me after we get in the car.

"That went well, and I expected it to be much worse. Jane was nice, and we made a wonderful team, remember" I laugh.

"So, the last thing on the schedule finished. Are you ready to head back home, to the city"?

As much as I want to get back to my routine, this week away has been good for me and us. It brought us back to our friends before we started dating other people. I am not ready for it to end just yet.

"If it is all right with you, can we stay just one more night? I do not care if we just stay in for the night. I think the city and normal life will not miss us if we stay one more night."

Ryan smile. "I was hoping you would say that. I do not have anything I need to get back for, and if you want to stay, then we will stay."

"Now that we settled that, what should we do"? I ask

"I think I have an idea of something we could do," he says, looking over at me.

When we got to the guest house, Ryan suggested we order pizza and take a walk down to the beach while we waited for it. So, while walking along the coast, we talked about all the stuff we did while here, laughing at the bad luck we started with, and I told him how he was right about me liking Dan. He is the sweetest older man in love with his wife. I joked about how he plans to make an arch when he has never worked with a saw a day. We talked about how planning this wedding for them was not as bad as we thought it would be and how great it was that we reconnected after these odd few months of our friendship. We took a fantastic walk and returned to the guest house right before the pizza arrived. Ryan thought it would be fun to watch The Breakfast Club together, considering he was all wrong about the movie's ending, so we started that while eating pizza on the couch.

"You know you are nothing like the Claire in this movie," Ryan says while we finish watching the movie, my head lying on his lap while we are on the couch.

"Yeah, I agree. We are not alike. I would say I am more like Emma Stone from Crazy, Stupid, Love."

"I see the Emma Stone resemblance. I have never seen that movie, though."

"Well, there is another movie we should watch sometime. In the movie, she falls in love with a heartbreaker who is Ryan Gosling. There is a scene where they reenact the part of dirty dancing where Patrick Swayze holds up Baby at the end."

"We should try it; we should go down to the beach and see if we can nail it." He says with excitement.

I sit on the couch, "oh, I know we can nail it, but it is late and dark out now."

"That makes it even more challenging, and I know how much you love a challenge, so we are going down to the beach right now, and we are going to nail this."

"Fine, but if you drop me in the water, I will dunk you."

He laughs, "I will not be dropping you. Now come on."

Instead of changing into our swimsuits, we stay in lounge clothes, but I throw on a cardigan because it is a chilly night. We get down to the beach and decide to practice in the sand and only move to the water if we cannot get it down. I stand ten yards back from him, and he is laughing, "Come on, Claire, we can do this" he holds his hands out, ready.

I hesitate for a minute before running towards him full force. He grabs my hips but does not get me up, so he sets me back down. "Ugh... Let us try this again."

I walk back but get more yards away from him, "This is it, Claire. We are getting it this time."

Running at him as fast as I can again, he grabs my hips, pulling me up, but his arms give out, so he sets me back down.

"This is not as easy as I thought. I think we should move to the water. I will get knee-deep, and you run as fast as you can to me, and I know we will get it this time."

I nod, and he walks into the water, getting more than knee deep, and his shorts are wet.

"Ryan, you went further than I thought."

"It is okay, just come on. We can do this" Ryan is holding his arms out again.

I take off my cardigan, tossing it into the sand. I back up and start laughing.

"Claire, now. Come on," he is laughing now.

"Ryan, I do not think this is going to work," I yell.

"You do not know that until you try it," he says, just waiting for me.

I breathe in and out and then run as fast as I can, splashing around when I hit the water. Ryan grabs my hips and holds me up precisely like in the movie. I hold my arms out and start giggling. Ryan then drops me straight into the water.

When I returned to the surface, "You were not supposed to drop me."

I wipe my face, and he laughs hysterically when I look at him. So, I push him, and he falls back into the water but grabs me with him, and we both fall. He still holds me when we come back up, "We did it, Claire."

"We did it" we are staring closely at each other.

It is then that Ryan puts his hand on each side of my face, then kisses me as he has always wanted to, and I do not stop him but instead give into his kiss, wrapping my arms around his neck, bringing us closer together, and wrapping my legs around him.

We continue for what feels like minutes, but it is only seconds. I realize we should not be doing this even though it feels right. We could be damaging our friendship by trying to go a step further. What if this never works out between us? Could I lose him forever? I pull away, "I am sorry," and start walking out of the water, back to the beach house.

"Claire, where are you going"? From the sound of it, he is following behind me.

"To the guest house" I feel his hand on my arm, and he turns me around.

"What about what just happened, Claire? Admit you felt it, that there is something there between us.

I shake my head and start walking again. "I just got caught up in the moment, Ryan."

"So, it was just something that should not have happened. Is that what that was to you"?

I turn around, and he has not moved since I walked away from him. "I am sorry, but I caught up in the moment. I do not know what else to say"

"Say you want this too, Claire."

"Ryan… we can't. I am seeing someone, and so are you. We are friends, and we both know we would not want to risk our friendship. We could fail Ryan, and that would be the end of us, forever" I walk back to the guest house, and he never says anything else.

Heartbroken, that is what I am, but this is what is best for both of us. The kiss, though, is something I do not want to forget, even though I ruined the moment by ending it.

There was no coffee or breakfast this morning and no Ryan. He came in last night, grabbed clothes from his bag, and went to stay with his parents. I know I am to blame, but there will be a time when he sees that what I said was right. He came in while I was showering to finish packing up his bag, and I caught him down at the beach through the window while I spent getting ready. I packed my bag and looked around before walking outside to ensure we had grabbed everything. I will miss this place, and the memories Ryan and I made this week. I walk outside, and Ryan stands by the jeep with his arms crossed.

"Good morning," I say, handing him my bag.

"Morning, you got everything" he takes my bag, walking to the back of the jeep.

"Yes, I did" I open the door, and coffee is waiting for me.

He gets in the car, and we buckle up for the road trip back.

"Thank you"

"Thank you for what"?

"For the coffee," I say.

"That was mine," he says and then smiles.

It is good to see him smiling, and hopefully, he thought about what happened last night.

"Are we good because I do not want what happened last night to make things odd between us again? We had such a fun time together this week and…."

He interrupts, "Claire, we are good. I promise."

"Good because the thought of us having issues makes me miserable."

He reaches over and places his hand on my arm so I would look at him, "Look, I am sorry for last night. We were both at the moment. Things are good and will always be good between us."

He may have said that, but the silence between us on the way home tells me a different story. I do not know if the silence was because he was not ready to go home from our week away or if he was thinking about last night still. I do not know if what he said last night about his feelings towards me were real or what he said at the moment. I have had my best times with Ryan, but we have always been friends, so I have never thought of Ryan as more than a friend. Plus, he has always been seeing someone, so I would have never considered what he said last night was real. You do not see other people when you have feelings for someone else.

Ryan dropped me off at my apartment building, took my bag in, and walked me to my door. He has always done this, so it is nothing new to me. We said our goodbyes, and I told him I would see him later because I will. I know this moment from last night will fade and not be something hanging between us after a while.

I enter my apartment and immediately plop down on my couch, leaving my bag at the front door. Taking my phone out of my pocket, I call Emma to let her know we are back and to tell her how things went. I have not heard from her or Reid since I was gone.

"Claire, I missed you! How was the trip with Ryan"?

I find it odd she did not ask how the wedding planning went first.

"It was fun. We stuck to the schedule and got everything done" Emma does not need to know about the flower issue.

"Did you all do anything fun while you were there"?

"We went to the beach a couple of times, swam in their parent's pool, he took me to ice cream at this amazing parlor, he cooked almost every night, and I think that about sums it up."

"I am glad you got a week away together. I know it has been a while since you two have had time together."

"It was good for us. So, how was everything while I was gone? I cannot wait to get back into the shop to work again."

"It was just a normal week, nothing special. I cannot wait till Monday, and we are back together."

"Well, I am going to get off. I need to unpack, and I will call it a night soon. I am tired."

"See you Monday, Claire."

"You too," then I hang up the phone.

Before putting my phone down on the coffee table, I thumb over Reid's text thread, thinking if I should let him know I am back in town or not yet. I did not even hear from him while I was out of town, and he knew I was away, so maybe he just did not want to bother me. I decided to message him tomorrow and place my cell phone on the coffee table.

Chapter Seven

Ryan

Last week with Claire did not end the way I wanted it to, but Claire was right. We are in no way ready for a relationship with each other. I need to cut things off with Lena, and I hope things with her and Reid do not get any more serious. I need more time to prove to Claire that we are perfect for each other, and if that means being just friends for a little bit longer, then that is what I will do, but I need to prove to her I am capable of more than being more than her friend.

After our moment on the beach, I wanted her to know we were good because that is what we are. I do not want any more awkwardness in our friendship. Suppose anything I want to show her there is more to us. When she left me on the beach, I saw my parents were still up for the night, and I always talked to them about Claire. They are very aware of how I feel about her, and it is good to be able to go to them for help. They planned this weekend for our next volleyball tournament, and as always, Claire and I will be partners, which is the perfect time for us to have another fun time. We slay every match as partners, which is one of my favorite things to do with her. She fits in so well with my family, better than any girl I have ever brought home to them.

I called Lena to make sure she could be in town this week so we could talk. We made plans to meet on Thursday, and that is when I plan to end things with her. We have never been official, but it is correct if I make sure she knows this will never work out between us. I don't want to do it over the phone, so I would rather we talk about it in person.

Claire and I also made a lunch plan this week. Since she was gone last week, she has been busy every day, so we have not been able to go. I told her just to let me know when a fun time was, and she has not responded with a day yet. This week has been a long week for me, and I have not even been able to work in the office. I have had meetings all over town, so I have not been able to stop by the flower shop to bring Claire coffee or see her. I usually do both at least once or twice a week, and after last week with her and being able to do both every day has been hard for me.

I am finally in the office today, the first time I have seen Baker. I stop by his office on my way.

"Good morning" I peek my head through his door.

"There you are. How was last week"? Baker asks while sitting at his desk.

"It went well, and we did everything you asked" I walk in, taking a seat in his chair.

"Did you and Claire have a fun time"?

Baker knows Claire, and I are only friends. We do not usually share our life, so he has no idea I have a thing for Claire.

"It was a fun time; we just did what was on the schedule."

"Nothing else"?

I laugh.

He does not need to know about anything.

"Nope. I am going to get to work now" I get up from the chair.

I leave his office and walk into mine across the hall from his.

My office is almost identical to Bakers. It has a large dark wood desk and two camel-colored leather chairs for clients to sit. I do not have meetings in my office, and I mostly meet clients for lunch or at their buildings, so my office is always a mess. Months back, Claire brought me a plant for my desk, which I have kept alive. It was on the verge of dying, and she swore she did not know what she was doing wrong, so she trusted me to bring it back, and now it is thriving. She knows plants better than anyone, so she just wanted to gift me an office plant and made an excuse to give it to me. It was her way of thanking me for helping her move into her new place. I gave the plant a name, which is the most responsible thing to do, so even though the plant is green, I named it Red, after Claire.

I start my workday; I do not have plans to do anything but stay in my office all day to catch up on work. I water Red and then take a seat at my computer and make any needed phone calls. Since I wanted to spend all last week with Claire without interruptions, I put more work to the side than I should have, but I do not regret it. I am deep into paperwork and all sorts of things when I hear a knock on my door.

"Ryan, I missed you," Lena says, walking in, tossing her bags in the chair, and taking a seat in the other.

"Lena, what are you doing here? We are not supposed to meet until tonight."

She has never come to my office before, so I am surprised to see her here.

"I did not want to wait any longer to see you" she gets up to come to sit on my lap.

"I am busy today. Now really is not the time," I say, annoyed.

She wraps her arm around my neck and gives me a quick kiss.

"Lena, we need to talk but not right now. We need to get together tonight."

"Why can we not talk now"? she gives me a pouty lip.

I try to push her up from me, but she does not budge.

"I am working, and we already have plans to meet tonight. So how about you go shopping or whatever you need to do, and then we will have our conversation later."

She does not answer me before I hear another knock on my office door. Who now, I never get visitors? I move Lena over, and when I look up, it is Claire.

"Oh, I am so sorry," Claire says before walking out the door.

This situation is not good.

I get up from my chair, and Lena falls to the ground. I chase after Claire, who is at the front door.

"Claire, wait. I am so sorry."

"I was going to ask if you wanted to get lunch, but it looks like you are busy."

"She was not supposed to be here. Hold on, and we can go to lunch."

Claire stays there, and I turn around to walk to my office to tell Lena to leave, but she is already making her way toward us.

"I do not think today is a good day. I will just see you this weekend Ryan" Claire says

"What is this weekend"? Lena asks, coming up behind me.

Please do not say it, Claire. Please do not.

"The volleyball tournament at The Hayes in the Hamptons."

"I love a good competitive volleyball game," Lena says excitedly.

She does not have a competitive bone in her body unless it involves money.

"Looks like you have a new partner, Ryan," Claire says before walking out the door.

That was not supposed to happen at all.

I walk back to my office, and Lena follows closely behind me.

"Ryan, why did you not tell me about this weekend"?

"You want to know why? Because Lena, this between us is over, and I was supposed to talk to you about it tonight, but you know what, I do not want to wait anymore. I am sorry, but this will never work out between us, and I do not think we should see each other anymore," I say, taking a seat at my desk.

She stares at me, shocked. Then she picks up her bag to leave.

"Good. It was over long again when you would not sleep with me, anyways."

"Lena, I am sorry, there has not been anything between us in a long time, if ever, and I hate that I wasted your time, but I do hope the best for you."

She does not reply, and she walks out of my office. I feel relieved that that is finally over, but now I need to find the time tonight to make things right with Claire and let her know that she will still be my partner this weekend.

When I left the office, the flower shop closed for the day, and I did not get a chance to stop by to talk to Claire about what had happened this afternoon. I decided I would go to my apartment, and maybe I could give her a surprise visit after something to eat and change my clothes.

I moved apartments shortly after Bakers and Emma got engaged. I lived in the same building as Baker but moved after Claire got her new place. We were always together, and I knew she would need me, so I bought an apartment just a couple of blocks down from her. It is much smaller than my penthouse, but I like it better. It is a newer two-bedroom, two-bath, all modern black cabinets, white walls, and all one story. It is just quiet all the time, and I do not think I have ever had anyone over besides Claire. I have felt that I should get a dog. At least I would have something to come home to and an excuse to take walks by Claire's apartment.

Since it is just me here all the time, I do not cook, so every night, I come home to pop a meal prepped meal in a container into the microwave. Another thing I always used to do was go out after work and spend a ridiculous amount of money on food and alcohol, something I did not miss. This new me may be boring, but honestly, it has been refreshing not trying to be something I am not.

After eating, I change into gray joggers with a white t-shirt and take off from the front doors of my apartment building towards Claire's apartment. I have not spoken to her since she left my office, but I am sure she is at her apartment. She spends her nights at her apartment watching movies and eating takeout. I am about a block from her apartment when I spot a couple holding hands, walking down the sidewalk in my direction. When I look closely, I notice it is Claire and a guy that must be Reid.

I back up and hide behind the corner of the building.

I can hear them talking in the distance, "I am going to the Hamptons this weekend."

"Are you going to their parents"?

"Yes, you should come. I need someone to be my teammate."

I can hear them right beside me, so I back up further down the building so they will not see me. I am still trying to listen to Reid and Claire's conversation when a car stops at the stoplight and honks its horn. They walked across the crosswalk, still holding hands, but I did not hear what he said to her.

Oh no. I wipe my hand down my face and then through my hair, resting them on the back of my head. Can this day get any worse?

I want to follow them, but that is so wrong, so I walk back to my apartment. If Reid shows up with her at my parents' this weekend, that means I need to up my game. That will be easier for me now that Lena will not be coming.

Raindrops drop down on me on my way to my place, about a block from the building. I raise my hands, "Oh, come on, seriously" this is just the icing on the cake for today. I pick up the pace and start jogging towards my building, still soaked from the downpour. I make it through the doors. I am wiping my feet on the rug before heading into the elevator up to my floor. I walk into my apartment and instantly take my shirt off, throw it into the laundry room, and then head to my bedroom to take my wet joggers off to slide on a pair of shorts. I grab a towel in the bathroom to dry my hair. Then take a seat on the side of my bed.

I think back to seeing Claire with him holding hands. I did not like seeing her with him; I knew it would be worse to see them together at my parent's house this weekend. I lay back on the bed, and since it was getting late, I should stop for the day and go to bed. I brush my teeth and then pull my covers down from my bed when I hear a knock at my door. It is just my older neighbor, Jim. He sometimes comes by at night asking for things he needs so he does not have to run to the store. I gave him toilet paper, paper towels, sugar, and eggs; he once asked for tv because he went out. Since he is older, and it is harder for him to get out, I always get him what he needs, even if that means if I must go out to get it, and yes, I lent him a tv once.

I walk to the door, and a very wet Claire stands when I open it.

"Hey… come in."

She walks in, and I close the door behind her.

"Thank you"

"Let me go get you something to change into."

I walk to my room to grab her clothes.

"You do not need to do that. I was just out, and it started raining. Your apartment was closer than mine, so I hope I could stay here until it stops."

I grab a shirt and sweatpants for her from my dresser and then head back to where she is in the living room.

"Of course, you can. It may be a while before it stops, so if you need to stay, you are more than welcome to."

"Well, thank you, but I do not think I need to stay."

I know I can offer her a ride home in this, but she is here, and I do not want her to leave. I need to know how he is not with her anymore in such a short time since I saw her.

I hand her over the clothes, and she heads into the bathroom to change. So, I turn on the tv and make her hot tea since I know she is cold. She was wetter than I was, so I know she walked much farther than I did.

She comes out of the bathroom, her damp hair pulled into a messy bun, the gray sweats rolled at the top, and my old football t-shirt tucked into the front of the sweatpants. Everything is enormous on her, but she looks cute wearing my clothes.

She sits on the white sectional in the living room, and I walk over a mug of hot tea to her.

"What were you doing out"?

She grabs the tea from me, and then I take the blanket folded over the back of the couch to cover her up.

"Thank you, Ryan. You did not have to do this."

"It is no problem."

"I was just out walking…" she bites her bottom lip.

"Just walking. It is late."

"I was walking with Reid."

I don't particularly like it when she says his name, but at least she is talking about him to me.

"Where is he"?

"He met me out front of my apartment building, and we walked to get something to eat. He got a call and said he needed to leave, so he got a cab, and I just thought I could at least still get something to eat, but then it started raining, and I ended up here."

She will not admit it, but when he left her, I was the first person she thought of, and it felt good.

"Let me get you something to eat" I get up from the couch and head to the fridge.

I open the fridge a pull out a couple of the meals I have ready.

"What sounds better? Chicken with rice and veggies, or Beef taco bowl with rice and veggies"?

She turns around on the couch so that she can look at me. "Hmmm… I was on my way to tacos so let us go with the Beef taco bowl."

"Good choice" I raise the bowl to her and then pop it in the microwave.

I go back to the fridge to grab her water. Then take it to her on the couch, sitting next to her.

"So, did he not say where he was going"?

"No, he said it was an emergency, so I assumed it was the fire station. He got the call and left quickly"

"You know, I do not want to be mean, but I do not like that he just left you alone."

"I know, I did not like it either, but I know it was probably something important."

The microwave goes off, so I get up to grab the food for her. When I bring it to her, I take a seat closer to her this time and then grab the remote to change the channel on the TV. She starts eating while I find us something to watch.

"This is good. Where did you get this"?

"It is from that place over by the flower shop. I go in there on Mondays and grab dinners for the week. It is just me here always, so I do not cook. They are just easier for me."

"I may have to stop in there to get me some"

"Or you could just come over here, and I can cook for us."

She smiles and continues eating. I finally decided on Ted Lasso for us to watch, starting on episode one.

"I have always wanted to watch this show, but I do not have an Apple tv."

"I have already seen all the episodes, but you are more than welcome to come over here to watch it anytime you want. I can share my meals with you, also."

She finishes her bowl, then places it on the coffee table. Then she lays a pillow beside her, lays her head on it, and then puts her feet by me.

"I do appreciate you this. I did not mean to show up, but it was raining so hard, it was impossible to text you."

"Anything for you, Claire."

She rolls over to face the tv better and places her hands under her head on the pillow. I pull the end of her blanket over my legs, and she puts her feet on my lap. Episode two starts when I pull out my phone to check the weather. A storm is coming toward us, so the rain will not let up anytime soon. She is into the show, so while on my phone, I pull up Reid's social media pages to see if I can find any other information on him. If she is going to be with him, I want to ensure he is not hiding anything from her. I had looked him up before and did not find anything, but I feel like I need to double-check.

A Love That Blooms

When I look over, Claire is asleep on the couch, so I continue my search for a mister who leaves Claire alone in the pouring rain and finds him tagged in a post on Instagram last week by a girl named Blair. It looks like he was out at a club, and she looks like she could be the server or his date. They look cozy. I click on Blair's account and find more pictures of them together last week, at various places than the first one, making me think they are seeing each other or just friends. I know he can do that, considering Claire and him are not official, but she will not like that he has been seeing someone else while she was out of town last week. I wonder if his emergency tonight was with this woman or work. If this guy shows up at my parent's this weekend with Claire, I will not be a happy man, and I will pull him aside for a talk. I need to know if she is cared for, if not with me.

I am calling it a night, and I do not intend to wake Claire. She can just stay here for the night. I cover her up with the blanket well, then place a kiss on the top of her head. I turn the tv off before getting a blanket and sleeping opposite her on the couch. I do not want to leave her alone in the living room.

Chapter Eight

Claire

The smell of breakfast and coffee wakes me up, and I realize I am still at Ryan's apartment. I must have fallen asleep while watching tv with him last night. Sitting up from the couch, I see my dry clothes folded on the table with coffee in a to-go cup sitting next to them.

"Good morning," I hear Ryan say, and I turn around to see him in the kitchen, leaning up against the kitchen counter, drinking coffee from a white mug, still shirtless from last night.

"Good morning," I say, getting up from the couch.

"What time is it"? I ask him, picking up my clothes from the table.

"It is early. I will drop you off at your apartment after you change, and you should have time to get ready before you need to be at work."

"You can take me in these clothes unless you want them back"?

He smiles, "No, you can keep them."

Ryan heads to his room, I assume to throw a shirt on so we can leave, and I pick up the coffee he made before sliding on the sandals I had on last night.

Ryan comes down the hall, "Ready"?

"Yep," I say as we walk out the door.

It takes not even five minutes for him to pull up outside my building since we live so close to each other. I thank him again for letting me spend time together last night and then open the door to his jeep.

"Hey, do not forget this" he hands me the breakfast sandwich he made for me this morning.

"Thanks for keeping me fed," I laugh. "See you later."

I get out of his jeep and shut the door. He rolls his window down, "If I do not see you again today, I will see you tomorrow in the Hamptons, right"?

"Yes… Bye, Ryan."

"Later, Claire" he rolls his window up and drives off.

I get to my apartment and start the shower as soon as I get through my door. I take off the clothes Ryan lent me last night and fold them up on the end of my bed. I plan to sleep in those again tonight, they are comfortable, and I do not know if they are old or because they smell like him, but I am keeping them.

Last night turned out to be a great night considering the disaster it was turning into before it started raining. I did not lie to Ryan; Reid did suddenly leave last night before we even made it to dinner. When I went to have lunch with Ryan yesterday and found Lena there, it upset me, and the fact that she would be joining us this weekend made it even worse. So, before leaving work, I texted Reid to see if we could go out to dinner. He said he was free and would stop by to get me. He waited for me out front of my building, and we were on our way to dinner when I asked if he would want to join us this weekend so I could have someone as a partner. Reid said he did not want to stay the night there with us but could meet me there Saturday if I wanted him to come. I tried to get him to ride with us, and we could stay in the guest house together, but he insisted he did not want to, and that is when Reid got defensive and then, after pulling his phone out from his pocket, said he needed to leave. He did not even offer to walk me back but instead just got a cab and left.

The only person on my mind when he left me alone to walk back to my place was Ryan, and I knew I needed to see him because he is the only person who can put a smile on my face when I am down about something, but I knew I could not tell him what had happened. I also hoped that Lena would not be at his apartment. I did not want to have to face her again. Of course, it would start raining after Reid left me, but I wanted to see if Ryan was home instead of just going back to my place, which was a shorter walk. So, I ended up getting more soaked than I had intended, but it was worth it when I got to Ryan's place, he was so welcoming, and he lent me his clothes. As always, he made sure I was comfortable, fed me dinner after I had not eaten all day, and put a smile on my face. And I had not intended to sleep there last night, but I cannot complain about waking up at his place.

I get out of the shower, dry off, and then wrap my towel around me to blow dry my hair.

Once finished, I dress in my closet, picking out the same thing I wear daily: jeans paired with my Bloom shirt and white sneakers. I head to the kitchen to warm up the sandwich Ryan made me when I hear my phone go off. I pick up my phone off the counter.

Reid-I wants you to know I am sorry for last night. I will come with you this weekend if you want me to.

A Love That Blooms

I know I need to make things right with him before he joins us this weekend. I do not want the next time I see him after a little fight.

Me-Can we talk after I get off work today? Let us say around noon.

I plan to leave the shop at the same time as Emma today so that I can ride with her and Baker to the Hamptons.

Reid- Yes. I will meet you at the shop when you get off.

I do not know if I still want him to come, but I can at least make whatever this is between us right before I leave town. I do not want to feel left out since Ryan has Lena joining him. I will see what he says when we talk and see if I still want him to come.

I walk out of my building with the coffee that Ryan made me and walk to the shop. I cannot wait to see Emma and get help from her about what I should do after what happened last night. We do not see each other much anymore outside of work since she got engaged, so I always look forward to our chats at work.

First, at the shop, I unlock the front door and then lock it behind me after I walk in. Emma should be here shortly, and I can talk to her before everyone shows up. I turn on all the computers and then check the front desk for today's orders. I start on the regular flower orders for today at my workstation. I start on a couple of bouquets when I hear the front doors open.

"Hey Claire"

I turn to see Emma walking in.

"Hey, how are you today"?

"Would it be bad for me to say I am ready to get out of here today"? she laughs.

"I am with you; this weekend will be fun."

Emma and I grew up in Florida, so anytime we get the chance to go to Baker and Ryan's parents in the Hamptons, we look forward to it. We could spend hours on the beach.

"How was last night with Reid"?

"About that… it did not go that great. I asked Reid to go with us as you told me to, but he got mad when I asked him if he wanted to go with us and stay. Then he pulled his phone out, saying he needed to go, and took a cab and left. We walked a couple of blocks from my apartment, and then I ended up at Ryan's."

"What? What do you mean ended up at Ryan's"?

She comes over to where I am and sits on the workstation.

"Please tell me everything."

I stop working on the bouquets and lean against my counter to look at her.

"Okay, when Reid left me blocks away from my apartment, the only person I wanted to see was Ryan. I knew he was someone that would never do something like that to me, and he always knew how to make me smile, so I went there even though my apartment was closer, and it was pouring rain."

"Did you tell Ryan that"?

"No way! I just told him I was out walking, Reid had an emergency, and his apartment was closer, so I just wanted to hang out until the rain stopped, but after he made me something to eat, I fell asleep watching tv with him."

"Claire, you have feelings for Ryan."

I shake my head. I do not have those feelings for Ryan, and we are friends.

I never told Emma about what happened between Ryan and me while we were away. It was personal between just Ryan and me, and I have thought about it every day since. There were moments this week where I thought about that kiss with Ryan and felt butterflies, but it is just because it has been so long since I have kissed someone. He came to my mind first last night because he genuinely cares about me.

"Emma, we are friends, and even if I have feelings, I do not want to break a friendship with him. He has been there for me for a year, and I am so thankful for everything he does. If we had any type of relationship that was not friends, I just do not know if it could work. My relationship history is horrible."

"He is the first person you thought of when you were alone last night. You more than care about him" she jumps off the counter and walks towards the back office.

I will not admit it to her, but she could be right. I never thought about Ryan as more than a friend until that one night he kissed me and expressed that he may feel something for me, but he admitted the next day that he caught up in the moment, and since then, nothing has been different with our relationship.

I returned to what I did while Emma was in the back office. I stack flowers on sheets of brown paper and then wrap them up when I finish, wrapping twine around one bouquet to hold it together, and light pink ribbon around the next. Then I place them in the cooler until they are ready for pick up. I go back to the front counter and check if there is nothing else I need to do when I see Ryan pull up in front of his office next door. He gets out of his Jeep, wearing fitted khaki-colored dress pants, a white button-up with the first couple of buttons undone, and brown dress shoes. Ryan looks so handsome, and I secretly wish he was stopping by to see me even though I know I had already seen him this morning. He looks over at the shop and then walks into his office building. I frown and then turn around to see Emma standing behind me.

She is shaking her head and laughing.

"What"

"Oh, nothing besides the fact I just caught you checking Ryan out."

Okay, I was, but there is no need for me to admit it when she already knows.

"I did not tell you, but Reid is meeting me here when I get off. I already packed, so once I finish talking to him about last night, I will meet you at your place so we can leave"

"You are still going to try something with him, and I do not know if that is a promising idea considering he got weird on you last night. He is hiding something."

"You do not know that. I should meet him. At least let him apologize to me in person for last night and see what his excuse was. Then if I accept, he will still meet us this weekend. Ryan has Lena coming, and I do not want to feel left out."

Emma does not get to respond; the phone starts ringing, and she answers it. I walk away to go back to making more arrangements so I can finish early today.

As I stand outside the shop waiting for Reid, who is either running fifteen minutes behind or forgetting that he said he would meet me here, I contemplate just going home and forgetting about him altogether. I am pacing back and forth, looking at my phone, and thinking there is no way I will message him. He is the one who needs to tell me if he is coming or not.

"This is ridiculous, and I am going home," I whisper.

I start walking in the direction of my apartment building when I hear someone say my name from behind me. I turn around to see Reid running towards me.

"Hey, I am so sorry. I got tied up at work."

I do not answer him, but instead, I keep walking.

"Look, Claire, I am sorry for running late, and I am sorry for leaving you last night. I should not have just left you out alone. They called me into work, and I needed to be there. I want to make it up to you if you let me."

I stop walking and turn around to him.

"I did not like that you left me, and how do I know that is something you would never do to me again? What if we were in a relationship? Would you do it then"?

"I can promise that is something that I will never do to you again. I am also sorry for how I acted last night, work has been tough lately, and I just had things on my mind. I want this to work between us, and I missed you all last week. I should not have been that way towards you. You have been nothing but nice to me."

He genuinely feels terrible for what he did last night, so I should give him another chance.

"I forgive you, but can we not have another night like that."

He takes both of my hands in his.

"I promise we will never have another night like that again" he smiles

"Do you want to walk me to my place? I must ensure I have everything I need before we leave town."

He lets go of one of my hands, and we start walking down the sidewalk together.

"About that, do you still want me to come with you"?

"If you want just to come tomorrow, that is good with me. I can text you the address tonight. If you leave in the morning, you should be able to make it for volleyball, and then we always do dinner outside afterward."

We reach my building, and he stops outside the door like he usually does. He has yet to come up to my apartment since fixing my sink.

"So, I will see you tomorrow"? he asks me, letting go of my hand.

"I will see you tomorrow" I smile

And just when he is just going to leave like he always does, he places a small kiss on my lips. I was not expecting it, so I pulled away before he did.

"Bye, Claire"

"Bye," I blush and open the front doors to my building.

We pull up outside The Hayes residences, and Jack and Catherine are always waiting for us out front. They love when we all visit as much as we love coming out here to see them. They have replaced my family, which I rarely see anymore in Florida, and I love them so much. They have welcomed me with open arms even though I am just Emma's friend and, well, I guess you can say Ryan's too. I rode down here with just Emma and Baker like I always do, and Ryan had things to do before he left the city, so he should be arriving later tonight. I am sure he is running late because of Pamela; I mean Lena.

Baker parks the car out front, and we all get out.

"We are so happy you all are here," Catherine says.

I grab my bag from the back and run to greet her with a hug.

"We are all happy to be here. How are you"? I ask her.

"Better now that I got that hug."

I run to Jack and hug him, "Awe, you are too sweet, Catherine… Hello, Jack"

Baker and Emma follow behind me, giving them both hugs before we make our way inside.

"We have dinner waiting for you. After you all put your bags down, just go ahead and join us in the kitchen. Ryan should be here soon, and Audrey, Clark, and the kids will be here in the morning."

"Thank you," I say before running up the stairs.

I walk down the hall and into Ryan's old room. Here is where I always stay when I come. Ryan always stays in the guest house since I use his room, which was his idea. I place my bag on the bed before looking around the room. This room has football trophies, jerseys, and signed footballs from famous football players. Ryan used to play all through high school and was playing on scholarship when he suffered a career-ending injury during his freshman season in college. He finished school with a bachelor's degree in Pre-Law but collaborated with Baker instead of following in his dad's footsteps. Ryan realized he did not want his dad's life while going through school. He is excellent at what he does now, and I could not imagine him as a lawyer.

"Hey, you," Ryan says, walking into the room.

"Hey… I was not expecting you here yet," I say, surprised.

"I had to finish a meeting with a client. It ended quicker than I expected, so I was not far behind you."

I sit on the bed, and he sits beside me.

"Where is Lena? Was she supposed to come with you"?

"Remember when you stopped by my office, and she was there? Shortly after you left, I finally broke things off with her. I had plans to do it for a while now, and I did not want her coming here this weekend since you so kindly invited her"

Now I feel terrible for inviting Reid, and I should have made sure she was coming or not before asking him. Ryan will play all by himself tomorrow when playing in the tournament.

"I am so sorry, but I thought she was coming with you, so I invited Reid to join us tomorrow, so I was not alone on a team."

"Just call him to tell him he is not needed, and it will solve that problem."

"I wish it were that easy. I did not tell you last night that we had a little fight before he left me alone. He wanted to make it right with me, so I met him before coming here today, and he apologized for how last night went. So, I cannot just say sorry you cannot come anymore."

"You most definitely can tell him. Why did you not tell me about the little fight? What exactly happened"?

"When I asked him to come here because I thought Lena was coming with you, I tried to get him to come down with us and stay overnight. He got irritated and defensive when I asked, then he checked his phone and left."

"Claire, come on, seriously. You do not need this guy."

Baker asks in the doorway, "You two coming down for dinner"?

I instantly stand from the bed, "Yes."

I start walking towards the door when Ryan grabs my wrist and pulls me back into him.

"We are talking about this after dinner."

"Why do we need to keep talking about this"?

He spins me around to look at him, "Because I care...."

I look him into his eyes and then pull myself away from him to head down the stairs for dinner.

He does not follow behind me, and he must still be in the room when I enter the kitchen and see that everyone else has made a plate and they are all gathered at the table eating in the dining room. I still feel warm where he touched me, and I cannot shake the feeling of being in his arms. I know I can text Reid and give him an excuse not to come here, and I contemplate it while making a plate. This weekend will go smoothly if he does not come because now that Ryan knows the truth of last night, he will have a tough time. I finish making my plate and pass Ryan with his phone in his hand, leaving through the front door on my way to the dining room to join everyone else.

"Claire, there you are. Where did Ryan go"? Catherine asks.

"He went out front, and I think he had a phone call to make," I say, taking a seat by Emma.

Everyone at the table is in conversation and laughing, and I am looking out the front window to check on Ryan while he is on the phone. I do not want to talk about Reid to Ryan anymore. I push my food around on my plate and do not want to eat anymore. I need to figure out what I want to do. Do I want to spend the weekend with Ryan, or do I want to spend this weekend with Reid?

Chapter Nine

Ryan

Baker and I are on the patio, sitting in the lounge chairs, drinking coffee, and watching the girls take a walk together along the beach. Audrey, my sister, and her family should be here soon so we can start the weekend. I have not talked to Claire since last night, she found any way she could to ignore me, and I know it means she invited Reid to join us today.

"You want to tell me what is going on"? Baker asks me.

"Do you want to know"? I lift my sunglasses to look at him.

"Yes, I want to know."

He will find out soon, so I better talk to him about it now.

"I like Claire, and in more than a friend way."

"I already knew this… Emma and I have known for a while, and we were just waiting for you to admit it. Does Claire know"?

"When we were here last week, there was a moment with us, and I told her then, but she turned me down, so I told her I was in the moment. She has been seeing this other guy, and he is coming here today."

"Yea, Emma told me this morning he would be here today… If you were more honest with Claire, she would give you a chance over this guy."

"I have tried being honest, and she has friend-zoned me. She is scared that we would not work out and she would lose me as a friend."

"Show her you care and want to be with her. She will come around soon, I promise."

I watch Claire as she is walking on the beach still with Emma, and they are in a deep conversation.

"You think they are talking about us down there"?

"Oh yeah, they are talking about us," he laughs.

I hope Claire is talking about me. If Baker said they have known for a while, I could only hope that Emma would help Claire realize it is me she needs.

When the girls start heading towards the house, I take that as my sign to head back to the guest house where I am staying so Claire does not get to talk to me. I know she wants me to see that he is coming, but I do not feel like talking about it now. I take the stone walkway to the guest house, and once inside the door, I lock it behind me.

It takes me half an hour to shower and prepare for the day. I would think by now, and everyone else has arrived, so we can get on with this tournament and get this day over. I have no desire to introduce myself to this guy, and I will have to be teammates with my sister since Clark always produces a reason not to play.

I walk to my parents' backyard and see everyone gathering around the volleyball net and talking. I see Claire on the other side, introducing Reid to Baker. Audrey sees me coming in the distance and starts walking towards me.

A Love That Blooms

"Hey, little bro, I hope you do not mind being with me today," she says when she catches up to me.

"I kind of figured it would be me and you," I say as we walk together.

"How have you been doing lately"?

"I have been better. How about you"?

"Same," she says, looking out in the ocean.

We walk up to everyone else, and my mother has a handful of shirts in assorted colors. She always gets new shirts for us because she feels we all need to look professional during these games. She starts reading names off the back of the shirts and hands them to whoever the shirt belongs to.

"Here are your shirts, Audrey and Ryan," she says, handing us bright pink shirts.

"You are kidding, right? Why do we have to be pink"? I say, holding up the shirt.

"Audrey picked it. Just wear it," my mother says.

I pull my shirt off over my head and then slip on the ridiculous pink shirt. Now I look embarrassed in front of this man. Thanks, Audrey.

"Okay, first up is Emma and Baker, against Claire and Reid," my mother yells out to everyone.

So, Audrey and I take a seat in the sand to watch. If they start, we will play against my parents, and then the winner of both will play the best of the three. Then whoever wins that takes the whole tournament. The prizes are always different; they have given out dinners and spa days. Claire and I once won a couples massage, but I let her and Emma have it one weekend when they had a girl's day.

I watch Claire as she pulls her shirt over her head, only wearing a sports bra and short black gym shorts, and then slips on the red shirt my mother gave her. Claire and I are always on the red team, so now I am annoyed that Reid is wearing my color.

Everyone gets in their positions, and Reid gives Claire a good luck kiss on the cheek before my mom tosses him the ball to start. I cannot help but roll my eyes, annoyed.

Mom blows her whistle, and they serve the ball.

It starts slow between the two teams, just back and forth hits until Baker smashes one right in front of Reid that hits the ground before he can dive for it. I show no emotion because I want Claire and him to take this so I can show Reid up.

Baker serves the ball over to them, and it is once again just a boring game. We can win if Reid plays like this against Audrey and me.

Their game is going on forever, and they sit tied at nine to nine right now. We play to ten points, so I want Reid to blow this one out right now so we can get this whole thing over. Baker serves the ball and goes straight to Reid, who falls to the ground after he sends it back over. Emma hits it back, Claire jumps to smack the ball over the net, and it falls to the ground before Emma can get back to it. That is my girl. Claire and Reid win.

They all cheer for them. Reid gives Claire a bear hug, picking her up and spinning her around.

This game sucks already, and it just started.

Before we get to our spots to play our game against my parents, my mother yells out

"Your father and I are sitting out today, so Audrey and Ryan, play Reid and Claire."

A Love That Blooms

I do not mind this one bit; we were going to play them anyway.

"Sounds good, Ready Audrey"? I look over at her as we get to our spots.

"Yep. I am ready," Audrey says

Audrey is very fit for someone who has had two kids and is good at volleyball, but I wish I could have told her beforehand how I do not like this guy so she could help take him out.

My mother tosses the ball to me, and I throw it up a couple of times to warm up before she blows the whistle. I need to play my best game. Even though Claire knows how good I am, I need to prove myself.

Mom blows the whistle; I throw the ball up and serve it over the net.

Reid steps forward to hit it back over, Audrey jumps to hit the ball, and it falls straight into the net.

"Audrey, what was that"?

She shrugs, "Sorry, my bad."

I shake my head and get back into position.

Reid throws the ball to Claire to serve, which goes right over the net.

I toss it back over, and Claire jumps, hits it, and goes right between Audrey and me.

"There you go, babe," Reid says to Claire

Now I want to punt the ball right into his face, and I do not want to hear him call her another name.

"Time out" I hold up my hands and pull Audrey to the side.

We walk over to where no one can hear us.

"Look, I do not like this guy at all. You think you can help me a little bit" I look over at her.

"Ryan, I am trying, but I mean, you are not looking any better" she laughs

"Just help us win, and you can have the prize all to yourself."

I pull her back over to the net and give her a look. She rolls her eyes.

"Okay, we are ready," I say.

Reid throws the ball up and serves it over.

I jump up, hitting it the hardest I can, and it goes straight into the sand—one point for us.

We go back and forth for about thirty minutes, and the scores tied at nine points apiece. Audrey is finally helping me out, and Claire is doing more work than he is.

It is our turn to serve; all we need to do is win. Well, there are still two more games, but this win would mean only one more fun because I will beat this guy again.

I throw the ball up and serve it over. Reid hits it back, and then I do.

Just me, and he goes back and forth, irritating me. I need to finish this guy off.

He punches it over, and I punch it back but lightly.

Claire is standing back, and it is like she wants to see who would win between us. Audrey has not even been trying to get in on this action, so I continue this war with Reid.

I finally get tired, and I just want to end this, so when he punches it over, I try to punch it as hard as I can, and then that is when Claire finally decides to jump in.

A Love That Blooms

Boom, the ball hits her right in her nose.

"Ahhhhhhh… RYAN!"

Oh no.

I run over to her, and she pushes me away.

"What were you doing"? Audrey yells out.

I am speechless. That did not turn out the way I planned that. Why did it have to be Claire to take the ball to the face?

Reid takes Claire into his arms, and everyone gathers around them. Emma takes her shirt off and puts it on Claire's face, which means she has a bloody nose.

I stand back while they deal with Claire, and I feel terrible.

She pushed me away; I knew I was the last person she wanted to see right now.

I need to figure out a way to have better luck because lately, I feel like my life is rolling downhill.

I need to get out of here, but first, I need to change out of this hideous shirt.

After going into the guest house to change, I get into my jeep and drive off to I have no idea where but as far away from here as I can get. I cannot go back to the city without saying goodbye, and at least trying to apologize to Claire, but I need to make sure Reid is gone before I do. All I need right now is to find something to do to take my mind off what happened and to give me time. I know just the place.

Pulling up the driveway, I get out of the jeep and shut the door. I walk through the tall grass and to the shop in the back. When I walk through the door, "Dan, you in here."

I see him sitting on his stool and working with wood. "Ryan, how are you"?

"I am doing the best I can. How are you, Dan"?

He pushes his glass back and turns on his stool towards me as I sit on the seat next to him. He is wearing his regular denim overalls and white shirt.

"Good. Where is that pretty lady of yours"?

"Claire is back at my parents' house. She could not make it here with me today. I just thought I could stop by, check on you, and see how you have been doing"?

"That is nice of you, but I do not need someone to check on me. I am doing very well. I work out all day, make these boxes, and think about my Susie."

This man loved his wife more than anything in the world, and I could learn something from him about what it is like to love someone.

"You want to tell me about Susie"?

He continues working on a box, and I just watch him.

"I met Susie when she was nineteen. She worked at the ice cream shop in town, and you know the one still open."

I shake my head. He must be talking about the ice cream shop I took Claire to. He continues.

"I would go in at a closing time to get a scoop of vanilla on a cone, and I would wait for her to get off work. She had a boyfriend back then, but it did not bother me. Anyways, I would always wait for her to finish closing, and then when she came out, I would talk to her and ask her out, but she would always turn me down for Steve. He was a bad guy, but I was not scared of him. She was the only thing that mattered to me, and her beauty, I knew I needed her."

He pauses to cough and continues to work on his box.

"One day, I found her crying on the bench outside the ice cream shop, and I put my arm around her and told her it would be okay. I knew she was crying over that other guy, but I showed her what kind of man I was, and it was at that moment that she kissed me. She never left my side after that day, and we married two weeks later. We were married for fifty years before Susie left me. I still count every year as another because if she were still here, we would still be happily married."

"Your story is awfully like Claire and me, but I do not think I will get the successful ending you got. Claire is my friend, and she does not know I have feelings for her. I feel like no matter what I do to try to get her. It always just backfires on me."

He looks at me, "Have you tried being honest with her? You need to let her know how you feel, and if you want her bad enough, you never give up."

Here is the second time today someone told me to be honest with her.

"I tried being honest with her, but I am not good with words. She is scared that she will lose me as a friend if we have a relationship since she has had bad luck with boyfriends in the past."

"If you think she is your person, and if she is, she will find her way to you. Just be honest, and never give up."

I watch him continue his box, and he makes it looks easy. Here was where I needed to come to take my mind away from what had happened.

109

"You want some help with that box? Could you show me a little bit of woodwork before I come to make that arch"?

"I would love to show you."

We spend the next few hours working on a box. Dan showed me how to cut the wood, sand it down, and put a new wood box together. He gave me more advice on how I could try to get Claire and even told me some more sweet stories about him and Susie. I only wish I could have a love like theirs. When Dan says the day is over for him, the sun starts to set, and I help him back to his house. Once I get him settled, I get back into my jeep and head back to the house. I can only hope that I was gone long enough that Reid is gone from my parents, and Claire is still awake.

When I pull up to the house, it looks like no light is inside. I park in front of the guest house, but when I get out, I walk to the back of my parents' house. I slide open the back patio door and close it behind me after I walk in. I just need to know if Claire is still awake. I tip top up the stairs so no one can hear me, and when I reach my old room, the door is closed. I turn the handle quietly and then crack it open. The room is dark, and it looks like Claire is already asleep. It seems like I am too late. I pull the door closed, but before I close it, I hear Claire say, "Ryan"?

I open it back up, "Yeah."

"You can come in," she says as she sits up and turns on the side table lamp.

I walk in and close the door. Then take a seat on the end of the bed.

"I want you to know I am sorry for today. I did not intend to hurt you."

"It is okay. I know you did not mean for it to happen."

Now is a perfect time for me to be honest with her.

I sit down on the bed and take her hand in mine. "Claire, I lied last week when I told you I was in the moment. It was not at the moment. Kissing you was something I had wanted to do for a long time. I like you so much, Claire. It scares me sometimes. I want more than a friendship with you. I know you are too scared to take a chance, but I want to promise that I can make you happy."

She turns her eyes away from me and bites her bottom lip.

"Ryan… Reid asked me to be his girlfriend before he left today."

I get up from the bed and throw my arms out to her.

"What did you say"?

"I said I do not know, but I would like to see where it goes."

I pace the room; this is not something I was expecting her to say. They have only been seeing each other for a couple of weeks, and I do not trust this guy.

"Claire, what do you want"?

"I just want to be happy. I want to be the world to someone and not just Claire, who never gets that second date. Can I have that with you? I do not know. We are friends, Ryan. Not just friends like best friends and the thought of losing you guts me. I do not want to take a chance, and then you are gone from my life forever. Then there is the thought of you being with someone else, and I lose you too. It is so complicated for me to decide on what I want right now."

"So, you want to be just friends then"? I sit back down on the end of the bed.

Minutes pass, and she shakes her head no and still does not answer my question.

"Listen, you do not have to decide right now, but I wanted you to know how I feel. Will I be waiting around forever for you? I do not know, but I feel what I feel for you right now, and it is not going away anytime soon. I do not want you to be the one that got away. I want you to be the one."

I get up from the bed and open the bedroom door to leave.

"Ryan"?

I turn around to her.

"Thank you for being honest with me."

I nod to her and then walk out of the room.

Chapter Ten

Claire

Two weeks have passed since that conversation with Ryan at his parent's, and nothing has changed since then besides the last conversation I had with him. When we returned to town and returned to work after that weekend, we had not seen each other once. Of course, I watch him walk into work mornings from the windows while standing in the shop, and there have been times I have come into work with my favorite iced coffee waiting for me on the front counter, but seeing him face to face, just has not happened. I do not know if he is giving me space to think about what he told me or if he is upset that I did not know what I wanted.

Reid and I have gone out, but I am with him sometimes and think about what Ryan is doing. Things with Reid have been going well, but I am still not ready for the next step with him, and I do not know if that is because of Ryan's confession or the fact that I do not know if I want a future with him. When did my life become a decision? It is not a decision that needs making, and the answer is right in front of me, but I do not see it. And when did my life get so confusing?

Tonight is our monthly meeting, and we have it at a restaurant. We are just two weeks from the town's gala for businesses, and I know the guys will want to talk about that, considering we are now decorating for the event. So tonight, I get to see Ryan and speak to him for the first time, and honestly, I am nervous. I wonder how he will act around me, what he will want to talk about, and I am worried because I miss him and what if he does not miss me.

"Claire! Hello"? Emma says to me, waving her hand in front of my face.

"Sorry, I was…." I take my hand off my chin from my elbow, resting on the counter.

"Thinking about tonight. I know you have not seen Ryan in a while."

"It is scary sometimes how well you know me" I laugh and then return to work.

Emma knows about the confession. When we got back into town, I hosted a girl's night with just the two of us at my apartment, watching Golden Girls and eating ice cream. Something we used to do every weekend. I hosted it because I was down about Ryan and needed to talk to her. She so kindly insisted that I give him a chance. She and Baker have known about his feelings towards me for a while, and they are rooting for us. I told her it was not easy. While I do feel things for him, I do not know what that means for us. She told me to stop overthinking things and just live for the moment. She wants to see me happy more than anyone else, and I know she is right.

So, if she is correct, then what is the hold-up? Why do I not just go for it and give Ryan a chance? That is because I once had a thing for Ryan, and he shut me down. I developed a crush on Ryan long before he did for me. A year ago, Ryan and I went to the Gala together, we held hands, and he was kind and sweet to me all night. I had started developing feelings for him before then and thought there was something there. That was until it was time to leave, and I could not find him anywhere, and that is when I caught him outside with another girl. He went with her that night, and I was heartbroken and alone. Granted, Ryan is not the same person he was then, and no one then knew that I had something for him because anytime someone asked, we would always say we were just friends. What if Ryan has not changed, I mean, he has been dating while I have, and I have seen him kiss other girls. What if I give Ryan a chance and then decide I am not what he wants? Then he goes right back to the Ryan he used to be. Not only will I be heartbroken again, but I will also lose the best friend I gained these last ten months.

Still, to this day, no one knows because it just happened that the day after the Gala was when Baker and Emma split over the secret the guys were keeping, and I had my secret to share with Emma then, and it was not that one. I plan to tell Ryan one day, but I want to when the time is right.

"You want to walk together to the restaurant soon? The guys are running late but wanted us to get the table."

"Sure. I am finishing now; if you want to go," I put the last bouquet in the cooler.

I grab my things from the back office, and Emma meets me there to get her stuff so we can leave. It is closing time, but the other employees close the shop for us on Friday nights. We walk out the front door, and I see the lights are still on in the guy's office building, so I know they are still working and hopefully will be joining us shortly.

"Ryan will be happy to see you tonight. He has been asking Baker about you since you two are not on speaking terms now."

"We are on speaking terms; we do not talk to each other. What all has Ryan been asking"?

"Just the normal. How are you, and are you still seeing that guy? Do not worry. Baker always tells him to ask you, but I guess he has not"

"That would be a no… to him asking me."

We arrive at the restaurant; Emma walks up to the host and gives her the table's name. Then we follow her to a booth at the back of the restaurant.

"Here you go, ladies. Enjoy"

I just stand there while Emma takes a seat.

"What are you doing, Claire"?

"Can I sit with you? If not, then I will sit by Ryan."

She laughs, "Claire, sit over there. He does not bite."

I slide into the booth, "But it will be awkward."

Emma picks up the menu and looks it over. So, I do the same while we wait.

"Hey, sorry we are late," Baker says, taking a seat by Emma.

When I look up, I see Ryan, and he gives me a slight smile before sitting down next to me.

"Hi," I say to him.

"How are you"? he asks me

"I am good" I nod

But the truth is I have been better.

The server comes to the table, and everyone gives her their drink and food order. Baker wants to start talking business when she walks away from the table.

"Okay, this year's Gala theme is under the stars. Have the two of you thought about what you want to do for the centerpieces this year and what the plan is"?

I let Emma take this question because, honestly, she has been talking to me about her plans, and since my mind has been in other places the last couple of weeks, I have not been listening.

"Yes, we will do all white flower arrangements for every table. I ordered gold stars to stick in the arrangements, and then we will have the delivery driver pick them up the morning of the event, and then we will be there to decorate the tables" she looks at me, and I nod in agreement.

"Have you girls gone to get your dresses yet"? Baker asks.

Last year Emma and I went shopping together to get all the things we needed for that night.

"I was hoping we could go this weekend; would that work for you, Claire"? Emma asks me.

"Oh, about that. I am not going this year," I say.

"What! You are going," Ryan says

"I do not have a reason to go. Emma will be the one to present them with our donation. I do not have a date or want to get fancy for just one night. You will have fun without me."

The memory of last year is why I do not want to go.

"You are going with me," Ryan says.

"I am sorry, but I do not remember you asking me to go."

"Claire, will you go to the Gala with me"? He turns to me when he asks.

"No… I already said I am not going."

Ryan is getting irritated with my decision not to go. Honestly, his reaction is not bothering me.

"What are you two donating this year"? Baker asks to try to change the subject.

I once again just let Emma answer, and then it dawned on me that I did not even need to be here for this meeting.

"We are going to do the same thing as last year," Emma says.

The server comes to the table with our food. After everyone gets plates, the guys want to continue the business.

"The old shop has not been doing very well lately. I was hoping one of you could go there next week to check on things and help the other girls get it back in order," Baker asks

"I will go," I say.

"Thanks, Claire," Emma says.

Me working at the old shop next week will hopefully help me take my mind off Ryan since I will not be watching him walk into work every day.

"I will check in with Emma daily about what has been going on there."

"Thanks," Baker says.

Ryan has not said a word, and I know it is because he may be upset with me, but I am not changing my mind. Going to the Gala will bring me back to the heartbroken feeling I felt last year, even if Ryan takes me.

So, this next week at the old shop, and when I return to the new shop, we will be working on centerpieces for the Gala, my mind should not be wandering for the next two weeks. While everyone is having fun at the Gala, I will get ice cream and watch romance films on Netflix.

Once we are all done eating, Emma and Baker are the first to leave, leaving me with Ryan at the booth. He typically walks me home afterward, so this is normal. Last month though, I did go to the meeting to meet Reid for dinner. I have no plans tonight.

"You ready to go home"? he asks me.

"Yeah"

When we leave the front doors, we walk down the sidewalk together to my place in silence.

"You do not have to walk me in."

"I do not know what is going on, but I do not understand why you think things need to be different today than they normally are. Like you not going with me to the Gala, and now you are telling me not to walk you in. What is the deal"?

I shrug my shoulders, "we have not exactly been talking to each other the last two weeks, and I do not know if that is my fault or yours. I just thought since things were different between us that things were changing"

"Nothing has changed with me, has it with you?"

"No, besides the fact that I have missed you. Also, my mind has been all over the place since the last time we talked."

He shakes his head, "So you have been thinking about it"?

We reach my building, and he opens the front door for me and then follows me to the elevator.

Once we are inside the elevator and going up, I tell him. "Yes, I have been thinking about it."

He smiles at me, and then the doors open.

119

We walk to my apartment door together, and I search around my bag for my keys. That is when I look up, and he is already unlocking the door with the key I gave him.

"Thanks," I say as he opens the door for me to walk in first.

After shutting the door, he sits on the couch, and I drop my bag on the kitchen counter before joining him on the sofa.

"You missed me. So, now that I am with you, what do you want to do"?

"Sleep, I want to sleep."

"You want me to stay here tonight," he asks with a smile.

"You can stay here till I fall asleep. I will be right back."

He has walked me home times and stayed till I fell asleep. He has never stayed all night, but he has remained into the wee hours of the morning.

I walk into my room, changing into shorts and the old football shirt that he gave me when I stayed at his apartment weeks ago and when I come back into the living room, he has it all set up with a blanket, pillow, and a movie on tv.

He pats the spot on the couch next to him, "Come here."

I sit, lay my head on the pillow on his lap, and cover up with the blanket. He started Crazy, Stupid, Love, and it made me smile that he remembered the movie from the week we stayed in the guest house.

"You want to come with me tomorrow? I am getting a dog," he asks me while playing with my hair.

Surprised by what he said, "You are getting a dog"?

"It gets lonely at my apartment these days, so I thought I could get a dog. I am rescuing a golden retriever named Tuck, and I am picking him up from the airport tomorrow afternoon."

I sit up on the couch so I can look at him.

"I would love to come with you tomorrow. My parents never let us have animals growing up, so I have never had a dog. We should get him all the special stuff after we pick him up."

"We can do that too."

"I am so excited. You will officially be a dog dad tomorrow," I say, laying my head back on his lap.

He laughs, "I guess I will."

We continue watching a movie, and I do not make it exceedingly long into it before my eyes start closing, and I try hard to stay awake.

When I wake up the following day, I am in my bed. Sometime during the night, Ryan must have picked me up off the couch and brought me to my bed. I look over to the clock on my side table to see the time, and there is a note there that says,

Good morning, Claire

Be ready by eleven

I will pick you up so we can get Tuck

See you then

121

Today will be such a good day for Ryan and me, and I am thrilled for him. I think I will see a side of him I have never seen before when he gets Tuck today.

After dressing, I slip on shoes, head down to the lobby of my apartment building, and wait for Ryan to pick me up. I stand against the wall, waiting when my phone goes off, and it must be Ryan telling me he is on his way.

I open my phone, and it is Reid.

Reid- I will be off tonight if you want to go to dinner.

It has been days since I saw him, and while I would like to go to dinner, I do not want to mess up a good day with Ryan. Today is a big day for him, and I want to be there.

Ryan pulls up outside, so I meet him out front.

"Are you ready"? I say, getting in and shutting the door.

"So Ready," he says as we drive off.

The airport is close to town, and we both stay silent the way there. And I know it is because Ryan seems nervous. Heck, I am even anxious. What if Tuck does not like me, or what if he thinks I look mean? Today is a big day for me, too, because I could potentially be a dog mom for Tuck. I mean, Ryan and I are not together, but since we are friends and live close to each other, I could dog sit and walk him when he needs to go out, or at least I would like to think that Ryan would let me do those things.

We pull up outside the exit at the airport and park the car by the sidewalk. We are meeting the air transporter with Tuck at the baggage claim, so once we get there, is it just a waiting game for them to show up?

Ryan seems calm, but I can tell he is just ready to meet him. He keeps looking around the room. Anytime someone

A Love That Blooms

passes by with a pet carrier, Ryan gets a smile. Bags start coming through the baggage carousel, and I know we are getting close. I start looking around, and I spot a man pushing a per carrier on a rolling cart. The cage is giant, so I know it must be him.

I nudge Ryan, "I think this is him."

He turns to me with a nervous smile, and the man walks up to us.

"Ryan Hayes"?

"That is me."

"Here is your new dog."

The man opens the door on the carrier, and a dark golden retriever emerges.

We both get down low to the ground, and Tuck instantly goes up to Ryan, licking him on the face, and it is the cutest thing I have ever seen in my life. Then he comes over to me and licks me on the front, and we cannot control our laughs.

"Hey, Tuck. It is so nice to meet you," I say, petting him while he licks me.

Ryan gets down on his knees and holds Tuck's leash so he does not run away.

"Here is the paperwork, sir, and if you have any questions, the contact number is on the paperwork." The man tells him, and Ryan takes the papers.

"Thank you so much," Ryan tells the man before he walks away.

I continue to pet Tuck, and he has taken us well.

"You ready to go? We can take him to the pet store and grab some lunch."

"Yes, sounds good."

Ryan takes him by the leash and listens well when we tell him to stay down while we walk to the car. He is so excited that he just wants us to love him.

"I will ride in the back with him if you want me to."

"Yeah, that is a clever idea."

I hop in the back, and Ryan lets him in with me before shutting the door. He jumps on my lap to look out the window, and then when Ryan takes off, Tuck lays his head on my lap while we drive.

"So, what is the information on him"? I ask

Ryan looks at me through the rear-view mirror. "They think he is three years old, and they found him abandoned and were close to having to put him down because they did not have any more room for animals. I found him on the internet and knew I needed to save him."

I frown, the thought of them putting this sweet boy down breaks my heart, and Ryan is so dear to save him.

Tuck is asleep on me when we get to the pet store, but I was so impressed with how well he rode in the car, and I am sure the trip here was exhausting for him. I take him by the leash, and we make our way inside.

"I need everything, so I'll grab a cart," Ryan says.

While he gets the cart, I take Tuck down the toy aisle and let him pick out anything he wants. He sniffs around and then picks up a long blue rope with knots. We are talking like a five-foot-long rope, and he starts dragging it down the aisle, happy, so I just let him. We round the corner, and Ryan is laughing.

"He picked it, and it could not tell him, no, so I guess he wants to take it home" I shrug.

"If that is what he wants."

We all walk the store together, Ryan throwing food, bowls, a bed, and a crate in the cart. At the same time, he let me pick out the collar and a new leash. We payout, hoping we got everything we needed, and then load the jeep. I get in the back again and let Tuck lay his head on me while we make our way to Ryan's apartment.

When we get out of the car, I take Tuck for a walk in the grass across the street from Ryan's apartment building while he unloads the stuff. I want Tuck to like his new home, so I let him sniff around for a while and do his business before we go up the apartment.

"Come on, Tuck, you want to see your new home" I tug on the leash, and he comes.

We take the elevator, and Tuck seems unsure of it, but he still does a beautiful job as a good boy. And then, we walk into the apartment. He gets excited when he sees Ryan and tries to tackle him on the couch. We both start laughing. Then Tuck starts walking around the house, sniffing around, while Ryan and I stay on the couch.

"Thanks for coming with me today."

"It is no problem, and I like him."

Tuck comes back into the living room and jumps up on the couch, lying between us. I lost track of time today helping Ryan, and when I look down at my watch, I notice that I still have time to meet Reid for dinner.

"Well, I should probably get going," I say, giving Tuck one last loving before getting up from the couch.

"Already? There is still daylight left," Ryan says, looking at his watch.

"I know, but I have plans tonight. I can stop by later to tell Tuck goodnight."

Ryan smiles, "I think he would like that."

I tell them goodbye and head to my apartment to get ready for my date with Reid.

Reid wanted me to meet him in the park, so we could eat at the food stand just like we did on our first date. He said he was running late and could not walk with me from my place. I have been waiting on a park bench for about thirty minutes, and if Reid does not show up soon, I will walk to Ryan's apartment to see Tuck. I send Reid a message to make sure he is not bailing on me, and he sends me one back that says turn around.

"There you are. I was getting worried you were going to be a no-show," I say, turning around.

"I have never done that to you before. Why would I do that now," Reid says, taking my hand for me to get up and walk with him.

We make our way to the hot dog stand, ordering the same thing we ordered the first time we came here, and then sit back down on the bench to eat.

"I am going to see my grandmother on Monday, and you think you could make a bouquet for me to take"

"Emma can make one for you. I \will be working at the old shop all week, so I will be across town," I say and then take a bite.

A Love That Blooms

We finish eating quietly and then walk through the park, holding hands. He is not his usual self; tonight, it is like he has something on his mind or does not want to be here.

"What did you do today"? I ask him.

"I went to the fire station to wash the trucks, and that is about it," he says.

I wonder why he was late if that was all he did.

"What did you do today"? He asks me.

"I went with Ryan to pick up his new dog," I say.

He shakes his head, clearly annoyed.

"Why do you still spend time together with him? Do you not remember how he treated you the weekend I visited his parents? How could you forget the nosebleed"?

"He is my friend, and he was sorry for those things. You just were not there to see him apologize. Today was a big day for him, and I wanted to be there."

We continue walking, and I do not want to keep talking about Ryan because Reid does not understand.

"I would not be friends with him," he says

"You do not have to be friends with him."

Because the truth is, I know they do not like each other, and I do not want them to be friends anyway. It would be too much for me.

Chapter Eleven

Ryan

It is getting late, and I figured I would have heard from Claire by now if she were going to stop by. After she left earlier today, I let Tuck get used to the place, and after taking him outside for a walk, we both took a nap together on the couch. He misses having Claire around, he keeps looking at the front door of my apartment, whining, and I know it must be because he is waiting for her to return. Me to a friend, me too.

I was not expecting her to leave so early today, and I knew where she was going when she said she had plans. When I chose to give her time to think, leaving the room after being honest with her, I did not expect her to end things with Reid, and I knew she would continue to see him while she thought about what she wanted. What did surprise me, though, during her thinking time, was the fact she did not want to go to the gala, and even though I should be happy that she was not taking what is his name, I was not taking it well that she did not want to go with me? There must be a good reason for her not to want to go.

"Come on, Tuck, let's go for a walk" I grab his leash from the kitchen island, and he runs to me, ready to go outside.

After hooking it on him, we get in the elevator, which is fun, considering Tuck does not like to ride in it, so he always acts silly when we are in it. He runs right out the elevator door when it opens and pulls me through the front doors. He loves taking walks, and I am happy that I finally have a reason to get out every night.

He takes off once we get out the building doors.

"Slow down, boy," I say as we walk towards the park.

He does not slow down; he walks like he is on a mission to find something.

"Tuck," I say, trying to pull on the leash to see if that would help him slow down, but he continues to go on his mission. He just likes the park.

We come close to the park, and he is almost running now, so I jog to keep up with him. He stops, sits, and starts barking when we get through the park entrance.

"Tuck," I hear someone say, and when I come around the corner, there is Claire and... Reid.

"Hey, he must have smelled you from way back there. He dragged me here," I say, trying to catch my breath.

Tuck has jumped up on Claire, and she is petting him while he licks her face.

"I missed you too, Tuck," she says.

Reid looks annoyed, and Claire does not seem to care.

"Well, I am sorry to interrupt your date. Tuck and I will continue our walk. You two have a great night," I say, pulling Tuck towards me by his collar.

"Thank you," Reid says, taking Claire's hand.

"I will see you two later. Goodnight, Tuck," Claires says, giving him one last pet on the head, and then takes off with Reid out of the park.

I try to continue my walk with Tuck, but he turns around and starts whining for Claire to come back.

"I know, Tuck, but we got to keep going," I tell him, and he lays down.

I peeked out of the entrance to see what way they went, and it was in the direction of my apartment. So, I wait a bit to make sure the coast is clear, and then I get Tuck to walk with me knowing he will at least have a little of Claire's scent and I can get him home. When I took her today with me to get Tuck, I did not realize that he would love her more than he does me.

I finally got Tuck back to the apartment, and since we saw Claire at the park, I do not think she will be stopping by. Plus, it is late now. Instead of making Tuck sleep in his crate for the night, I know he misses Claire, so I let him sleep in bed with me to get comfortable. While he falls asleep quickly, I can not help but lay there and think about what Claire sees in Reid. I have been trying to track him from his Instagram account, and in the last week, I have not been able to find anything new, but something tells me he is hiding something.

Since we are back to the work week, I had to leave Tuck in his crate for the day. I did stop by on my lunch and take him for a walk before heading back to work. I have a dinner meeting tonight with clients, and since I may be gone for a couple of hours, Claire is coming to my apartment to play with Tuck and keep him company.

Playing with him has become a full-time job, and I am so glad that Claire wants to help take on the responsibility of taking care of him too. She came over yesterday and spent the day with us. We went for a walk through the park, played catch, watched movies, and I even got a cute picture of the two of them taking a nap on the couch. She is mom to him, and I honestly could not be happier right now besides the fact that there is still someone else in Claire's life, and as much as I want her to myself right now, it is just not possible. There is still a choice for her, and it will be him or me.

I am getting ready for dinner while Claire and Tuck hang out on the couch. This dinner is at a fancy place, so I needed to come home to change before going. I put on a nice black suit jacket, fitted black pants, and a white button leaving the top buttons undone. I look at myself in the mirror to fix my hair and walk into the living room.

"Alright, do you have everything you need for the night," I ask Claire before I leave for dinner.

"Yes! We will be fine, Tuck" she pets him, and he lifts his head before laying back down.

"Okay, hopefully, I will not be late. If there is anything you need, call me."

"Ryan… we will be okay. You can go."

I take my keys off the island and, for a reason, have an urge to kiss Claire goodbye, but I sadly ignore it and head to the door.

"You two do not have too much fun without me."

"Hey… you look nice, by the way," Claire says with a smile.

I answer her with a smile before shutting the door.

This meeting tonight is just a typical business meeting with other real estate brokers in the area, and we talk about ways we could make the city better. A year ago, this was a meeting I would not be having since I wanted Hayes Reality to be the best in the city. So glad that my perspective of my life has changed for me. I just wish I knew then the things I know now. Baker is not meeting with us tonight, and I am to take care of our side of this meeting myself, which is another thing that has changed. I used to put Baker in charge of everything and sit back and watch.

I pull up to the restaurant, and the valet driver takes my keys to park my car when I get out.

"Ryan Hayes, I am here for the meeting," I tell the host.

She walks me back to a secluded room towards the back of the restaurant, and when I get in, I am the first person there.

This restaurant is one of the fanciest places to eat in New York City, and I have only been here once before for the same type of meeting. The restaurant's setting is dark, and all the tables have white table clothes. You need a reservation, and it will take weeks to be able to get in. We usually schedule our reservation for the meeting months in advance.

I sit to wait for everyone and pull out my phone to see Claire send me a photo of her and Tuck watching a movie. I have only been gone for minutes, and I already miss them and wish I were there.

When I look at my watch, I see that I have some more minutes before the meeting starts, so I get up to use the bathroom, so I would not have to go while we have the discussion. I walk out of the room and down a hallway to a bathroom. I use it quickly and then wash my hands. Taking one more look at myself in the mirror, I fix the buttons on my sleeve and then leave.

I walk back down the hallway, and before I reach the door, I notice a guy at a table with a woman holding flowers that I have seen before. I take a closer look, and sure enough, it is Reid. Before I open the door to the room, I try to look at the woman he is sitting with, and her flowers have to come from Bloom. Since I am here for a meeting, I do not want to cause a scene. I go in the door, take a seat, and try to produce a plan in my head that is not me punching him in the face but something better.

People for the meeting start coming in, and while I say hello to all of them and listen to their conversations, my head is elsewhere. I need to get out there and confront Reid and find out who the woman is. Everyone is here for the meeting, and the server starts all of us off with a glass of wine. We all order our food, and everyone but me starts talking business. I try to listen the best I can and put thoughts in occasionally, but I know I cannot wait too long to go back out there, or he will be gone.

"Excuse me, everyone, but I will be right back" I stand up and nod.

When I leave the room, I see he is still there and does not even notice me. I wait for a second because I do not want to get rude to him, I need to keep calm when I talk to him, because this may be a friend or something, I mean Claire and I spend time together all the time, and he has not thrown a fit yet.

I walk over to him, and he finally notices me, and his face says it all. He is shocked, and this is a date. He puts his head down and hands over his face.

"Hey, I am Ryan Hayes. And who might you be"? I ask the woman sitting with him.

She takes a long look at me and then Reid before she answers.

"I am Hannah Anderson, and this is my husband, Reid."

He's married. I would have never guessed, but this is not good.

"We are separated but still married," Reid says, and the woman does not like that answer.

"Look, Hannah, I know your husband here, and if you do not mind, I would like to have a word with him outside."

Reid gets up from the table and tells her he will be back. Then we walk outside.

"What is going on here"? I ask him.

"I moved here because of her. She left me over a year ago, and I followed her here, hoping she would not want a divorce and we could work on our marriage. We have seen other people occasionally, and I did not mean to bring Claire into this, but it just happened," he paces while talking to me.

"What do you mean it just happened? You could have told her at any time this last month that you were married. You are here tonight with your wife, with flowers that you got from Bloom, where Claire is the one that made them. What does Claire think when you come in to order flowers"?

"She thinks they are for my grandmother. I have lied to Claire, and I do not mean to, but I cannot let her know the truth. Claire was someone that I was interested in from coming into the shop, and she is great, like great, but I could never tell her that I was married. I am still married, but Claire means so much to me."

"You need to call Claire tonight. You need to confess everything to her, and you need never see her again. You hear me because if you do not do it, then she will be hearing this from me, and I do not think she would like that." I tell him to his face.

He puts his head down, "I will tell her tonight. I promise"

"Good," I say and then head back inside the restaurant.

A Love That Blooms

I feel like I managed that well, but Claire will not be managing that very well at all. I think this is a moment I should be happy, that Claire will finally not be with him, but it is not. She will be heartbroken, and it will be the same broken she was when she never got a call back for a second date while dating on the dating app. She will fall into a dark hole again, but I need to be there for her more than before.

I finished the dinner meeting, and I still have not been able to take my mind off what happened here tonight. I cannot say anything to Claire when I return to my apartment. It is not my business to be telling her, and I know I should say something as a friend, but it just does not feel right.

When I walk into the apartment, Claire and Tuck are passed out together on the couch. Marley and Me are playing on the tv. She made it easier for me not to say anything by being asleep, and I did not want to wake her. I told Reid to call her tonight, but I feel it could be tomorrow before he says anything. He already has explaining to do to his wife. I take a blanket and cover Claire up. Leaving her phone close to her on the coffee table in case he does call. After changing out of my nice clothes and putting on shorts, I join them on the couch, where we all will sleep for the night.

When I wake up in the morning, they are still sleeping in the same position they fell asleep, and as I thought, I never heard Claire's phone go off last night. I get up to shower, and I plan to wake her when I finish so I can take her to her place so she can get ready for work. It is early, and the sun has not even come out yet, so she will have time before she needs to be at the shop across town.

When showering, I replay the conversation with Reid in my head, and I hope he takes care of this today because I do not want to have to tell Claire. I get out of the shower and hear a knock on the bathroom door, and when I open it, with a towel wrapped around my waist.

135

"I have to go. I just wanted you to know before I left," Claire says with a frown.

"Let me drive you."

"I will get a cab but thank you for the offering. I need to leave right now."

She starts to walk out of my bedroom.

"Is everything okay"? I say, following her out of the room.

"I do not know, but I will talk to you later, okay"? she gets to the door.

"Okay, I will check on you later," I tell her before she leaves

Reid must have contacted her while I was in the shower, and while I would generally demand to find out what was going on, this time, I already knew. I need to ensure I check in on her throughout the day and want her to know I will be there for her.

We get to lunchtime, and I still have not heard anything from Claire. Baker called us for lunch and said Emma would join us in the conference room, so we would have room to eat together. I somehow sense that they know about Claire and want to tell me. It is then that I realize I do not know if I should say to them or not that I already know. There could be a chance that Claire could find out, and then she would hurt even more.

I walk to the conference room, and they are talking and eating, so maybe this is all of us having lunch instead.

"Smells good. What did you order"?

"Sandwiches from The Sandwich Shop. Emma stopped over at the old shop and grabbed us lunch before coming back," Baker says while Emma is busy eating.

"How is the old shop doing"? I ask while taking a seat.

"Claire said Lexi and Liv have not been getting along, so we are going to split them up and bring one over here to work," Emma says.

"Does that mean Claire is staying over there"

"Yes. Today Claire volunteered to stay over there until we get someone to fill the spot. It should not take long considering we have so many people to choose from at the new shop to fill the spot. It is just figuring out who," Emma says before taking another bite of her sandwich.

Claire, not working with me for who knows how long makes me sad. I have gotten so used to being close to her.

"We need to talk about Claire, actually," Emma says.

"What about Claire"? I ask as if I know nothing is going on.

"She needs you."

"What do you mean she needs me"? I am suddenly not hungry.

"This morning, Reid called her and told her he is married. He lied to her about multiple things and came to town to get his wife back but somehow ended up dating Claire. She is not good and has been upset all morning while working at the other shop. We think you need to be there for her, and since we know how you feel about her, you are the perfect person to get Claire back to herself."

"It is not that easy… I knew about this"

"WHAT!" Emma says.

"I found Reid at the restaurant last night with his wife while attending that meeting. I was the one who told him he needed to be the one to tell her, and if she found out that, I knew she would be even more hurt, but it was not my place to tell her. Also, he saw other people while talking to her, and I found things on his social media."

"Why did you not tell her anything? You could have saved her long ago, and she would be with you now instead of feeling hurt."

Emma is not happy with me right now.

"It was not my place to say anything. Claire would not have believed me, considering she knows how I feel about her. She would think I was telling her that, so she would be with me instead."

"Which is not a terrible thing. You could have saved her from all this heartache."

"I did my job, I told her how I felt about her, and she has not responded. We have continued just being friends."

Baker is just sitting back and enjoying all the words Emma and I are sharing.

"Ryan… will you please be there for her? She needs you more than anyone right now."

I cannot help but think Emma is saying this because she knows the feeling that lies between Claire and me. Claire has not said she has feelings towards me, but Emma would understand if she did.

"I will do my best, but I cannot guarantee anything. Why do you want me to be there for Claire when you are her best friend and a girl so you can deal with this situation better than me"? I say before finally eating my food.

"I tried this morning, and she did not want to talk about it. I asked her if she wanted to get together tonight for a girl's night, and she said she was not interested. I then tried anything, telling her she should go to the gala with us next weekend and we could get dresses Saturday, but she would not budge and got even more upset. She has been around you more in the last few months than anyone, so I think you should try something."

"I will figure something out, but I am sure she just needs time to process everything."

"Do you know why she will not go to the Gala? I have tried asking her since she told us the other night she was not going, but I cannot figure out why," Emma asks me.

"No, I have no idea why."

I still want to talk to her about this, but now is not the time to.

We finish our lunch, and Claire does not come up again.

When I get back to my office, I send Claire a quick message to check on her, and if she is as upset as Emma says, I do not believe she will get back to me today. The last time Claire was upset over the dating app thing, she spent days to herself in her apartment before she finally wanted to talk to someone about what was going on, and I would consider this situation worse.

I return to work on my computer when I hear my phone go off.

Claire- Can we talk later tonight?

I was not expecting her to want to talk now about what was happening, so I was surprised when I read her message.

Me- Of course, come to my place when you get off.

Emma was right, and I am the only person who can be there for her right now.

I left work early because I wanted to take Tuck on a walk before Claire showed up to talk, and I wanted to make sure I had a clear mind when she showed up so I could be there for her. I do not know if she wants to talk about Reid or something else on her mind. For all I know, she could just want to see Tuck put a smile on her face.

After our walk and mind-clearing, Tuck and I wait for Claire to show up by playing a game of catch in the living room. Every time I throw the ball, he brings it back to me and then will wait by the door, and it is like he knows she is coming over.

I hear a faint knock, and then the door opens. Tuck runs to the door, tackling Claire before she can even get in. "Hey buddy, how are you doing"? she says to him.

"Sorry, I think he was waiting for you," I tell her while she closes the door.

"I think I miss him as much as he misses me all day," she laughs, and it is good to see she is all right.

She sits her stuff down on the kitchen island before taking a seat by me on the couch with Tuck sitting on her.

"You want something to eat or anything, we can call in some dinner"?

"That is okay, and I am not that hungry."

I take that as a sign, as maybe she is not staying that long.

"So, what did you want to talk about"? I ask her.

She gets Tuck to calm down and lay on her, then sits back, takes off her shoes, and puts her feet on the couch. She is getting comfortable, which means this could be a serious conversation.

"I have a secret that I think I need to tell you."

"A secret"? I say, surprised.

I do not know where this is going.

"There is a reason I do not want to go to the Gala this year."

This conversation is not about Reid.

I nod for her to go on.

"Last year, we went together, and I had the best time with you. We had been spending time together for weeks, and I had developed a little bit of a crush on you. Anyways, that night I had planned to tell you when we left that I was starting to catch feelings. When it came time for us to leave, I used the bathroom, then chatted with the other guest, and then went looking for you, and that is when I found you outside with someone, and you left that night with her, and I went home, alone, and heartbroken. I was sure you could sense I was feeling a way for you, but I was wrong. So, I do not want to go this year because I am scared it will return the memory of last year. I just wanted to let you know why I told you no, and I am sorry, but I still do not want to go."

Wow. I do not even know what to say, and this is unexpected.

"Claire, I am so sorry. I had no idea at all. I hate that I did that to you. I was a different person then than I am now, and I wish I could take back that feeling from you. I do."

"I felt that you did not know then, and I cannot be mad at you for it because you did not know. I had been holding that secret for a long time and felt I needed to tell you."

I did not know Claire had a thing for me then. We were spending time together but considered ourselves friends to everyone, and it was not long after the gala last year that I started developing more than friends' feelings for her. I wish I had known before that night because I would have never left her alone that night, and the thought of leaving her hurts. I used to be oblivious to everything in my life then; honestly, she changed me.

I will regret this, but I need to share mine if she wants to tell me a secret.

"Claire, I have something I need to tell you."

I take her hand in mine and hope for the best.

"I know about Reid…."

She interrupts me, "I do not want to talk about him to you anymore. We do not see each other; he does not matter to me."

"I saw him at the restaurant last night with his wife."

She lets go of my hand, "Why did you not tell me"?

"Because it was not my place to tell you. I pulled Reid outside and told him he needed to call you could confess everything to you. I felt there was something with him, but I never expected him to be married. I have seen him in pictures with other girls but never with her. I feel like if I had been the one to tell you, you would not have believed me and thought I was telling you because I have my feelings for you."

"What do you mean seeing him in pictures with other girls"?

"I saw weeks ago that he was in photos on social media with a girl from the club. I did not know if it was just the server or if they saw each other. You two were not official, so I thought I did not need to tell you because we had been spending time together, shared a kiss, and I did not know if it would be important to you."

She shakes her head and then gets up from the couch like she is going to leave.

"It would have been nice to know those things, Ryan, and I would not have continued to see him. Those are not qualities I look for when talking to a guy. You knew this guy was a jerk the whole time, and you just continued to let me see him. I do not understand."

"I cannot tell you what to do and not do. That is not who I am. That is why I would have been thrilled for you not to see Reid anymore is not a choice I could make. I needed you to figure out who he was yourself. All this time, I have wanted nothing but you, and yes, I could have made it easier for you to pick me by just telling you about him, but I wanted to be a choice. I wanted you to choose me instead. I want to mean something to you, and you to look at me like you want to be with me."

"We are friends, Ryan. I would have thought you had my back on something like this"

"So, is that all you want to be, just friends? Because if that is the case, then yes, I will have your back next time. I will make sure that you never date another guy like him. I figured I could have done that by just being with you to ensure you never had to be with anyone else anyway."

"Maybe just being friends is best for the both of us," she says.

She gives Tuck a goodbye and then walks out the door.

I pick up Tucks ball and throw it at the wall. That conversation did not go the way it should have.

Chapter Twelve

Claire

I made a mistake, and I regret it. Did I mean to tell Ryan we should be friends? No, I did not. At that moment, I was angry at him for keeping a secret from me, but when I realized I had kept one from him, I knew I should not have acted that way. So now things are weird between the two of us again. I miss him, and I miss Tuck. Since I was the one who screwed up this time, it is on me to find a way to make it up to him. I think the most responsible thing I should do is apologize and then go from there.

I have been thinking about this all week, considering I needed to give myself time to produce a plan because I learned the hard way that you cannot just say things at the moment when you have a difficult day. You see, when I went to Ryan's house to tell him my secret, it was the same day Reid called telling me all about how he was married and trying to get back with his wife, and he did not mean to drag me into the mix, but it just happened. While upset then, I realized that I have terrible taste in men and that you should not keep secrets. I calmed myself down for the day and went to Ryan's because he needed to know why I would not go to the gala since it had to do with him. I was not expecting him to have his secret, and while I was mad at him then, I have thought long and hard about everything he said this week. He was right about everything, it was not his place, and I am glad I learned about Reid on my own because I would have accused Ryan of saying something like that to get me.

What I did not realize then, and I do now, is just how Ryan cares about me. He cares so much that he could have taken the uncomplicated way to me and told me about Reid, but he did not. He is right, and he should be a choice for me to make. I should choose him. That has constantly been on my mind since I left his apartment.

First, I am going to see if I can see Tuck. Ryan would not be able to tell me no because he knows how Tuck and I miss each other. Then when I get to see them, that is when I will apologize. It has been a week, and since I am still at the old shop working with Liv, I have not even been able to catch a glimpse of Ryan.

I take a minute in the back office and pull my phone out to text him. I take a deep breath.

Me- Hey. I was just wondering if I could see Tuck tonight. I miss the little guy.

I sit back in the desk chair and just wait now.

And wait.

Wait some more.

When did one minute feel like thirty?

My phone pings with a text, and my phone is still in my hand.

Ryan- He misses you too. Come by later tonight.

Me- Thank you

Well, that turned out to be easier than I thought it would be. Now I look forward to closing the shop for the day to go home. This last week has been a lonely one, and besides going to help Emma pick out a gala dress one day, I have just been lying around my apartment thinking about Ryan and, of course, Tuck.

Speaking of the gala, I will finally be back with Emma later this week at the old shop. We are going to be working on the arraignments for the event. Last year we made them, and then Baker and Emma set them up. Since I am not going this year, I volunteered to set everything up and do the decorating. I figured it would help me prepare for Emma and Baker's wedding in just a couple of weeks.

It is crazy to think we are so close to them getting married and being spouses even though they are already. Ryan will need to go to the Hamptons soon to make the arch with Dan, and I cannot wait to see how it will look. Ryan and I need to be back to where we were as friends before wedding week, and I know we can get there with time.

I close the shop with Liv and take a cab to get home. I will be happy when I am back to being close to my apartment and can walk home when getting off work. When I get to my apartment, I quickly change into a sundress and slip-on sandals before leaving and walking down to Ryan's apartment building.

I knock and wait for him to answer when I reach his door. I can hear Tuck bark, but Ryan is not answering the door. I pull my phone out of my bag and dial his number to call to make sure he is there. It rings repeatedly, then goes straight to voicemail. I dig around my bag for my keys. Ryan gave me a key to his place, just like I gave him a key to mine. I find his key and open the door. Tuck is so happy to see me. I notice his bed in the crate has stuffing coming out the side, making me think that Tuck has been in there all day.

I take Tuck out, put on his leash, and then after I grab my phone, I walk him downstairs to take him on a walk. I have no idea where Ryan could be and why he has not been home today.

When we get to the park, Tuck immediately uses the bathroom, and while doing his business, I try to call Ryan again. I still do not get an answer. So, I try to call Emma to see if she is still at the shop, and she can check to see if Ryan is still in the office. It continues to ring with no answer.

"Where is everyone," I say to myself.

When Tuck finishes, I take him for a walk around the park and just wait for someone to call me back. After thirty minutes pass by with no one calling me back, I head back to Ryan's apartment to see if he will show up there. He could have had something happen to his phone, which is why he could not contact me.

We get up to the apartment, and Tuck brings me his ball to throw, so I throw it, and he brings it back to me. I feel anxious and keep looking at my phone, waiting for someone to call me back. Tuck finally stops playing catch, so I watch a dog movie on tv. He jumps on the couch beside me and lays down.

An hour has passed before my phone finally rings, and when I pick it up to answer it, it is Emma.

"Hey, where are you"? I ask her.

"Claire… we are at the hospital. Something is wrong with Catherine."

"What happened? What hospital are you at"?

She tells me they transported Catherine to a hospital in the city close to Ryan's apartment. They do not know what is wrong with her, but everyone is at the hospital waiting for answers. I tell her I am at Ryan's apartment and will be on my way there before I hang up the phone.

I put Tuck back in his crate and told him I was sorry before grabbing my bag to leave. When I go to the sidewalk, I hail a cab to take me to the hospital. I could have walked, but my nerves could not take the time it would take me to get there. I need to be there quickly.

Thankfully, traffic was light, so it did not take long for it to drop me off at the emergency entrance. I walk through the door and try to remember where Emma said they were inside the hospital. I walk through double doors into a waiting room, and that is when I see Jack standing with his arms crossed. When I walk toward him, I see everyone else standing. Ryan sees me when he turns around, walks toward me, and I open my arms. He falls into me, and we hold on to each other for minutes.

"I am so sorry, Ryan."

He pulls back from me, takes my hand, and we sit.

"Have you heard anything yet"? I ask him.

"Not yet. Dad thinks it could have been a heart attack or a stroke, but he is unsure. The doctor should be out soon with answers."

"I went to your apartment and let Tuck out for a walk."

"Thank you, and I left my phone at the office. Dad called us around lunch, and we came straight here."

Everyone in the room is quiet; we just sit and wait for the doctor.

Minutes turn into hours before someone finally comes out.

"Hayes family," a nurse comes out.

Everyone gets up from their seats when they hear her say the name.

We all gather around her to hear the update.

"Catherine just got out of surgery. She had a heart attack and required emergency surgery. We did a procedure she seems it be doing all right."

You can feel in that moment how relaxed everyone became just from her saying those words.

"When can we go back to see her"? Jack asks.

"Well, since it is late, we will let one of you go in tonight, and the rest of you can come back tomorrow. We would like to keep her here for a couple of days to keep an eye on her"

"Thank you so much," Jack says to the nurse

When she walks away, Jack turns around, and Baker and Ryan embrace him.

"You all go home for the night; it is late, and I will update you on anything if something happens. The nurse said she would be all right, so you boys get rest," Jack tells Baker and Ryan.

"Are you sure, Dad? We can spend time together here if you need us," Baker says.

"I will be fine; you all go home, and I will see you tomorrow."

"If you need anything, please let me know. I will be here first thing in the morning," Baker says, taking Emma's hand for them to leave.

Jack nods to him, and they walk out the waiting room doors.

"I should probably get going," I say before hugging Jack.

"Thank you for coming, Claire," Jack says to me.

Ryan takes my hand to stop me from walking away. "I'll come with you," he says

"I will see you in the morning," Ryan says to his dad.

Jack starts walking towards the hospital rooms, and we leave.

We are walking in silence, and I know Ryan has things on his mind. Even though the nurse said Catherine would be all right, Ryan would still be apprehensive about her.

"I will take you home," he says to me.

"Thank you," I say as we walk to his jeep.

We ride the whole way to my apartment in more silence. I do not know what to say, but I want to be there for him. Catherine is Ryan's world, and she also means so much to me. I know the thought of being close to losing her today will be running through his head. It has been going through mine.

We pull up outside my apartment building.

"Want me to stay with you… tonight" I ask Ryan.

"You want to"?

"Of course, I want to. I will get my stuff for work tomorrow."

"I will wait for you."

I get to my apartment and pack everything I need for tonight and tomorrow. This is a new feeling staying the night with him since this is the first time I would be staying without just falling asleep there.

When we get to Ryan's place, he takes Tuck out for a walk while I get ready for bed. We decided we would have a sleepover in the living room on the sectional since we would only be sleeping a couple of hours. It is late, and why I would like to go to the hospital with Ryan in the morning to check on Catherine, I need to be at the shop. We are shorthanded at the old shop, and I know Liv could not manage the place alone. We also cannot get behind on orders with the gala coming up in just a few days.

I am in the bathroom, taking out my contacts and putting on my glasses, then throwing my hair up in a ponytail to sleep in when Ryan returns from taking Tuck on a walk. I can hear him talking to him and apologizing for making him stay in his crate all day. Just the cute conversation puts a slight smile on my face. When I join them in the living room, Ryan already has our pallets made on the couch, and he is lying in his spot, my pillow behind his. So, I lay down behind him, and Tuck jumped to lay down by my feet. The lights are off, and Ryan has on the tv.

"Claire…"

"Yes," I say, looking up at the ceiling.

"Thank you for staying tonight and coming to the hospital."

"You are welcome."

I close my eyes to try to fall asleep, but I can tell Ryan is struggling.

"Your mother is a powerful woman who will get through this, Ryan."

"I know… Today was a wake-up call for me. What if…" He rolls over his stomach to look at me, "What if it was worse than it was, and I never got to see or talk to her again."

I roll over on my stomach so I can look at him. "But she is still here and going to be all right."

He takes my hand, "I am sorry for last week."

"If anyone should be sorry, it should be me. I said things I regret."

"Well… Goodnight, Claire" he rolls over on his back, pulling his blanket up.

"Goodnight, Ryan," I say, rolling over and closing my eyes again.

Today is the longest working day I have ever had. Ryan wanted me to go with him to the hospital this morning, but it was not possible with work being busy, and I feel terrible. I have tried checking in on him as much as I can throughout the day, and he even face-timed me with Catherine. She looked great for everything that had happened to her in the last twenty-four hours, and she was in good spirits, making her feel much better. They said she is doing so well that she can go home today, which is fantastic. She is to rest for weeks, so it looks like Jack and she will miss the gala this weekend too.

Ryan and Baker tried to get Catherine to stay in town at one of their places, but she insisted she just wanted to be home, so when she got out, Jack would drive them to their house in the Hamptons. Ryan wants to be with her, so he will load up Tuck and follow behind them.

Liv is working on arrangements, and I work on ordering flowers for this shop before I leave for the day. I have one more day here, and I feel I have done a decent job getting everything back in order. Liv and Lexi had a fallout, resulting in the shop falling behind. I miss this place sometimes and the memories we made here, but I feel like this place holds my past, and the new shop is my future.

I am on the computer in the office when I hear a familiar voice.

I look up, and it is Ryan. "Hey"

"Hey," I say, surprised, "What are you doing here"?

"I was heading home to pack and load up for the next few days. I thought I would stop by to tell you bye."

"Well, you could have just called me to tell me that," I say.

Ryan sits in the chair across from the desk, "I know."

"How is your mom? Is she already getting to leave?"

"She is doing good. They are letting her leave in an hour, so I figured that enough time for me to come to talk to you and pack up to leave."

"What did you want to talk about"? I cross my arms and lean back in the desk chair.

"I want you to change your mind about the gala and go with me" he gives me his best, I am serious look.

"I will think about it," I say.

He smiles at me and then gets up from the chair to leave.

"Will you call me every day to keep me updated on your mom? I will be busy, but I promise I will answer your call."

I get up from the desk chair, and we walk together out of the office to the front.

"Of course I will."

When we reach the front door, he turns to me and wraps his arms around me in an embrace.

"Let me know when you make it there… Bye Ryan"

He lets out of the hug, "Bye, Claire."

I wave to him as he walks out the door, and when I turn around, Liv is staring at me with a grin.

"What" I laugh.

She shakes her head, "oh, nothing."

I get back into the office to finish flower orders and whatever else I need to do before I leave for the day. I will not admit it to Ryan, but I am sad he will be gone for a few days. Luckily I have a full schedule to take my mind off him being gone. Since everything I am doing for the next few days has to do with the gala, I do not think I will be able to take Ryan's question off my mind. Do I want to go with him? I am still very unsure. We could have had a fun time, but those memories of last year are still very there for me.

When I walk out the doors of the flower shop, my phone rings in my bag, and I immediately think it is Ryan, letting me know he made it to his parents. I dig around my bag and pull it out, not looking at who it is, while I hail a cab to take it home.

"Hello," I say, waving my hand in the air.

"Claire, what are you doing"?

"Emma! I am trying to track down a cab. What are you doing"?

"Do you have any plans? Baker left for his parents for the night and will not be back till tomorrow. Do you want to have a girl's night"?

A cab pulls up, and I get in. "Yes… Come to my apartment. We can get takeout and drink wine like we used to."

"Okay. I am just leaving the shop. I will be there soon."

"Same. I will see you in a bit," I say before hanging up the phone.

Walking into my apartment, I toss my stuff on the kitchen counter and head to my room to change. I am looking forward to this night since it has been a long time since the last time we had a girl's night. I am pulling my shirt off when I hear the front door open.

"Claire," Emma calls out.

"I am in here," I yell before slipping Ryan's old football shirt over my head.

She walks into my bedroom and looks at me. "Nice shirt"

"Thanks, it is new," I laugh.

She sits on my bed, and I notice she has brought a bag.

"Are you staying the night"?

"The next time we will get a chance to do this is the night before the wedding."

I frown; I did not realize until this moment that we would not be able to do this for much longer.

"Well, we need to make the best of this night."

I order us takeout while Emma calls Baker to let him know she is staying over for the night, and then I go to the cabinet to find us wine.

I am looking all around and cannot find a single bottle.

"Looks like I am fresh out of wine. You want something else"?

"Water will be perfect," she says.

I open the fridge and grab two bottles of water.

"So, tell me how things are going lately,"? she asks me, taking a seat on the island.

"Besides the fact that Ryan and I got into a little argument a week ago, Catherine had a heart attack, I was working without you for over a week now, and Reid turned out to be married, I would say things are going well.

She laughs, "Okay, so I would say you are managing all that well. What exactly did you and Ryan get into a fight about"?

I take a seat next to her. "Do not get mad at me. You were going through a lot then, so you never got to hear this, but last year when I went to the gala with Ryan, I developed feelings for him, and that night he left with someone else, and it left me heartbroken for a little while. That is why I do not want to go this year. After Reid confessed all his lies, I knew I needed to tell Ryan about what I had been keeping a secret. Then he told me he knew all about Reid, and I got upset about it, but we are good now."

"Wait a minute, that is why you already had ice cream when you came to my apartment after I found out about Baker's secret. You were not only keeping the secret of what happened at the shop but also the secret of liking Ryan. We are just all full of secrets, crazy."

I wonder what she means by we are all just full of secrets, but I do not get a chance to ask because she talks before I can even get a word out.

"How are things going with Ryan now that you are good"?

"Well, he came by the shop earlier before he left town to ask me to go to the gala with him on Saturday, and I told him I would think about it," I say, then take a drink of water

"If you had to ask me, I would say go. It will be a small table without Catherine and Jack already, so you should come to have fun with us," she says enthusiastically.

157

"I will think about it still. I have my work cut out for me this week, and on top of that, I do not even have a dress."

"You should have got that amazing dress you tried on."

When I went shopping with Emma, she begged me to try on dresses too, so I did, and fell in love with this long fitted navy blue, v-neck thin strapped dress, with a slit on one leg. I felt beautiful in it, but I put it back on the rack because I knew I wasn't going.

"I know," I say.

I hear a knock at the door.

I answer the door, and it is the food. I pay the guy before bringing food to the kitchen island and setting it down. I grab plates from the cabinet and set them by the takeout Chinese food we ordered. Once we plate our food, we sit in the living room to eat and turn on our favorite thing to watch together, Golden Girls.

Just like old times, which I will miss so dearly soon. We do not speak while eating; we laugh when something hilarious happens during the show. I finish my plate when I hear my phone on the coffee table. I see Ryan's name, and his picture flashes on the screen. Emma looks over to me, "Answer it"

I set my plate down and picked up my phone.

"Hello"

"Enjoying girls' night"? he asks

"Most definitely am, thank you. How is Catherine"?

"Mom is doing good. I slipped out of the house for the night and came down to the beach with Baker. It made me think of you, and I realized I never called you when I got here."

"It is okay, I have been spending time with Emma since I got off, so I forgot I told you to call. I am glad you made it," I say, and Emma is just watching me while I talk to him with a massive smile on her face.

"Well, I guess since you know I am here, I will get off and let you enjoy your night," he says

While it is awkward talking on the phone to him while Emma is staring at me, I am not ready to get off the phone with him yet, so I try to think of something to say.

"How is Tuck doing"? I ask him.

"He is having fun with all the running room in my parent's yard, and he is not sure if he likes the sand or not. He walks in it like he has something stuck between his paw, and it is funny to watch."

"So, it sounds like he has the time of his life."

"Have you thought more about what I asked you earlier today"?

I have thought about it, but I do not believe he needs to know.

"Maybe, just a little."

Emma is looking at me and mouthing to put the phone on speaker, but Ryan would know if I did and that she was listening, so I shake my head no at her.

"I will let you go now, Claire. I will call you tomorrow."

"Okay, bye, Ryan," I say and then hang up the phone.

I set my phone down on the table and put my plate away.

"I wanted to listen. What did Ryan say"? Emma says, watching me walk into the kitchen.

"He only called to tell me he made it to his parents," I say.

"I wish we were there with them."

"Me too"

I do wish I was there. Not just for the beach, but to help Catherine and to be there with Ryan. That night with him on the beach comes to my mind, and I am sure it is on his too.

Chapter Thirteen

Ryan

There has not been a moment in my life where I felt terrified, worried that I would lose someone when I got my father's call about mom. My whole world got dark then, and I somehow ended up at the hospital, just waiting to know that she would be okay. While waiting for what felt like hours, I never saw the light at the end of the tunnel until Claire walked through those doors, and I just wanted to hold her until this whole thing was over. She was my haven that day. It was then that I knew this was it, I could not lose her, and I needed her to know I was not giving up. There will be no more games between us, and I will give it to her straight and make her realize it is me that she needs. I am starting with what I hope will be our first official date, the gala.

I need her to change her mind about going, and if that means I will have to come up with a plan, then that is what I will do. What am I going to come up with? I do not know, but I only have one more day to devise the most excellent plan.

When my mother naps, and I know someone is around to check on her, I sneak trips down to the beach, and they have been helping me through my time here. Thinking back to the night here with Claire, I wish I could return to that moment. Sometimes I wish I could have changed what I said then. Maybe we would be together today if I had just talked to her lightly about it. I know our lives then were different, and the time was not right for each of us. Going through this with my mom has been my wake-up call not to waste another day just living, doing, and going for what I want. That day Claire walked away after having a heated argument between us, and I never had the chance to see her. Tell her I am sorry. I would never be able to live with myself. From now on, I will never let her leave me without talking, fixing any issue, and letting her know how I feel.

The last few days here, I have not let a day go by without calling Claire, filling her in on how mom is doing, and asking her about her day. She will not admit it, but even though she has been the busiest, she misses me there, and I can hear it in her voice. It's the low whiny tone when she asks me, "what are you doing" that I listen for when on the phone with her, and it always brings a smile to my face. I know she is hoping I will answer that I am thinking about her or standing in the spot where we kissed, wishing I was still with her, but I cannot be here without her and telling her those things. When I tell her exactly what is on my mind, I want to be right there looking into her big green eyes and ending the moment with a kiss.

I have dreamed about many moments I want to have with Claire while away. All of them have ended with her in my arms. Please let it be accurate to me when I do see her Saturday, and she ends the night with me. I need to prove to her this year at the gala that last year was just the past and that she is my future.

It is my last night here, and I am lying across the bed when my phone rings in my pocket. I fish it out and see Claire's name across the screen.

"Hey, you. What are you doing"? I ask her.

"Just leaving the shop, and since it is late, I did not want to walk home alone, so I figured talking to you while I walk home was the safest option."

I look at my watch to see the time, which is almost eleven.

"Good choice. Why exactly are you leaving this late, though"? I ask her while I grab my pillow and tuck it under my head.

"Arrangements needed finishing for tomorrow. Then I started on some of the decorations for tomorrow to get a head start. Time just got away from me. It is not like I had something to do tonight anyways," she says, and she said that last part with the tone.

"I will be back tomorrow, then you will have something to look forward to," I say with a smile, hoping she says something sweet back.

"About that, I hate to do this on the phone, but I know you want me to go with you, but I have nothing to wear, and I have no time to find something. I cannot go, Ryan." She says, and that is not what I was wanting.

I sit up on the bed and put my feet over the side.

"Claire, I am sure you have something in your closet, right? Does Emma have something you could borrow? You know you could wear anything, and it will be just fine. I just want you to be there with me."

"I am in my apartment, just saying so you know I made it home," she says, and I can hear her shut the door and lock it. "Look, I will try to see if I can find something. I still do not want to go, but I am trying to want to for you," she says.

I looked at my watch again, not because I wanted to get off the phone but because I knew it was close to a specific time.

"What time is it"? I ask her, knowing it is precisely 11:11.

"Uhhh…" she says, and I know she is probably looking over at her stove clock. "Ryan, you know what time it is," she says, and I can tell she is smiling.

"Claire, I cannot wait to see you tomorrow."

"Same to you… Ryan," she says.

I still do not want to end our conversation, but I know it is late.

"Goodnight," I tell her.

"Goodnight," she says before hanging up the phone.

After she ends the call, I set my phone down on my nightstand and then check on Tuck sleeping on the floor before finally getting ready for bed so I can get to tomorrow.

When I get into town, the first thing on my to-do list is to check on the progress for tonight's gala at the ballroom Baker and I own, which they use yearly for the event. Hopefully, there is a chance Claire will still be there setting up, so I can see her.

When I get out after parking, I notice they already have the red carpet on the front door for entrances and the backdrop with all the sponsors' names. Last year, when Claire and I walked in together, our photo was on the newspaper's front cover, titled "New Couple Alert." It did not go over well with the woman I went home with that night the following day, but now it is something I want to see on the front page tomorrow morning.

I walk through the doors and see all the floral arrangements in the middle of every table. The tables are in dark blue clothes, and each flower arrangement has a variety of white flowers, with gold stars sticking out around them. Several strands of string lights are strung across the ceiling to imitate stars in the sky. The ballroom looks finished, besides people sitting on the dance floor. I see Emma and Baker placing place cards on tables, so I make my way towards them.

"Hey, it looks great in here," I say.

"Hey… You can thank Claire for all of this. She set it all up herself," Emma says when she turns to see me.

"Where is she? Is she still here"? I ask.

Emma walks away to set down a place card, so Baker answers me.

"No, she left a long time ago. It seems like everyone at the shop came down with some sickness, so she is filling in there."

"A sickness"?

Emma comes back to us to look at the list again.

"Yeah. We initially thought it was food poisoning, but now everyone is sick, so it must be a stomach bug or virus. Claire is the only one besides me not sick, so she is going to work at the shop until we close tonight," Emma says.

Well, this is something I was not expecting to happen today. I figured Claire would set up for the gala, and then she would have time to get ready and find something to wear. The flower shop does not stay open too late on Saturdays, so there has to be something I can do to make sure Claire gets to this event tonight.

After standing there watching them for just a few minutes, something crosses my mind.

"You guys think you can help me with something"?

Claire

This day started great. I was able to set everything up at the ballroom early, and I thought I would have time to look for something to wear tonight just in case I decided to go. I had plans to raid Emma's incredible closet that Baker gifted her, but it was not one minute after setting up the ballroom that everyone came down with what seemed like a stomach bug at the shop. Only one person could fill in there, and that was me. So, I am taking this as a sign that I should not go and order a pizza for one when I finish here today and binge some tv.

Since I have not heard from Ryan since he texted me that he made it back today, maybe he has forgotten that he asked me to go. I was expecting him to come by to see me sometime before tonight, but Emma called to check in on me not long ago and said she ran into Ryan at the ballroom. She said he told her he had a list of things to do, and she suspected he would not have time to come by. The day of the gala can get busy with Baker and Ryan, considering their ballroom holds the event, and they help with the whole thing.

Luckily the shop orders for today have been low, and I have been passing the time with cleaning so I could shut this place down early tonight. While sweeping the floor, I cannot help but think of everyone getting ready and dressed up in their extravagant formal wear. Then here is me wearing jean shorts, a shirt, and hair in a ponytail, looking like I just threw some clothes on before decorating this morning because I did. Last year's gala came into my mind, and I felt so pretty for one night, thinking that I was going to land this awesome guy, and instead ended up alone.

I hear the front door open, and when I look up from sweeping, I see Ryan dressed so handsome in his tux. He is wearing a dark navy fitted pants and jacket, with a white button-up, and the top buttons undone, paired with some tan leather shoes.

"Hey," he says.

I set the broom against the wall and met him at the front counter.

"Hey…You look handsome," I say.

"Thank you. How much longer do you have here"? He asks.

I look over at the clock on the wall and then turn my eyes to him.

"Not much longer."

"What are you going to do when you leave here"? He asks me.

"I will probably just go to my apartment and order a pizza, the usual. I am sorry I can not make it tonight. I know you wanted me to come with you, but then I got called in and did not get time to look for anything to wear. You will have fun without me. Eat some amazing desserts for me."

He chuckles, "It is okay. I know this has been a long day for you."

He came around the counter to hug me, and I missed his embrace while he was gone.

"I will talk to you later, alright," he says.

"Okay," I say with a frown in a sad tone.

Then he walks out the front doors, and I wave to him as he leaves.

I spend the next hour finishing up the cleaning. Tonight is a nice night, the shop is quiet, and it is almost as if the whole city is at the gala with how slow the city seems to be tonight. I lock the front doors and walk down the sidewalk to my apartment building.

The first thing I do when I walk into my apartment is grabbing a glass and pour myself some wine. The wine I restocked after Emma stayed at my place a few nights ago. Instead of tv, I turn on the Spotify playlist that Ryan shared with me when we went on our trip to the Hamptons. I even noticed he added my favorite song to it.

I take my glass of wine to my bedroom, where I plan to start a nice hot bath in my bathroom and relax. I am singing along to the music, setting my glass down on the bathroom counter, and looking at myself in the mirror while my water fills the bathtub. I look like I got ready in the dark this morning, and I am not even shocked that I went about my day looking this disheveled. I take my hair down, shake my head, take off my clothes, and throw them into my bedroom floor. I get into the bath and unwind back. Tonight is what I needed to end this day.

A Love That Blooms

I have been in the bath for at least fifteen minutes when I hear my phone go off. I look around when I realize I forgot it on the kitchen counter. Who could be messaging me when everyone is at the gala? I slip out of the bath, wrapping a towel around me. When I walk out of the bathroom into my room, I see a dress bag hug up over my closet door, with a note tapped on the hanger. What is this?

I tightened my towel and then grabbed the note to read it.

Claire

Make me the luckiest man at the Gala.

Put on this dress and join me for the night that you deserve.

I owe you

Xoxo

Ryan

I toss the note card on my bed and unzip the dress bag to find the navy dress I tried on with Emma.

Chapter Fourteen

Ryan

The plan was a horrible idea. When I asked Emma and Baker to help me out, Emma said she knew of the perfect dress for me to pick up for Claire, so why is she still not here? I felt like I wrote the right words on the note, but I have been sitting here at the gala for almost two hours, and she still has not shown up. This year's table is just me, Baker, and Emma, and I am starting to get tired of watching them make out all night. We had already finished dinner, and while Claire said to eat dessert for her, I was hoping she would be here right now to share a plate with me. I have not been on the dance floor once. I am so close to heading home for the night, heartbroken and lonely. Then I realized the exact feeling Claire must have had last year. What a jerk I was, then.

Emma and Baker sit across from me, feeding each other cheesecake and laughing. "She will come, Ryan, I promise. Just be patient," Emma says to me when she realizes I am still looking over at the door, just waiting for her to walk in.

"You said this plan will work"

"It will just wait. Maybe Claire didn't see the dress hanging up."

I knew the closet was not the place to hang it, but Emma insisted that she constantly changed when she got home so she would see it there.

I look over at the door and then down at my watch. I rub the back of my neck, anxiously waiting for Claire, and then I hear Emma cough to clear her throat. When I look at her to ensure she is okay, she nods to the front door. I turn my head, and there she is.

Claire looks stunning, wearing the dress I got her, and it fits her in all the right places, perfect on her. Her hair is down, curled, and on one side is behind her ear. She is wearing the perfect amount of makeup, and when she spots me across to room, she is wearing the most beautiful smile.

I get up from my chair to meet her halfway.

She throws her arms around me when we meet in the middle of the room

"I tried to get here as fast as I could. I am sorry, but I did not see the dress."

"You are here now, and that is all that matters," I say as I take her hand and we make our way to the table. I pull her chair out for her, and she takes a seat. Then I sit right next to her and take her hand in mine again, but this time I intertwine our fingers, placing them on my lap, which gets me a surprised look from her.

"About time you join us," Emma says to Claire.

"Well, I was not expecting this. I came home, poured myself a glass of wine, got in the bath, then when my phone went off, I saw the dress when I got out. Then when I got my phone, I saw Emma's text asking me where I was, so I got ready as fast as possible," she says to Emma. "Thank you for the dress, by the way," she nods.

"You look amazing," I tell her, and she blushes.

Emma and Claire converse about the shop and what has been happening with everyone who has been sick. I sit back and listen to them talking, but I want to scoop Claire up and take her to the dance floor. I want a moment with just us. When I think their conversation will finally end, Baker asks Emma to dance, and this is my chance to ask Claire the same. She accepts, and we make our way to the dance floor. She leads the way, and I follow with my hand on the small of her back.

When we get on the dance floor, we position ourselves the exact way Jane taught us when we took the dance class in the Hamptons, but there is no space between us this time. She rests her head on my chest as we dance. "I missed the silent auction, didn't I?" she asks while we continue our steps. "Yeah, you sure did," I tell her. I do not tell her that I already bid on and won the same self-care package she bid and won last year, along with a date night dinner and movie night for the two of us. It is something I can surprise her with later. We danced for two more songs when Claire asked if I had dessert yet, and of course, I did not since I was waiting for her.

We get over to the dessert tables, she picks up two plates and tries to hand me one, but I put it back down. "You do not want anything"? she asks me, "We are going to share a plate," I say to her with a smile. "Sharing is better than eating it alone; you pick what you want." She smiles and starts loading our plate with brownies, cake, and cheesecake. We get back to the tables. Emma and Baker are still on the dance floor, so we have the table to ourselves.

Claire scoots the plate between the two of us so we can share. She starts with a bite of cheesecake. "Come home with me when we leave here," I ask her. Her eyes get wide, and she almost spits her taste, but she manages to swallow it instead. "I guess so, and I have missed Tuck."

"Tuck is not there, sorry."

"What, where is he"? she asks me, worried.

"He is still in the Hamptons with mom and dad. He loved it there and laying with mom while she rested, so I left him there, and I will go get him sometime this week."

She has a mouthful, so she does not get a chance to answer, so she nods.

"I want you to stay with me tonight," I whisper.

She pushes the plates closer to me.

"Are you asking me this because you owe me a better night than last year"? She asks.

It hits me then that I never once thought of it that way, but I see what she means.

"No, I would never do that to you. I am asking you because this night means so much more to me. We have been apart all week, and I am just not ready for this night to end with you."

She looks down for a second to think about it, and then her eyes turn back to me.

"Okay," she says.

"Okay"?

"Yes, I will stay with you."

I smile at her, she smiles back at me, and then I take her hand. Tonight will not be our normal sleep on the couch sleepover. It will be a night when she will fall asleep in my arms.

I guide Claire back to the dance floor for one more dance before we leave. I wanted to do much more with her tonight, but we did not have the time. Emma and Baker dance beside us, and I catch Emma giving Claire a thumbs up. At this moment, I realize how good this all feels to me, to finally have her (not officially, but it feels like it). My brother and her best friend are getting married soon, all of us being family soon. It is a feeling I did not know I was looking for, but it feels so right.

All four of us are the only guest left in the ballroom when it comes time to end the night. Claire and Emma are helping pick up the mess left on the tables while Baker and I stack some of the chairs. We have people who clean up the next day, but we are all too lovely to leave it too messy for them. After I stack the last chair, I run up behind Claire, putting my arms around her shoulder, and ask her if she is ready to leave. My move surprises her, but I am not surprised to hear her say she is prepared to go. It is late, and I know she has had a long day.

We say goodbye to Emma and Baker and walk out the front doors. The red carpet is gone when we get outside, but the backdrop is still up, so I pull Claire over to me and stand in front of the backdrop. "What are you doing"? she asks me. "We did not get a picture coming in together. We need a picture from tonight." I put my arm around her, bringing her close to me, and she puts her cheek up to mine. I take my phone out of my pocket and snap a quick picture of us laughing and smiling. "There, now we have proof we went together," I say as she shakes her head and giggles. I take her hand, and we walk to the jeep together.

Once inside my apartment, she immediately sits on the couch and takes off her heels. She sets them to side the side and then lays down. I slip off my shoes by the front door, unbuttoning my jacket, take it off, and place it over the back of the couch. "You want anything to eat? I know you did not get to eat dinner with us."

"I am good, thank you," she answers, placing her hands under her head to get comfy.

"If you want to, we can get ready for bed, "I say, sitting down by her feet.

She is slowly closing her eyes, and she has them fully closed when she says

"You get the pillows and blankets, and I will just wait here."

I laugh, "Oh, we are not sleeping in here. We are sleeping back there."

She opens her eyes quickly. "We are"

I get up and walk over to Claire. I slide my arms underneath her, pick her up from the couch and start walking to the bedroom.

She is laughing, "I can walk, I can walk."

"Too late. We are already there," I say.

I slowly lay her down on my bed when I walked into the room with her in my arms. Then look in my dresser for something for her to wear.

I pick up a shirt and toss it to her, "Here you go."

She sits up from the bed, picks up the shirt, and holds it up. "I need pants too."

Of course, she wants pants, and I do not want her thinking we will be doing anything special tonight. I go back to my dresser and pull out some sweats for her and a pair of shorts for me. After I toss her the pants, I head into the bathroom to change. I brush my teeth for the night. When I open the door to the bathroom, she is lying in bed. Under the covers and already changed into the clothes I gave her.

"You are quick," I tell her, coming to the other side of the bed to join her.

"Well, I do not have anything to do in my nightly routine here, and I just hope my contacts do not bother my eyes while I am sleeping." She says as she lays her head down on her pillow when I get into bed with her.

"I guess we should have stopped by your place before we came here."

"It is okay."

I roll over to look at her; she already has her eyes closed again. I slide my arm under her and pull her closer to me. She does not hesitate my move and instead places her head and hand on my chest as much as I want to talk while we lay here. I get that she has had one of the longest days and needs her sleep. I will be happy when I wake up and she is still in my arms.

It is still dark when I wake to a sound coming from the bathroom. Claire is no longer lying next to me, and when I open my eyes, I see she is not in bed. I sit up fast and hear her throwing up in the bathroom. She caught the bug.

I rush out of bed and knock on the bathroom door.

"Claire, can I come in"

A Love That Blooms

She does not answer immediately, and I hear her throw up again.

I am unsure at this point if she would want me to walk in and see her in the state that she is in, but I cannot just let her go through this. I feel like I need to take care of her.

So, I open the door and find her lying on the floor.

"Claire, babe. Are you okay"?

She just shakes her head and covers her eyes with her hands.

I get a washcloth from under the sink and rinse it with cold water. I squeeze the extra water out before getting down on the floor and placing it on Claire's head. I brush the hair away from her face. Then run my hand up and down her arm to get her to relax some.

"Let me go get you some water," I tell her getting up off the bathroom floor.

I head down the hallway to the kitchen and grab water from the fridge before heading back into the bathroom. When I return, Claire sits up, head resting on her knees.

"Here, try to take a drink," I say, unscrewing the cap and handing it to her.

She takes the water from me, drinks it, and then hands it back to me.

"You have anything else in there to get out, or do you want to try to get back into bed"? I ask her, hoping she won't be throwing up.

"I think I am good for now," she says, still resting her head on her knees.

I feel her forehead, and she feels warm to me. I get up off the floor and hold my hand out for her to grab so I can help her.

When I get her off the floor, I help her onto the bed and then cover her up. She does not look good, and I am sure I will not get any more sleep once she gets comfy and looks to fall back asleep. I see that it is five am. My apartment is at the bare minimum right now regarding medicine and food. I know she will need fluids until she can keep food down. She will also probably want some things from her apartment to feel more comfortable. Emma would be the person to talk to, and I hope she has not come down with the same bug. I pick my phone up off my nightstand and ring Baker.

"What do you need," he says when he answers the phone.

"Please tell me Emma is not sick and can help me out," I say as I look over at Claire, who is sound asleep.

"Is Claire sick? Emma started throwing up an hour ago, and I just got her back into bed."

"Ugh… it is the same situation here, and I have no one to call for help besides you two. So, it looks like I am all on my own," I say with a slight panic in my voice. I have never had to take care of a woman before, let alone get into her apartment to get the things she would need.

"Look, it is early, and if she just went back to bed, then now would be the perfect time to get out and pick up what she needs. Claire will never know that you left."

I contemplate what he is saying, but I feel horrible leaving her alone. What if she wakes again?

"Got it…well, hopefully, you have everything you need for Emma because this is not going to be fun for me," I say, walking over to my closet to find a shirt to throw on.

"You can do this, Ryan, and then she will appreciate it."

"I sure hope you are right," I say before hanging up the phone.

A Love That Blooms

I checked on Claire one more time before putting on my shoes to leave. I grab her apartment key off my hanger and walk out the door. I feel so bad leaving her alone, so I need to make this a quick trip.

The first stop is her apartment, and once I get inside, I notice how messy the place is. It must be how she lives when she is busy, and I can understand, but I feel like I should be cleaning this place up for her, but I need to keep my head straight. Just get the things I need. I walk into her room, grabbing an overnight bag off her door handle. I open her dresser, knowing she will need clothes, and the first drawer I open brings me a lot of underwear. I pick up the ones that look most appealing to me and throw them in the bag. The next drawer I open is leggings, and while I do not see her wearing these often, I know they must be comfortable, so I put two in the bag. Once I have a couple of shirts from her closet. I grab all her contact stuff and glasses in her bathroom. Remembering that was one thing she mentioned she wished she had last night. Holding the toothbrush, and toothpaste next, then follow with any products she has in her shower because I know she will want one of those later. I feel like I am doing alright.

I walk past her kitchen and realize I could make this easier by checking if she has anything to drink besides water and wine, two things I know she always has. When I open her fridge, I find some fancy electrolyte drinks that I know would be perfect, and since they came from her place, I know she has had them before. I search for crackers in her cabinet and find a ridiculous amount of those, so I grab a couple of boxes. Is Claire always sick because I just shopped her kitchen for everything I needed for her, and she had every bit of it, or maybe she suspected she would be catching this bug?

I think it took me ten minutes to get everything I needed for her and walk out of her building back to my jeep. It is turning

179

out to be much simpler than I imagined. Now I need to care for her today and keep her close.

When I walk back into my apartment, it looks like she has not even moved an inch and is still sleeping peacefully. I set her bag I packed on my dresser, took out her bathroom things, and put them in my bathroom, so she would know they were there. I set a drink, and crackers on the nightstand by her, in case she wants them when she wakes. I take the rest of the stuff to my fridge in the kitchen and then check the time. It is not even six am, and I am beginning to think I could crawl back into bed with her and get some sleep. I do not see either of us being able to leave the apartment today, and I am not even upset about it.

I take off my shirt and then slide back into bed quietly. I want to wrap my arms around Claire and comfort her, but I do not know where her comfort zone stands when she is sick.

Chapter Fifteen

Claire

Not only did I catch the stomach bug going around the Blooms, but I also just realized I was sick at Ryan's. I am embarrassed. This morning, he was great when he caught me in the bathroom getting sick, but I was horrified. It is not something I wanted after such a perfect night with Ryan. The gala turned out to be incredible, just what I imagined it would be with him, but when the night ended, I was catching myself getting increasingly tired. I was not sure if it was because the week caught up to me or if I was coming down sick. While lying in bed with Ryan, I wanted to talk and be close to him, but sure enough, I passed smoothly out, only to wake up with the sensation of needing to throw up.

I woke up after falling back asleep and found Ryan sleeping soundly on his side of the bed, and I wish he had been closer to me to comfort me at that moment. Fortunately, I did not need to throw up anymore when I woke up, but I did find a pleasant surprise when I used the bathroom. From the looks of it, Ryan went to my apartment to get some of my things. It looks like he raided my fridge on his way out. When I first caught wind of this bug going around, I stopped at the store to get anything I needed because there could have been a chance I would be alone during it. Thankfully I am not, and I could not appreciate Ryan more for thinking of all the things I would need today.

Since he was still sleeping, I decided to take a shower. I feel gross from this morning's events. I still feel fragile and sick but could not think of anything more I would want now than to be clean. I start the water, place the clothes Ryan grabbed me on the counter, and then get in. It does not take long before I hear the door open to the bathroom.

"Claire... Are you okay"? Ryan asks me.

I am rinsing my hair, "I feel about the same, just without holding my head over the toilet."

"You need any help."

What kind of help does he think I need right now?

"I almost finished, but thank you," I say, lathering up some soap to wash my body.

"Just yell at me if you need anything," he says before shutting the door.

I finish showering and dry off.

Braiding my hair in a side braid after I brush it, I slip into the leggings Ryan packed me but opted for the shirt he let me sleep in instead of the one he brought me. I take out my contacts and put my glasses on. I look like I could use some color on my face, but I know it will come back once I start eating and drinking again. When I open the bathroom door, Ryan is nowhere, but I can hear the tv playing up front. I grab the crackers and drink by the bed and walk down the hallway.

When I get to the living room, Ryan is already waiting for me to join him. He is in the corner of the sectional, with a pillow on his lap. When Ryan sees me, he pats the cushion for me to come to lie down, and there is a blanket over the back of the couch in case I need it. I set my stuff down on the coffee table and then lay my head down on him. He instantly comforts me with his hand brushing up and down my arm.

"Emma is sick too," he says to me.

"So, it looks like everyone got it. You might not want to be close to me today," I say.

"That is nonsense. I am not leaving your side," Ryan says as he continues comforting me.

As weird as it sounds, I feel like Ryan and I grew closer when he was away with his parents, helping take care of his mom. Our friendship is growing more, and I know this could be because of what happened to his mother or because we are both finally single at the same time. He took me by surprise yesterday, with the dress, the note, and how he was with me last night. We do not feel like just friends anymore, and I kind of like the feeling of this. I want to take it daily and see what happens with us, and today I am thankful for him being here with me while I am embarrassingly sick.

While watching a movie together, I can finally drink, eat a little, and amazingly keep it down. My eyes keep wanting to close, and I can not remember when I was this tired. While I was busy this last week, staying out late working since Ryan was gone, I do not know if the work or sickness is making me so sleepy.

We somehow managed to get closer throughout the day, lounging on the couch and watching movies after the occasional nap. We are now lying in the same spot on the couch. His arms around me, holding me close to him. I am finally starting to feel myself again, and I know we both are probably starving, but neither of us has said anything about it.

"Ryan, are you hungry"?

After asking him no less than a second, I hear his stomach growl and laugh.

"I guess you can take that as a yes," he says with a chuckle

"Let's order in something."

I sit up, and he follows my lead.

"Are you sure you are going to be okay eating something"? he asks me

I nod my head, and he gets up from the couch.

"Pizza"? he asks me as if he has been thinking about it all day.

"Yes, that sounds great."

It takes us no time to devour a whole pizza together, and I feel much better. We are hanging out on the couch still, and instead of sleeping. Thanks to me, I want to hang out and talk, considering we have not done much of that in the last twenty-four hours. It is late, and while we both have work tomorrow, neither is tired.

"Alright, let's play a game," I tell him.

"What kind of game"? he asks, looking confused.

"Truth or dare but without the dare, more like a get to know each other kind of game. And I know you will say we already know each other, but we are just playing for fun."

"I am in, I guess," he nods.

I pull my legs up on the couch and turn towards him.

"Have you ever gone skinny dipping"?

"No," he says with a smile.

I nod and then tell him it is his turn.

"Have you ever gone skinny dipping"? He asks.

I laugh, "No, but you cannot just always ask me the same question I ask you."

"Well, I could not think of anything yet," he laughs.

"What is your least favorite food"?

He thinks about it for a second before saying, "Lettuce. And I will not ask you because I already know your least favorite food."

"Really, what is it then"?

"Bananas, you have a thing with the taste and texture.

"Wow, I did not know you knew that," I say, impressed.

He is always paying attention to me when I do not realize it.

"What is something someone may not know about you"? he asks me, which is a good question.

"Even Emma does not know this, but I think traveling would be fun. Like taking a month or so off work and just living, exploring, and going places, I have never been but have always wanted to. I have only ever been here and home in Florida."

"You consider Florida your home"? he asks me.

"You get two questions"? I ask him.

He shrugs his shoulder, "I am just curious."

"Well, I consider it home because that is where I am from, and my family is still there. I just feel like I have not laid roots here yet. I feel like I have the shop and Emma here, and it has not felt like home to me."

He nods, and then I continue to think of something to ask him.

"What is something you would still like to do with your life"?

"Besides the obvious of getting married, having a family. I would love to move back to the Hamptons one day and be closer to my parents. Maybe open my own real estate office there. The city is not somewhere I would want to live when married and raising kids. Just like you consider Florida home, I consider the Hamptons my home. Here is just a place I came with Baker, and while I went off the deep end shortly after opening the office here, I am finally getting to a place in my life where I am ready for those things more now than ever."

I blush, just thinking about him saying that to me and knowing how he feels about me. Of course, I would want those same things soon, but I am unsure of the future. I cannot help but want to know when he wants those things.

"How soon"? I ask.

He scoots closer to me, "You get two questions"? he smirks

"Just curious" I smile at him.

He brushes a piece of hair away from my face, looking me in the eyes. He shrugs his shoulders as he answers and continues getting closer to me.

"Claire, I am going to kiss you right now, and it is not going to be a just friend kiss. It is going to be more than that."

I nod, and he brings his hand to my face, brushing his thumb across my bottom lip before going in with a kiss. He is right; it is not just a friendly kiss. I put my hand behind his head, bringing our kiss closer, and he places both hands on my cheeks. Our kiss moves slower, and he places tiny kisses on my lips before pulling back, keeping his hands on each side of my face.

"Go on a date with me"? he whispers

"Okay," I whisper back, and he smiles.

_____

When it came time for Ryan and me to get up and ready for work on Monday morning, it was not easy. Not only did we sleep most of the day on Sunday, so it took us into the wee hours of the morning to fall asleep, but we also just wanted to stay up talking. You would think we did not know each other until yesterday. We talked more about places I would love to travel to, and he told me places he had never been before that he would like to see. I want to stay within the US because the thought of being on a plane longer than a few hours makes me nervous, but Ryan talked about some places overseas. That is probably the first thing we do not have in common.

Thankfully the bug was only a twenty-four-hour thing for everyone, and we are all back at Blooms today, including Emma, who seems to be asking a lot of questions today since she heard from Baker that I was at Ryan's place. She said Ryan called Baker asking for help from Emma, but only for her to be sick herself. It made me appreciate more that he went to my apartment alone and could get everything I needed successfully. I may have stayed with him again, but I needed to be at the apartment first thing this morning to get ready for work. Even though he asked me to come over again tonight before I left, I turned him down. I am not prepared to make this a daily thing. If

187

I learned anything from past dating experiences and relationships, jumping into sleeping in the same bed every night does not work out for me in the end. Pretty sure James, my bad ex, started staying every night with me from day one, and we all know how that turned out. While I understand Ryan is different, that makes me want to take this slow and do it the right way.

"So, tell me again, when are you guys going on your first real date"? Emma asks me while sitting on my workstation so we can talk.

"He did not say. He just asked me last night," I say, continuing to work on an arrangement.

"Have you kissed him"?

"Seriously"? I say, giving her the side eye.

She throws her hands up. "Sorry, but I kind of need to know."

I continue working and not paying attention to her. Then I say quietly, "Maybe."

She yells out, "I knew it!"

The phone at the front counter rings, and Emma runs to answer it. She is talking to the person like she knows them, so I just continue working.

"Claire, it is for you," Emma yells.

Confused, I walk over to the counter and pick up the phone.

"This is Claire," I say.

"Hey"

"Ryan, why are you calling me on this phone"? I ask.

"You have not answered me on your phone, so I had no choice but to call you here. I was calling to tell you I have a meeting tonight."

"You are calling me to tell me you have a meeting"?

"Yes, an end-of-the-month meeting with work, so we probably will not be able to see each other tonight, considering you will not stay at my place."

"End of the month? Oh, shoot!" I turn away so Emma cannot hear me talking. "It is almost September, meaning the wedding is like weeks away, and I still have not ordered the flowers. I probably should go do that right now," I say as I hang up the phone.

I run straight into the office and lock the door behind me. Emma not only knows that the Hamptons flower shop could not order the flowers for her big day, but her best friend is doing a terrible job planning her wedding. I sit at the computer, and my cell phone rings from my bag. It dawned on me then that I had just hung up on Ryan. I take my phone out of my bag and answer it.

"Oh, my goodness, I am so sorry. I panicked," I told Ryan.

"Are you okay? Do you need me to come and help you"? He asks me.

I looked around my purse for the paper I had written down all the flowers she had asked us to order. I forget I am on the phone for a second and just keep searching. It is not in there.

"Hello, are you still there"?

"Ryan, the list is missing from my bag, and I have no clue where it is. I know for sure I put it in there." I am now in full-blown panic mode.

"Okay, do you remember what the list had on it? You know your flowers, so I am sure you could remember the names."

"I know she wanted all white flowers, with a few pink ones, and some greenery at lot has gone on in my life since I looked at the list."

"Just order what flowers you think would look good in those colors."

"Okay," I say, sitting back down at the computer.

"Okay, so are you good now"? he asks me.

"Yes, thank you for helping me out," I say, turning on the computer.

"Alright then, I will see you later tonight," he says.

"You just told me you had a meeting tonight" I throw my hands up and then start typing to website into the computer.

"Right, I was just checking to make sure you were listening to me," he laughs.

"Are you done with your jokes? I have important business I need to get done," I tell him as I start thinking about the number of flowers I am placing in this order. Is this all fit in a delivery truck to get to the Hamptons?

"I will call you later," he says.

"Okay, talk later," I say before hanging up the phone.

How on earth are we going to get this number of flowers there? I think we are going to need another delivery van.

I continue the order while trying to imagine how we will set everything up in my head. If I see it in my head, I can place the proper flower order. I am closing my eyes and thinking of how everything will look. There will be tables covered with white tablecloths and then white chairs for the ceremony. I would order flowers in many colors and varieties, but it is not what Emma wanted. I go ahead with the order of white flowers, some light pink, and greenery.

When I send the order in, I walk out of the office, and Emma passes me on my way back

I try not to look suspicious, "I was on the phone with Ryan. I just needed a little privacy."

She knows me well and may blame me for hiding something, but she will never know what I am hiding. I will never tell her the amount of bad luck we had planning her wedding. At the same time, this was not bad luck, more like an accidental moment, since I have had a lot of other things going on in my life lately.

Chapter Sixteen

Ryan

I spend one whole day with Claire, taking care of her, finally getting a kiss that she does not back away from, and then falling asleep with her in my arms, and now I am suddenly becoming obsessed. I called her to tell her I had a meeting because I was just looking for a reason to hear her voice. I was not expecting my phone call to put her in a full-blown panic, but at least I was able to help her through the whole flower order debacle.

She let me down cold this morning, telling me that she did not want to sleep at each other places every night, and I understand a little bit. We have not even gone out on a date, which I am still working on, but we know each other better than anyone else. Two, she has been trashed by men in the past that she basically lived with, and while we would not be living together, I do not see myself joining the list of men in her past.

I am sitting in the conference room at our office for the end of the monthly meeting we have with other real estate offices, and while everyone in the room is talking, I cannot understand a word coming out of anyone's mouth. My mind has been thinking about Claire since before this meeting ever started. I wonder what she is doing now, what she ate for lunch, where I should take her on our date, and whether she likes fried eggs or scrambled. What has gotten into me? I should already know the answer to the last one, but then again, I never ask her and just make her whatever. I guess she never complained, so I will continue making her eggs the way I think she likes them. Okay, this is getting ridiculous. I am a sick puppy waiting for its owner when I hear my phone vibrating in my pocket.

When I pull it out, I see that Claire is trying to call me. I hit ignore, sadly. I would love to answer the phone and talk to her, but I am stuck in this meeting. Instead of leaving her hanging, I decided to text her. She should remember that I had a meeting unless she forgot.

Me- In a meeting, I will call you when I leave.

Claire-*face palm emoji

Yep, just as I suspected. Claire forgot.

I look at my watch and see it is time for her to leave the shop and walk home.

What is that? Do I feel a fever coming on? Maybe a little stomach bug is coming over me. I touch my head while pretending I start not to feel well, and Baker glances over at me from across the table. He would be the one to believe that this little show I am putting on is real, even though it is not. I suddenly just want out of this meeting. I open my phone again to text Baker that I am not feeling well. I watch him as he opens his phone, reads the message, and then nods to the door for me to leave. It worked. Gathering my things, I get up from the table and walk out the conference room door.

After dropping my notebooks off in my office, I leave the office building. If Baker is in the meeting, then there is no reason for me to be there when my mind it other places anyways. I hop in my jeep and drive right over to Claire's apartment.

She is not expecting anyone, and I know she will not mind if I walk in, so when I get to her door, I expect her to be hanging out on the couch, but she is not. She is here, her bag on the counter, her wine bottle open sitting next to it, and my road trip playlist is playing on her tv. I do not want to scare her, so I do not call her name but instead head to her room. I come through the doorway, and just as I walk into the bedroom, I see the bathroom door open and Claire sitting in the bathtub with her head back and eyes closed. There are bubbles higher than her, candles lit on each end, and a glass of wine chilling on the side.

I walk to the bathroom and lean over on the doorframe. "Hey"

Claire opens one eye like she feels like she may be dreaming of me standing here, and when she sees me for real, she screams. "RYAN! What are you doing here? I am, I am naked under these" she throws some bubbles up with her hands.

I laugh, "SO… I left my meeting. "Sick," I say, doing quotation marks with my fingers before sitting on the toilet seat so I can be closer to her. "I also do not care if you are naked under there. I will leave the room when you are ready to get out."

She sits in the tub and ensures the bubbles are covering her everywhere. "Let me guess; you faked you had the stomach bug," she giggles.

"Exactly, and since Baker knows it was a real thing, he let me go. I do not feel a tiny bit bad I left; I have had you on my mind that whole meeting and could barely concentrate."

She blushes and starts playing with the bubbles like she is nervous.

"I will be upfront waiting for you. Do you have anything to eat, cook, or want me to order something"?

After telling me she has no groceries, we decide to order something, and then I head to the kitchen. She has a drawer full of just takeout menus that we have used before, and I know she uses them at least twice a week for herself. It takes me back to a memory of when she moved in here and had me come over every day for a week to help her decorate and build furniture. We ate so much take-out that week. I cooked for myself at my apartment every night for a month. I could not stomach eating another takeout meal. One of Claire's favorite places is sushi, so I order that for the two of us to be delivered, then turn on a movie on the tv while I wait for her to come out of the bathroom.

While sitting on the couch waiting, I try to think about the perfect date for Claire; she is more than just a night in or dinner. We have done these things as friends, and I do not know if she would see that as a suitable date. I am not asking her to walk in the park and eat from the hot dog stand. Those were dates she had with that married guy. Just when I think I have a perfect idea, she comes out of her bathroom wearing my old football shirt, sleeps shorts, and her hair up in a messy bun. I never realized until now how adorable she looks wearing that shirt. She joins me on the couch, and I cannot help myself at the moment. I turn to her, taking her face in my hand, and I place a single kiss right on her lips. And then another one, and another one. Each one took her by surprise and made her cheeks turn a lovely shade of pink.

"Come with me to the Hamptons this weekend. We can get Tuck, check on mom, stay in the guest house, and I can make you dinner. We can wake up drinking coffee on the porch together. It can be our official first date," I tell her.

She bites down on her bottom lip, "Emma is getting her wedding dress this weekend, and I need to be there."

"Then take off tomorrow, and we can leave in the morning the next day. Emma will not mind considering you worked by yourself on Saturday. I do not have anything going on at work that I need to be here for," I tell her, taking her hand in mine.

She picks her phone up off the coffee table and starts typing away at what I hope is a text to Emma telling her she will not be there the next few days. She stops typing, flashing me a smile before her phone goes off with a ping. "Okay, looks like we are going to the Hamptons tomorrow."

When we pull into the driveway of my parent's house, my dad, Jack, is already outside waiting for our arrival with Tuck. Claire gets out of the car first, and Tuck runs for her. He licks her all over her face and has her laughing so hard from him trying to jump all over her. I think it is safe to say he missed her. My dad comes over to greet us, and we all make our way inside. Usually, my mother would be the first person outside greeting us, but she has still been on bed rest and taking it easy from her heart attack. I know Claire cannot wait to see her.

"You two make yourself at home. Catherine is still sleeping, but I will tell you when she wakes up. If you need anything while you are here, just let me know," Jack says.

"Thanks, Dad, but I think we will stay in the guest house while we are here."

He nods to us and then heads upstairs, I suspect, to check on mom.

I take Claire's hand, guiding her through the kitchen and then to the back door so we can make our way over to the guest house. Could I have thought of a better first date for us? This time here means something to me, probably because last time, we were not together, and I wanted so badly to be hers then, and now I have the chance to redo our time here. I plan this time to make it a memorable one for us, and I have a little surprise for her. Here is one of her favorite places, so honestly, I could not think of anywhere else I would want to be with her.

"At least I do not have to worry about you asking me to sleep on the couch again," I say, hanging our clothes up in the closet.

She laughs, "We have come a long way since then."

"You have," I pause, "I still feel the same about you now as I did then. I just had to wait for you" I sit on the end of the bed, take Claire's hand, and pull her towards me. She falls on my lap, turning her face to me.

"I am sorry for making you wait," she says.

I tuck a piece of hair behind her ear, "Do not be sorry. You were worth the wait" I place a kiss on her cheek, "Even though it was not easy. Sometimes I thought I was never going to get you."

We both hear the front door of the guest house open, so we get up and walk into the living room.

"Hey, I just thought I would let you know your mom is awake."

I look over to Claire, "You want to go see her"? I ask her.

"Yes. We can go together,"

We follow my dad out the door, walk over to their house, and through the back patio door. I have seen my mom many times since her accident, and it still hurts to see her, not herself. Indeed, she is looking and feeling better than when I left here a few days ago.

When we get to their room, the door is already open, and I let Claire walk in first since I know how much she wants to see her.

"Claire, darling, how are you"?

Mom is sitting in her reading chair by the window. She has her feet propped up on the footrest and a blanket over her legs and feet. She looks so much better than she did days ago.

"Catherine, you look amazing," she says, going in for the hug. "How are you feeling today"?

"Believe it or not, I almost feel like myself again. You want to go for a jog later"? She laughs.

We all laugh, and Claire sits by my mother's feet on the footrest.

"I do not think you will be going for a jog or playing pickleball with your friends anytime soon," I tell her.

"So, what are you two doing here? I do not think Tuck was ready to go home yet. We love him so much, and I will miss him during my naps."

"We wanted to see you, and I have plans for us while we are here," I tell her, taking a seat on the edge of their bed.

Claire looks over at me; I know it is because she does not know I have something up my sleeve for her.

"Claire dear, before you two leave, I would love you to have a conversation just the two of us. Would that be alright with you"?

Claire pats my mom on the knee, "I would love that."

I know what my mom wants to talk to her about alone, which makes me a bit nervous because I do not want her to scare me or put anything extra into Claire's head. We are just starting this relationship.

"Well, mom, we are going to get out of your way for now," I say, getting up from the bed and walking over to them.

Claire gets up, giving my mom another one of her hugs, "We will be back to see you later."

"Yes. Well, you two have fun doing whatever you have planned."

"We will," Claire and I say in unison.

We walk out of the room, and once we are down the stairs, Claire asks me if I have an idea of why my mom wants to talk.

"She probably just wants to make sure you have the right intentions with me," I say, joking. Which then earns me a nasty glare from Claire and a nice little smack on the arm. I am laughing hard.

"Okay, I was kidding, but I am sure she has questions. A mom is always looking out for her son. She loves you, so I know she will take it easy on you," I say as we walk out the back door toward the guest house. "And she probably would want you to quit calling her Catherine and to call her mom."

"I know, but I always think the generous thing to do is call her by her name," she says as we walk in the door.

"Yea, but she hates it. You have been around here long enough to call her mom."

Claire falls onto the couch and puts her feet over the armrest, leaving me no room to sit with her. Considering I need to start working on what I have planned for us, I do not mind.

I plan to recreate the things we did together when we were here the week we planned the wedding and add a few new surprises. I want to make Claire dinner but set it up on the deck of the guest house with a nice little setup. After dinner, we can take a walk down the beach, and I have my dad set something there for her, hopefully not backfire on me.

Getting started in the kitchen, pulling out all the ingredients to make the same dinner I made for her, shrimp alfredo. When I look back to talk to Claire while I cook, she is napping on the couch. She still has not had a chance to catch up on the sleep she missed from staying up all night talking the other night. It was good that she fell asleep, so I could get everything done, and it surprised her when she woke.

I take a second away from what I am doing, draping a blanket over her—then placing a kiss on her forehead. Then get back to work in the kitchen. There is already a table on the deck. I find a tablecloth to go over it and candles for the center of the table. When I set up the table and chairs the way I want them, I get back into the kitchen to finish everything for dinner and constantly look up to check on Claire. Who seems not to be bothered by all the noise I am making.

I have my dad setting up on the beach just a short walk down from their house, and we are not to go that way until it gets dark. I had messaged him earlier in the day on the way here to ask him if he would like to help me with something meaningful, and of course, he said yes.

I am plating our dinner when Claire wakes up from her short nap and joins me in the kitchen. She wraps her arms around me from behind, and I place my hand on one of hers. "Smells yummy in here," Claire says before I spin around, wrapping my arms around her and placing a kiss on her lips. "Go change while I set up, and then join me on the deck," I tell her, giving her one more kiss before she walks away.

She will not be long, so I plate the rest of what I made up and then take the plates back. The view outside could not be any more perfect tonight. Sun is setting in the distance, and the waves are crashing in. When everything is ready, I stand by the railing for Claire, and she does not leave me waiting long. She comes around the corner, wearing a white sundress and slip-on sandals. She threw her hair into a high ponytail, which was a good choice since it was windy.

I pull out her chair for her, and she takes a seat. Then I sit right next to her.

"This is nice, Ryan. Thank you."

"Anything for you... I guess you could say I wanted a do-over. The last time I made you this dinner here, it was different for the both of us."

"So now that we are exclusive, you wanted to make this time special"? She says before taking a bite.

When she says the word exclusive, it gets my heart racing in a good way. That is not something we have talked about yet.

"Is that what you want, to be exclusive"? I ask her.

She blushes and then picks up her glass, taking a sip.

"I just thought that is what we were. There has been a lot of confusion between us regarding wanting to be with each other. First, I wanted to be with you, and then when I was not available, you wanted to be with me, and now that we can finally be with each other, we should not waste any more time not being exclusive. You called me at work to tell me you had a meeting. I would call that exclusive," she laughs.

"Everything you said makes sense. We have not talked about it, so I guess this is our conversation making it official."

She holds her hand out for me to shake her hand, and I laugh. "Are we shaking on this"?

She gives me a big smile, "We are shaking on an agreement. I feel like that is the most responsible thing to do as best friends who just agreed to be officially a couple. I am official yours, and you are mine."

This woman. I put my hand in hers and shook our agreement. Then pull her towards me for a kiss because that is the more responsible thing to do, in my opinion.

We finished our dinner, which took longer than I imagined because she had many things she wanted to talk about as a couple. She tried to set rules, and one of those still meant we could not have sleepovers but once a week. I rolled my eyes on the inside because I would hate for her to see how much I couldn't entirely agree with it, but I will always respect the things she wants. I know our time together will mean more, considering we will not be spending every waking hour of our days together.

After cleaning up from dinner, the sun has fully set, so it is time for our walk down the beach. Claire seems to be alone for anything and does not ask questions when I tell her we are going for a walk. I guide her down the walkway till we reach the sand, and then she takes my hand in hers as we start walking.

Neither of us talks much on our walk, just taking in the ocean, the stars, and the moment. Claire pauses for a second, slips off her shoes, and then picks them up from the sand to carry them. She lets go of my hand to walk closer to the water, getting her feet wet. We are close to what I had my dad set up for us, and while I can see it in the distance, Claire is not paying attention just yet. I walk faster to get there before her, and she still does not notice that she is further away from me. She continues walking through the water while I walk up to the two rows of candles lit and white rose petals spread around. My dad set it up exactly as I asked, and I hope this moment goes as I want.

Claire finally turns in my direction and pauses when she sees everything set up. She moves towards me or away but stands there like she is shocked.

"Claire Elyse Cassidy, get over here, now," I yell at her.

She stands there for another minute and finally decides to walk toward me.

A Love That Blooms

"Ryan, please tell me this is not a proposal."

Crap. This kind of looks like that, doesn't it?

She finally stands before me, and I take her hand while laughing. "Sorry... I did not mean to scare you like that. It is not a proposal. That moment would be more than candles and rose petals on the beach" I clear my throat; I feel like I practiced what I was about to tell her in the mirror a few times, but right now, my heart is racing, and I suddenly forget the words.

Her face looks worried still, and I need to get these words out quickly. "Claire... There was a time when I never thought this moment right here would be possible" I pause. "I meant it when I told you earlier that my feelings for you months ago are no different than the feeling I have for you now because of Claire... I love you, and I have for a long time. It was all those days I spent with you as your best friend. When inside, I wanted to be so much more than that"

She looks down at the ground, and it is then that I feel like this will not be suitable for me. She does not have to love yet; I can wait for her to have those feelings. I just needed her to know what I had wanted to say for months and months. I have never said those words to anyone, and I am glad I never did because those words have been hers all along.

I wrap my arms around her and hold her tight, "You do not have to say anything" She has her arms covered around me in return, and she has not looked me in the eyes since I told her those words. Is this moment turning into a heartbreaking one?

It is so quiet now that I suddenly start hearing her cry. That was not supposed to happen. I pull out of our hold on each other and pull her face up with my hand. "Claire, I did not mean to make you cry. I just wanted you to know. It is okay if you do not feel the same way right now. I get it. It is quick, but it isn't because I feel we have been like this long. It just took us a long time to get to here" I wipe away a few of her tears with my thumb. I have seen Claire cry but never like this.

She does not need to explain anything or say anything at this moment. I take her hand and start walking back towards the guest house when she stops me.

I turn back to her, "This is the best thing anyone has ever done for me," she says.

I walk up to her, taking her face into my hands and thumbing away the remaining tears on each of her cheeks before kissing her like she is the greatest thing to ever happen to me because she is.

We stop kissing, and I place my forehead on hers while her eyes are still closed. Then she whispers, "I love you."

"Wait a minute, I am going to need you to say that again," I say, pulling my phone out of my pocket and holding up one finger with my other hand for her to wait.

I scroll through my phone, looking for the perfect thing to one-up this moment.

I hit play on what happens to be Claire's favorite song, and when she hears what is playing "Just like a Dream" by The Cure. She gives me the biggest smile I have ever seen her wear and then says, "I love you" one more time. We spent the next several minutes kissing in pure bliss and taking in this unforgettable moment she said she wanted all those weeks ago while riding with me on the trip that would change us and bring us to where we are now.

Chapter Seventeen

Claire

I woke up this morning still wearing the smile I went to bed with last night. So, it was not just a dream, it was very accurate, and I got to live it. The set-up, and all the words Ryan said to me last night, was the sweetest, most meaningful thing anyone has ever done and said to me. I was speechless, and the tears, they were happy tears. When Ryan told me he loved me, I felt like I knew that long ago but did not want it to be correct or thought it was just because we were friends. Are things moving fast for us? Not when you wanted and felt this way for such a long time, it isn't.

Ryan was already out of bed when I woke up this morning and left me coffee, breakfast, and a note saying he was with his dad on the kitchen table of the guest house for me. I went ahead, got ready for the day, and saw Ryan and his dad down on the beach when I walked out the door to look for Tuck. I have not seen him since we arrived, and I know he has made himself at home within the week he has been here. I go through the back patio door to get inside the Hayes house and call for Tuck when I walk in, but he does not come running. I walk up the stairs, knowing he is probably in Catherine and Jack's bedroom, and when I walk by their door to peek in, I find Catherine sitting in her chair by the window, reading a book, and Tuck lying by the chair.

"Hey, I was just looking for Tuck. Sorry to bother you," I say, and Tuck comes up to me when he hears me say his name.

"Claire, you are not bothering me. Come in. I have wanted to talk to you," she says as she closes her book and lies it on the side table.

I took a seat on the foot stool in front of her. "How are you"?

"Do not worry about me, darling. I am doing much better than I once was and will get through this soon. I wanted to talk to you about Ryan," she tells me, and this is what I thought she would want to talk about.

"Are you worried about us"? I ask her.

"Oh dear, I am far from worried about the two of you. I want to thank you."

I am so confused, "Thank me? I am sorry, but for what"?

"Your friendship with Ryan changed him from going down the wrong path in his life. Ryan was so full of life, he loved playing football, and when he couldn't do that anymore, he took this opportunity with Baker. Ryan was only about the money, the women his money picked up, drinking, and he lost a lot of who he was along the way. When he met you, he was still going down this dark path. Then you asked him for help, and since he has become so close to you, he has turned into this man that I always knew he could be"

"I am flattered, but I cannot take credit for that. I know the Ryan I met and the one I know now are two different people, but I think he is the one who made himself that way. I think Ryan finally followed his heart and quit listening to what he thought he needed to be"

A Love That Blooms

"Exactly, he followed his heart, and Claire, you are his heart. You hold that for him, and to you, I am thankful. You saved him, and part of me knows he saved you too."

I smile because I know she is right; we did save each other. We met each other at the right time in each other's lives. Ryan kept me from countless nightmares and dark days when I thought no one wanted me, and he saved my heart. Tears fall down my cheeks, and I wipe them away.

"Honey, those tears just show me that I am right. You saved each other from the life you both thought you wanted, but your hearts showed you want you needed instead"

Continuing to wipe away my tears, I get up to hug her. "Thank you, Catherine,"

"Mom, you know better than to call me by my name," she says.

I laugh, "I know, I know."

I leave the room, and Tuck stays by her side instead of going with me.

"Claire," she says, and I turn back to her. "Yes"

"I think you two will live a delighted life together and with so much love that even I will be jealous."

I smile once again, "Thank you."

I walk into the hallway bathroom to fix my face from crying and then down the stairs. When I walk into the kitchen, Ryan sits at the kitchen island while talking to his dad, leaning up against the counter.

His face tells me he knows I have been crying when he sees me. "You okay"?

"Yes, I am good."

He holds out his arm to me, "Come here"?

I take his hand, and he pulls me close to him, placing a kiss on my cheek before looking into my eyes. "Are you sure"?

I shake my head yes, "I am perfect, promise."

He gives me one more kiss, this time on the lips.

"You want to go for a walk"? He asks me.

"Sure"

We walk hand and hand out the back door and down to the beach. Ryan is quiet, and I am sure this is something he has never had to navigate before with a woman, so he is probably just scared about what to ask me, so I decided to break the silence between us.

"Your mom is a good woman, you know," I tell him.

"I know… you want to tell me what the two of you talked about"? Ryan asks.

His tone made me change my mind, and it sounded like he was nervous about what was said.

"Honestly… not really. I feel like it was a conversation between Catherine and me, and it will always hold a special place in my heart. It would help if you did not worry, though. It was a good conversation."

We continue walking, and Ryan still seems to have something on his mind.

"What did you and your dad talk about this morning"?

"I told him about my plans, how I would like to move back here and open up my office, and the things we discussed."

"Are you wanting to do all those things soon? What did he say"?

A Love That Blooms

He does not answer me, and we just continue to walk, and I am not sure if maybe he and his dad's conversation just did not go as he planned it to go or if he is too scared to talk about how soon in the future he wants this stuff. I decided to stay quiet and not ask any more questions.

We circle back around and walk back to his parent's house. When we get to the guest house, he sits in one of the rocking chairs on the back deck and pulls me on his lap. The view from the balcony is the best, and to be with him here, makes it even better. One of his hands is resting on my thigh, and the other is brushing my hair off my shoulder.

"My dad said I should stay in the city for a few more years. He said I was still young, and he worries I will come out here and not be successful and regret that I ever left the city."

"I think you will be successful in what you put your heart to. I have faith in your dreams. I would hardly say thirty-one is young. It is the time to do the things you want in your life and do them for you. Once he sees how happy you are doing what you want to and how successful you can be, he will realize that he was wrong," I say, laying my head on his shoulder.

I love Jack, but I know how hard he can be on the guys regarding business. He built himself a very successful law firm so that he could provide for his family, and I know he expects Ryan and Baker to do the same. Baker said that Hayes Realty was built for his future and given to his children. What does that mean for Ryan, though? I know he went in on this to help Baker, and it used to only be about the money to him, but now that he dreams of owning his own, he should do it for his future and, hopefully, one day, his children.

"What did I do to deserve you"? he says, kissing my forehead.

"I have asked myself the same question lately," I grinned.

Today is the day we are getting Emma a wedding dress. Since Catherine is still not well enough to get out, it will just be Emma and me. So, today I get to not only play the role of maid of honor, but I am also filling in for all the other important people that cannot be here for her today. To say I am not nervous would be an understatement. Since Emma and I will be out shopping today, the guys have decided to go golfing after getting fitted for their tuxedos, and then Ryan wants me to come by his place later tonight. Since we are getting closer to the wedding, I know the time is coming when Ryan will need to head out back to the Hamptons and help Dan will make the arch. So, I know he will want to spend extra time together before he leaves, not knowing how long it will take him to make it.

I entered the bridal shop and found Emma sitting on a chair at the front, waiting for me. "Hey," she says, getting up and hugging me.

"Hey, you ready to get your dress," I ask her.

We are supposed to get my dress today, but finding a wedding dress is more exciting. Emma has an exquisite but girly color scheme for her wedding, which means she wants my dress to be a light pink silk dress, not my color, but I would only wear that color for her.

We follow the bridal consultant to the back room, where there are thousands and thousands of dresses. It is the higher-end bridal store in the city, and if she can not find a dress here, then I have no idea where we would go. This place should have every dress ever made. There are pink couches in front of huge mirrors for the brides to show off what they try on. The consultant has instructed us to find a few dresses to start with, and then I will wait for her to try those on. If none of those work, the consultant will help by suggesting dresses, and we will go from there. Emma is not very picky, and I know that tears will flow from her eyes once she puts the one on.

Emma and the consultant work together looking at dresses, and I walk to the side to look for her. She knows what she wants, so I am just looking through dresses to waste some time. I not only have this to do with Emma today. I also need to fill her in on what has happened between Ryan and me. She knows we have been spending more time together, but we wanted to wait to tell them we are an actual couple. Ryan plans to tell Baker while they golf today, and well, I am supposed to tell Emma here, but I think I will wait till lunch or something. I do not want to take away from this big day for her.

I see the consultant taking a whole load of dresses into a room, and Emma is still looking at more. I continue to pretend to look at dresses and waste some time before they work on trying dresses on Emma. When I envisioned getting married as a little girl, I always would say I wanted a substantial poofy dress like a Disney princess. That was until I found out fairytales are not real. That was probably the last time I remember discussing a wedding or getting married. There has not been one person to swoop me off my feet, making me think I was going to marry them. Ryan and I have only been official for like a week. Even though it feels more extended, and we know each other well, it is still too early to tell if he is the one I would marry. I want to think he could be, but I know Ryan has never thought about marriage.

I feel a tap on my shoulder, "You find anything"?

I turn to find Emma standing behind me, "No, what about you"?

She points in the direction of the consultant, "She is making me try on everything."

Looking in the direction of the consultant, I laugh. She seems nice, older with dark hair, and looks classy in some black suit pants and a white button-up silk blouse. I did not catch her name when we walked in, so I think I will call her lady.

"I am going to the dressing room. If you want to, sit on one of the pink couches out there to wait," Emma says, walking away.

I make my way over to one of the couches to sit. There is a possibility that we could be here for hours, so I better make myself comfortable. I pull out my phone to see if I have any messages from Ryan, and I find just one sweet text of missing you. Then he adds a picture of himself wearing his suit for the wedding. He knows how to put a smile on my face and looks so darn good in a tux. I text him a miss you too, and then slip my phone into my bag. I scanned the room, looking at other brides, trying on dresses, and I could not feel more out of place here.

Catherine insisted she wanted to be the one to set this appointment up, and she was funding the dress cost. So, that meant it needed to be at the most extravagant, classiest bridal shop. The ladies here have money, which I do not have a lot of, and Emma does not either until she marries Baker. That is one thing I enjoy about my relationship with Ryan. He has money and used to throw money away on ridiculous things, like cars, his penthouse, women, and trips. That was the old Ryan. Now he has a much smaller apartment, he sold two of his three vehicles, keeping just his jeep, and I know Ryan does not take any trips besides to his parents, and he does not spend a lot of money on me, and I am the only woman he is seeing. That is something I hope never changes between us. Coming here to open the flower shop was never about becoming wealthy. It was always about fulfilling a dream.

"What do you think"? Emma says, walking behind me and in front of one of the huge mirrors. She is wearing a strapless mermaid-fit wedding gown that fits her in all the right places. The dress is lace, and it may be just a tad tight because Emma's bust seems to be about to fall out the top.

"It is beautiful and looks great on you," I say, getting up from the couch to get a closer look at it.

"I love this one," she says, turning to the side to ensure she can see it from all sides.

"This is the first one, and when did you get these" I point to her chest "they look like they are going to fall out" I tug on the top of the dress, trying to pull it up.

Emma makes a confused face while watching me and finally just pushes my hand away. "Yeah, maybe the top is a bit much."

"I give this one like an eight. Go try on another one," I tell Emma before she walks back towards the dressing room.

The "lady" turns to me while walking away, "Claire, we have a room for you to try on bridesmaids' dresses if you would like." and then points in the direction of the dressing room.

"Thank you," I tell her before making my way to the dressing room.

Walking in is like a bubblegum nightmare, with pink dresses everywhere. Emma's wedding is testing me, and I never expected to have bad luck when planning it, almost forgetting to order a ridiculous amount of white and pink flowers and now pink dresses. I did not even know Emma liked pink so much. I close the door behind me and snap a picture to send Ryan of all the dresses before taking a deep breath, then going for the most decent dress to try on.

I slip on the palest pink dress silk dress. I look in the mirror, and this one is not that bad. It is a loose-fitting silky dress that dips at the top and drops just before my ankles. We are not wearing shoes since the ceremony is on the beach in the sand. This dress Is the perfect look for what Emma wants. Hopefully, she agrees, so I do not have to try many more dresses. My phone pings back with a text from Ryan.

Ryan- Yikes. That is a lot of pinks, but you got this, babe.

I smile and then walk out of the dressing room to see Emma wearing "the one," I begin to feel tears form in my eyes. She looks fantastic, in a white lace V-neck mermaid thin strapped dress, with a sweep train. It fits her like a glove, and the lady has already added a veil to her head. Emma sees me walking behind her through the mirror, and I see tears in her eyes.

"Emma, this one is perfect, twenty out of ten," I tell her.

She turns around and looks at me, so I spin for her to see the rest. "Claire, that one is perfect too."

I walk to her, giving her an embrace, and she starts crying, "You look like a bride, and I cannot wait to see you walk down the aisle in this one. Baker is going to love it."

"You think so," she says, wiping away tears and then looking at herself again in the mirror.

"I know so," I say, watching her.

Emma looks at herself in the mirror and tells the lady we are done here. She will get the dress, and I am glad I picked the perfect one first. Now that I have seen Emma, this all seems real and will happen soon.

When we finished everything at the bridal shop, Emma and I went for lunch at one of our favorite places, The Sandwich Shop. She seems always to want to eat here lately, and I do not mind considering we do not get to eat here as much as we used to while working at the original Blooms shop. We both order the same thing we always get and then take a seat at one of the booths.

"So, tell me, what has been going on lately with you"? Emma asks me, taking me by surprise.

"This is your day, and we do not have to talk about me" I blush, knowing she wants to talk about Ryan and me. I would love to talk about us, but I do not want to take away from her. We can speak of my life another day.

"Claire, don't be silly. Catherine slipped the other night on the phone and said, " Ryan, you are in love. We all knew this was going to happen, and honestly, I am surprised it took you this long for the both of you to figure it out. I am more than happy for you. It makes me excited for your future and our future as potentially being sisters-in-law."

"Hold up, what did Catherine say? And this is all new, so do not get too excited yet. Ryan and I have said I love you twice, and yes, I do feel that for him. We have both come a long way with each other. Finally, being together and feeling this for one another is one of the best feelings. That does not mean we are getting married like you and Baker."

She giggles and shakes her head like she is up to something but does not say anything. The waitress brings out food, and we both discuss dress shopping while eating. I finally gave in and asked what the big deal was with her wanting pink as one of her wedding colors, and she said it was something Baker wished to incorporate into the scheme. I would have never guessed him to be the one to choose that color as a wedding color, but he does seem on the feminine side. Baker has picked that color in the past. For the flower shop and the closet, which he had done for Emma.

We finish lunch and then go our separate ways. Emma said Baker and her have a date tonight, and the same goes for me. Ryan and I are making dinner at his apartment, and I am sure we both want to talk about things that happened today.

Chapter Eighteen

Ryan

Just finishing up nine holes of golf with Baker, I got a call from Claire saying she was done with Emma and heading to her apartment for a nap before coming over. After a day like today, I am looking forward to ending the day with her. I have plans to make us dinner and just watch a movie or something. Since coming back from the Hamptons, we have barely been able to see each other because of work and the fact that we sleep at our places each night.

After Baker and I finished our tux fittings this morning, we went out for a round of golf, knowing that eighteen holes would not happen. We all know what happened last time we did that. I needed to talk to him about Claire and me and was not surprised to find out that mom had already done the job for me. He said that they had been waiting for us to tell them. What I was surprised to hear from him was the talk of I need to make sure I am making the right decision by being with Claire. He thinks I could resort to my old ways and hurt her. He always thought he needed to take care of Claire, considering she and Emma are a package deal. He is looking out for his best interest of Claire, even though I am his brother. I understand that I have a past, but I know he has seen how I have turned everything around for myself this last year. I cut our conversation short because it bothered me to talk about my old ways. It makes me uneasy that I could ever be that person to Claire; she means so much more to me than that.

I take a quick shower and take Tuck on a walk when I get home. It was not an easy task getting him to come back home with Claire and me, but we missed him, and he will be going back with me next week when I need to make the arch so he can rest with my mother. I have been in touch with Dan since the day I went to his house after hurting Claire during the volleyball tournament, and his health has not been good. I am leaving sooner to go out there than I thought so I could make the arch and help Dan.

When Tuck finishes his business, we head back to the apartment, so I can start cooking dinner. To my amazement, Claire is already waiting for us when we open the door.

"Surprise," she says, greeting me with a kiss.

Tuck jumps up on her, as always, and she gives him some attention before taking his leash off for me.

"I was not expecting you this early. I was just about to start dinner," I say, heading into the kitchen to the fridge, and Claire follows me and sits on the kitchen island counter.

"I was just so excited to see the two of you that it was impossible to try to take a nap, so I just came on over. How did your day go"? She asks me while I pull out two steaks from the fridge and set them on the counter next to her.

She wraps her arms around my neck, and I place my hands on her legs. "It was good. How was yours"? I try to keep it short because I do not know if I want to tell her what Baker and I talked about while golfing.

"It was good" she gives me another kiss, and when I move my hands from her to start dinner, she jumps off the counter and lays on the couch.

I start cooking and see her flip through the TV guide for something to watch. Tuck is lying by her, and I know she will click on something for him. I watch her seasoning the steaks before putting them on the cast iron skillet to cook. She is still searching and then clicks on Cinderella. That is not what I was expecting.

"You watch cartoons now"? I ask her.

She sits up and turns around, hanging her hands over the back of the sectional.

"Today, while we were at the bridal shop, it got me thinking about how the last time I imagined what I wanted my wedding to look like, and well, it was when I was a little girl watching Disney princess movies. Then I remembered that was probably the last time I also watched a princess movie. Tuck would like this, so I turned it on for him," she laughs.

Confused, I ask her, "That was the last time. Like you never in your adult life had a vision of your wedding"?

"I might have recently remembered talking about it one night to Emma, but I do not remember the conversation very well. Maybe it was a dream I had," she says, putting her finger on her chin to help her remember.

Claire used to tell me about the dreams she used to have after the accident at the shop with her ex-boyfriend, so I am sure with all this wedding planning, it was just a dream she had.

She is still facing me, looking over the back of the sectional "I mean, I did imagine what kinds of flowers I would want the other day when I made the flower order."

"Really. What did you imagine?" I ask her because I genuinely want to know.

"Well, Emma wants everything white with just touches of pink. By the way, she said that was Baker's choosing. I find that strange…" she says, laughing.

"Yea, that does not seem like something Baker would choose. Tell me what you imagined"?

"Oh yeah, I imagined flowers of all colors, and maybe it was because she had everything white, so I just thought she needed more color or because that is what I would want."

My guess would be that is something Claire would want. She has her apartment decorated with many different colors, and she always wears colors, even pink, although she insists it is not her color. I think she still looks great in it.

I finish making dinner, and we eat together at the kitchen island. Claire continues talking about Emma's wedding and how wedding dress shopping went today. In the back of my mind is the conversation I had with Baker today. I know it is something I should talk about with her. I do not feel like darkening the mood right now, so it is something I will bring up sometime soon.

As I return to the Hamptons today, I can only think about Claire. Last night after dinner, we watched a movie on the couch with Tuck, and after she fell asleep, I carried her to bed and then fell asleep with her in my arms. I broke the news to her this morning that I needed to come back out here, and while she was sad, she knew it was coming soon that I would come back out here. So, while I am out here, she will finish the last-minute things she needs to do for the wedding there.

A Love That Blooms

After a quick trip by my parent's house to check on mom, drop off Tuck, and leave my bags at the guest house. I drive into town to the hardware store for the supplies I need to build the arch. It is not your typical wedding arch; this one is in the shape of an octagon. Once it is up, Claire will put flowers around a couple of the corners and order sheets of white and pink cloths to be draped over the top and hanging down the sides. The arch is going to be a dark walnut stain. It looks easy on paper to build, but I know I have my work cut out for me. Instead of using all of Dan's tools, I buy a few new ones, along with screws and the wood. On my way out of the store, I see a lawnmower, and I get it because I know Dan needs the help, and mowing is one of the things I know his house needs the most. So glad I borrowed a trailer from my dad before coming here.

When I pull up to his house, I am surprised to see him rocking in a chair on the front porch with a tea in hand. He waves when he notices it is me. I get out of the jeep, meet him on the front porch, then sit in the rocking chair opposite him.

"You are going to mow my yard too, Ryan," he says as he looks out in the yard, never making eye contact with me.

I laugh, "Yes, I am Dan. You know I came here to help you for a few days."

"No, you are here to use my shop. I do not need any help."

"I am here for your help, and I will return the favor by helping you. Since you are not feeling well, mowing today, and we can work in the shop tomorrow," I tell Dan as we both rock in the chairs on the front porch.

"I am fine. After you mow my yard, we can work in the shop together. I would like that today. I need to get out of the house."

I smile at him, getting up from my chair. "Sounds good, Dan. I am going to get started."

After unloading the mower from the trailer, I got started on the front, and Dan stayed on the front porch the whole time, watching me while he continued to rock in his rocking chair and drink his tea.

It takes me two hours to mow the whole yard, and when I walk back to the front, Dan must have gone inside because I do not see him anywhere. I start unloading all the wood, carrying it in loads to the shop, and then finish my trips with the saw. I place everything on the ground of the shop and look over it before rolling out the plans making sure I have it all here. I wipe my face with my shirt and, just thinking about all the work I am about to do me exhausted, but I want to do this for Baker and Emma. Claire and I have vowed to make this day the best day for them, and there is no going back now. I know I can do this.

I start organizing the wood, and when I look up, I see Dan sitting in his chair, watching me. It startles me, "Sorry, I did not see you there."

"I told you I was going to help you," he says straight-faced.

"Right, how am I doing so far"? I ask him, pointing to all the wood on the ground.

He pushed his glasses off the bridge of his nose and studied the wood I had just laid on the ground. Then his eyes look over at the saw I got at the hardwood store.

"So far, you look like you know what you are doing. I am impressed."

I laugh at him and then start looking over the measurements on the paper. He seemed to be watching me intensely, so I asked him some questions.

"How long have you been woodworking"?

He takes a tea drink and sits it back down before answering me.

"For fifty-five years."

He gives me a short answer, and when he says the number fifty-five, Claire comes into my mind.

"How did you know Susie was the one"? I ask him as I mark the measurement on the wood pieces lying on the ground.

"I just knew the moment I saw her. When she finally saw me for who I was, I never wanted to spend another day without her in it. I thought of not waking up to her or sharing my dreams when I wanted to be with her. She meant the world to me, and that is how I knew she was the one for me."

Which is what one person who was so madly in love would say, right? Do I feel I could say the same thing about Claire that Dan says about Susie? Absolutely.

"Do you and Susie have any children?

He looks down at the ground, and I immediately regret asking the question. I have been around Dan for years and years, and I have never seen family here or known anyone related to Dan.

"Sorry, you do not have to answer that."

He looks up at me and crosses his arms across his chest.

"Susie and I had only been married one year when she became pregnant with our son. The day he was born was the best day of his life. Well, besides the day I married Susie. When he was six, he got sick, and we did not have much money or insurance. Then after many trips to the doctors with no answers, he just got worse. He passed away just before his eighth birthday."

"I am so sorry to hear that, Dan. Did you ever figure out what was wrong with him"? I stop what I am doing and sit on Dan's stool.

"Doctors think he was born with an untreatable illness. Those eight years with him were not enough, but I still remember every day with him as if it was yesterday" he picks up his tea to take another sip.

"What is his name"? I ask him.

"Henry"

Instead of working on the arch, I sat with Dan and listened to him tell me stories of Henry and who he was. In the same wooden box, he once pulled out a picture of Susie to show Claire and some images of Henry to show me. Before we knew it, it was dark out, and although I did not get any woodworking done, I was more than pleased to sit with Dan and listen to his stories.

I woke up early the next day to head back to Dan's. I think I can finish the arch unless he is up for more storytelling today. When I arrived at his place, I expected him to be waiting for me on his porch since he knew I would be back today, but he was not there. I walk up to his door, knocking, and get no response. When I reach for the handle of the front door to see if it is locked, it is not, so I open it up. I yell his name while walking through his house and reaching his room. I find him lying in bed, still sleeping. I know I probably kept him up past his bedtime last night, so after I get closer to check on him, I leave him to rest and decide to get started on the arch by myself.

Since I have been here, Dan has seemed to be feeling better, and I hope it is not him just putting on a show for me. Before I leave, I want to ensure that he will be good until the next time I see him, which will be next week for the wedding.

I get started by sawing the wood pieces down to size and then lining them all up as I will need them. I start from the bottom, stand on each side, and work my way up, making an octagon shape on the front and back. I was almost finished with it when I heard someone clear their throat from behind me. I turn around to see Dan wearing his everyday outfit and sitting on his stool with a glass half full of tea.

"How long have you been there"? I ask him. I have been out here for hours and have been too busy to notice him.

"An hour, I would say" he picks up his glass, taking a drink.

I look at my watch to check the time; it is just after lunchtime.

"Well, what do you think"?

"I think you are doing a good job, I guess. I have never seen an arch like this one before, so I have nothing to compare it to."

I laugh, before grabbing the stain off the table with a cloth, so I can start staining it.

"You know Ryan; you have come a long way. You just made this without asking me to help you. I want to think there is a reason why this arch means so much to you."

"I wish, Dan; this is just something for my brother's wedding next week. They wanted us to have you make it, but I was happy to make it myself. I guess you could say it means so much to me because I wanted to be able to give them what they wanted for their big day. Maybe one day I can do the same for myself."

225

"How are things with the girl? She hasn't taken any more volleyballs to the nose, has she"? He asks me as I continue staining the arch.

I chuckle, "No, she hasn't... After being honest with her and never giving up, I finally scored the girl. So, thank you."

"You are welcome, but I do not think what I said helped you get the girl. I think you both finally realized you love each other," he says, still sitting there and watching me.

I turn back to look at him and smile. He then realizes he is right because he is.

"Well, I am glad to hear to finally figured out your love life."

Once I finish with the arch, I stand back, take in the whole thing, and admire my work. I am impressed. I look back at Dan, and he throws his hands up. "You did good, Ryan; you did well."

"Thanks," I say, wiping my hands together to clean them off.

Dan will let me keep the arch in his shop until the wedding day, so after cleaning up the mess I made and organizing his shop a little for him, we say our goodbyes for now. I head to the guest house for a long shower and to gather my things so I can get back to Claire. If this couple of days away from her has taught me anything. It is that I do not want to be away from her anymore. While I have been busy during my time here, she has always been on my mind, especially during conversations with Dan.

Chapter Nineteen

Claire

While I know where Ryan is and what he has been doing, his being away has not been fun, particularly when I do not know when he will return. When he woke me up yesterday morning to tell me he needed to go, I knew the time was coming. Next week, wedding week will be so busy for the two of us that I know Ryan wouldn't have time to make the arch then. He took Tuck with him, so when he offered to let me stay at his place while he was gone, I told him I would be fine staying at my place. I feel like the offer was sweet, and I would enjoy waking up to his smell every morning, but I would feel lonely there. Not like I do not on my own. I know this is his way of getting me to come around to the idea of staying together more, and well, it kind of worked. I would also like to say that I want to because his being away shows how much I miss and love him. I have hardly spoken to him since he left, and he gets the biggest kiss when he finally returns.

Things at the shop have been busy this week, now that we are into September. Some people love the fall season so much that they think if you order fall flower arrangements, then fall weather will show up, and it doesn't. I still love making the arrangements for those people, though. It does bring me the feeling of fall weather, which is my favorite season.

Since the wedding day is nearing, Emma has wanted to hang out more this week, and I have appreciated it since Ryan has been out of town. We have done lunch the last couple of days, and tonight she suggested we should close the store down together, just like old times. So, while I sweep the floors, she wipes all the counters.

"So, when will Ryan be back"? She asks me, and I know she already knows the answer.

"He hasn't said yet. I already told you this," I laugh, wondering why Emma is asking.

Emma and Baker think he went back to the Hamptons to check on Catherine. We never told them that Dan wouldn't be able to make the arch because of his health. So, they have no idea Ryan is the one who is making the arch. We have done well with not letting them know what went wrong during wedding planning.

"Did Ryan ever tell you what Baker told him"?

"What are you talking about"? I ask her, confused because Ryan never told me anything Baker said while the guys were together this weekend.

She sits on the stool at the front counter and watches me finish sweeping the floor. "Baker told me that he and Ryan had a little disagreement while playing golf. Baker wants to ensure Ryan's old ways are gone and that Ryan doesn't hurt you."

"Ryan didn't say anything, but I would like to think that he never returns to the person he once was."

"Will you talk to him about it? I want to know you are in good hands, which I am not saying you aren't, but I want to make sure that you and Ryan have a conversation about the future and where he stands with you and your relationship," she said, concerned.

I put up the broom and grabbed my things from the office so we could leave. When I get to the front, Emma is waiting by the front door for me to answer her.

"Yes... I will talk to Ryan whenever he gets back home, okay?"

She smiles, "Yes, thank you."

We say our goodbyes before Emma gets into her car to leave. I pull my phone out of my bag as I make my way home. I always like to talk to Ryan on my walk home, which is my way of feeling safe while walking alone. I dial his number and wait for him to answer. Since I haven't heard from him much while he has been away, I am not sure he will pick up. It rings three times before he answers.

"Walking home"? he says.

"Yes, I am. What are you doing"?

He sounds like he is doing something and does not immediately respond.

"If you are busy, I can let you go."

"Sorry... I am going to call you back. Give me just a minute," Ryan says before hanging up the phone.

I pull the phone away from my ear and look at it. Did that just happen? I slide my phone back into my bag and continue to walk home. If he is still working away in the Hamptons, he is probably busy, but I cannot help but think about what Emma told me back at the shop. He couldn't possibly be doing something he shouldn't, and I know I shouldn't feel like that about Ryan, but having the conversation with Emma fresh in my mind makes me think the worst.

I finish the walk to my building without talking to him on the phone and decide to text him to let him know I have made it home. Once I get out of the elevator and to my door. I get my keys out of my bag but notice the door is unlocked before sticking my key in. Did I leave it unlocked all day?

I open the door, expecting my place to look like it was robbed, but instead, I see Ryan holding a huge bouquet.

"Hey," he says.

I walk up to him, wrap my arms around him, and then kiss him. "You didn't tell me you were back" He sets the flowers down on the kitchen island and then wraps his arms around me in return.

"I wanted to surprise you," he whispers in my ear.

I kiss him again because I miss him so much; being here is comforting.

"Sorry, I got off the phone. I had just walked into your apartment when you called, and I wanted to pick the place up before you got here."

I laugh, letting go of him. "You didn't have to do that…Thank you for the flowers. Let me guess, Emma made them"?

"Correct, I told her not to tell you."

It makes me wonder why Emma brought up what she did, knowing Ryan was here and would be waiting for me at my apartment.

"Can I ask you something"? I say, getting a vase down from the cabinet and filling it with water from the sink so I can put the flowers in it.

"Sure," he sits at the kitchen island, watching me.

"Why haven't you told me about what Baker said while golfing"? I pick up the flowers and place them in the vase.

He looked at me like he didn't want me to know about their conversation.

"That is the reason why I am here actually…Well, that and being away from you for a few days."

"Okay"? I say, confused.

"Claire… Let's move in together," he says.

I did not see this coming, and most definitely not this soon. I do not understand how a conversation with Baker making sure this relationship is what he wants and a few days away brings him to want to move in together.

I walk around the counter and take a seat by him." I am sorry, but Ryan, this is crazy. One minute I think maybe you are out doing something you shouldn't, then the next minute, you are in my apartment asking us to make a big step."

"Out doing something I shouldn't. What are you talking about?"

"Emma had just asked me to talk to you about what Baker said before we left the shop, so when you had to get off the phone. I might have had the thought of you doing something."

"That I used to do," he interrupts me. "So, you think there is a chance that I would return to the old me"? He snarls, and it is then that I know I messed up.

"I didn't say that. It was just a thought that came to mind because of the conversation I had two minutes before with Emma."

He crosses his arms and sits back in the chair, shaking his head. I officially messed up a big moment for him and feel terrible.

"Look, I am sorry; I know this is not how you expect this moment to go."

He turns to me and takes my hands in his.

"You are right; this is crazy. We aren't ready to move in together."

"Ryan," I say, frowning because even though I wasn't sure if I was ready for that step in our relationship, I feel bad for ruining this for him.

"No, Claire, this is just too soon. I was gone, and all I could think about while there was you and how I never wanted to spend another day without you. I knew that meant I was ready for us to move in together and be together every day, but I should have thought about what you wanted first, and I know this is something you aren't ready for. We know each other well, but I think we still need time to figure each other out."

I feel a single tear fall from my eye because he is correct. We need to figure each other out. I shouldn't have thought of him doing something stupid like drinking or the chance he might have been out with another girl, but I did. I wipe away the single tear before he sees it. He gets up from the chair, takes my face in his hands, and gives me a single kiss.

"I love you, Claire."

"I love you too."

He wraps his arms around me and then says, "I am going to go."

"Ryan, you don't have to leave."

"I don't want either of us to say anything else that could potentially hurt one another, so this is goodbye for tonight. We both have things we need to think about."

I shake my head, and then he unwraps his arms around me. He gives me one last kiss on the forehead and then leaves. Once the door's closed, the tears start rolling down both cheeks.

Ryan

What I thought would be one of the greatest moments of my life went downhill suddenly, and I quickly learned that the one thing I didn't think Claire would think of me, she did, and she felt the worst. When Baker threw out the thought of me returning to the old me, I knew there was no chance that Claire would ever think I was that person anymore and think that she hurt worse than I could ever imagine. I felt like I had done everything I needed to prove to her that I would never be that person again, and I did. So why did she think I was out doing something I shouldn't? I want to blame Baker and Emma for bringing this up, but I can't because I know there will always be that thought in her mind that is who I once was.

I didn't want to leave. I never want to leave Claire, but I knew I needed to if one of us said something else we shouldn't have for the night. I couldn't change the situation getting worse, and I know we both have things we need to think about.

Last night I returned to my lonely apartment since I had left Tuck with my parents again. It didn't take me long to go to bed, try forgetting about everything that happened, and hope that today would be a better day. I did toss for a few hours, but the exhaustion from being away caught up with me, and I was asleep before midnight. I could have made it easy to message Claire, apologize for leaving, and make it all right, but I did not want to give in.

The first thing I do when I get up is sent Claire the usual Good Morning text and then hop into the shower for work. Generally, by the time I get out, she has sent me a response, but this morning I got nothing back, and I quickly realized that I hope I didn't screw this up. I change into work clothes and know I can stop by to see her before going into the office. It is nice her being next door to me while working.

I am walking down the hallway when I spot something on the couch, and when the living room comes into full view, I see it is Claire, peacefully sleeping on my couch with a blanket. There is a reason for no response. She is wearing the shirt I gave her, her hair is in a ponytail, and her glasses are still on her face. It looks like she got her early this morning, and I wonder why she only made it as far as my couch.

I sit on the coffee table and lean over her, brushing my hand across her face, moving some flyaway hairs back. "Good Morning"

She moans, rolling over but does not open her eyes. "Morning"

"Claire... When did you get here"?

She finally opens her eyes to look at me, "at two."

"Why are you on the couch"?

She sits up from the couch, pulls the blanket off her, and puts her hand on my leg.

"I couldn't sleep; I felt terrible for last night. I want to tell you that I am sorry for thinking that you would ever do anything to hurt me or anything that you used to do. I know you would never do anything like that to me, and you aren't that person anymore. I also want to tell you that my lease is up at the end of the month. I want to move in with you."

"That didn't explain why you are sleeping on the couch." I smile at her. "Are you sure that is what you want"?

"I am sure I want us to be together daily, and if that means living together, then let's do it. I don't want to spend another day not without you, Ryan."

I lean forward, taking her face in my hands, and place a single kiss on her lips.

"Same for me. Now explain why you are on the couch"? I put my forehead against hers

"I didn't want to wake you up" she looks down

I laugh, "And risk, giving me the best wake-up of my life. Hope you enjoyed that last time you will be sleeping on the couch."

She laughs. "Guess I will get ready for work."

She gets up from the couch, taking her bag on the floor down the hall to the bedroom.

I make a pot of coffee for us, wearing the biggest grin on my face. If Claire's lease is up at the end of the month, that would mean it has been almost a whole year of falling for Claire for me. It doesn't seem like a long time, but for me, it was. For nearly a year, I hid feelings from her, unhappily dated other women because she was dating, and fought hard these last few months to have her finally. If Claire said that she felt things for me before the gala last year, I missed her just weeks before I started developing my own for her.

Chapter Twenty

Claire

Since we agreed that I would move in after my lease. I have been staying with Ryan and slowly bringing my stuff to his. I am only starting with essentials, like my clothes. By the end of the week, I had enough clothes there for now and will worry about the rest later. Ryan surprised me with tickets he won from the Gala, so tonight we are going to dinner and a movie. A fantastic typical date night, and I am excited about it. A relaxing night together before the wedding chaos begins next week.

We are walking to dinner, enjoying the nice chilly night. The Italian restaurant for dinner is not far from the apartment. Ryan and I got dressed together for the evening. I chose jeans, a white shirt, and a thin cardigan to wear tonight. And Ryan chose jeans and a polo to wear. We have spent the week getting used to living together, and Ryan has learned to be patient when it comes to a woman getting ready. I like to take my time for no reason whatsoever. When Ryan finishes getting dressed, that means it's time to go. It has become a learning process for both of us.

Ryan is holding my hand while walking down the sidewalk. When we reached the restaurant, he opened the door for me to walk in first. The hostess takes us to our table, and Ryan pulls my chair out. I take a seat, and then he sits across from me. Ryan has never lacked in the generous category, and I love that about him. I feel like he always puts me first.

"Can I order your food for you"? Ryan asks me as he sets his menu down.

"Sure," I answer him. "But why"?

He grins, "I know what's good here, and we can share"

I set the menu down on the table. "Okay. I guess I trust you."

The waitress arrives, and just as Ryan asks, he orders food for both of us. I can't complain about his choices. They both sound great. The restaurant is a cute little Italian restaurant with an Italy feel to it. I have never been here before, but I guess Ryan has.

When I turn my eyes back to Ryan, he is wearing the biggest grin on his face.

"What"? I ask him with a smile on my face.

"You finally look at me like you chose me. You have looked at me like that for weeks, and I have loved every minute of it. What was it for you? What finally made you choose me"?

I lean forward, resting my arms on the table.

"It was you. I finally realized that my feelings for you were greater than a friendship. So, I knew it was worth taking a risk."

He leans forward, "Was there a moment you knew"?

I laugh, "You sure are asking a lot of questions."

"I am curious. I could tell you the exact moment I knew I wanted to be with you," Ryan says with seriousness.

"You remember the exact moment"? I ask him.

"Like it was yesterday," He smiles.

"Please share the details."

Ryan sits up, reaching for my hand across the table. I hold my hand out for him to take, and he brushes his thumb across my knuckles before telling me his story.

"It was almost a year ago. I was helping you move into your apartment, not because you asked me, but because Baker did. I will be honest. I didn't want to be there that night. I planned to go to club Deuce with friends like I had done every Saturday night before you. I showed up to help you, and it was only you there. I know we had spent time together before then, but this time was different. Your hair was messy, and you wore workout clothes even though I know you had never been to a gym. I helped you put your dining table chairs together, and you laughed at every ridiculous joke I said that night. We ordered takeout to end the day, and you turned on Golden Girls. A show I had never watched in my entire life, but we both laughed at every episode we watched that night. You laid your head on my lap because you have the tiniest couch and fell asleep on me. That moment felt like that was where I needed to be and belonged. After that night, I helped you the rest of the week. I never went back to the club again after then. I sold the penthouse, my cars, and everything else because I knew I wanted to be with you. That stuff doesn't matter to you, and I knew I needed to show you that I wasn't who you thought I was."

I interrupt him, "Why did you wait so long"?

"I was scared. I would lose you as a friend if I told you that you maybe didn't feel that way back, and I had never navigated that feeling before. I wasn't sure if it was something I felt then and would go away. I have never wanted to hurt you, and I was still trying to figure out how to be a nice guy then. The feeling never went away, and it only got deeper."

He is still holding my hand across the table. The room is starting to feel like we are the only two people at the restaurant.

"The conversation I had with your mother that day in the Hamptons. She thanked me for saving you from the path you were going down. I told her I couldn't take credit for it, but now it all makes sense."

"My parents have known about this since the beginning. I have always been honest with them about you."

"Why all the other girls, if you felt like that towards me"?

"You were dating, and I guess you could say I wanted to make sure these feelings for you were real. I didn't want to do it, but I couldn't just sit back and watch you date other people while I was alone. When you got with Reid while I was out of town, I lost it after that. I was done seeing other people and wanted to put all my focus on getting you."

I wish I had known all this sooner, but I am not sure if we would have made it if we had tried this relationship then. Ryan was still working on changing who he was, and I was going so focused on finding someone that I was not sure that would have been healthy for a relationship.

The waitress brings out our food, placing spaghetti bolognaise in front of me, and pasta carbonara in front of Ryan. When she walks away, Ryan picks up both plates and switches them.

I laugh, "What was that for"?

He points to the dish before me, "That one is better."

We both begin to eat, but I still want to talk about the sweet stuff.

"You want to know my moment"? I asked him.

He swallows his bite, then wipes his mouth with his napkin.

"Please tell me. I have been dying to know."

"It was our first kiss in the ocean. I will admit, though, that I tried to ignore there was something there after that night. That night Reid left me alone. The night it rained, and I showed up at your apartment. It wasn't a closer walk. I showed up there because when he left me alone. All I wanted was to be with you."

Surprised by what I said, Ryan almost spits out his bite.

"The night of the kiss in the ocean. Claire, I wanted that to be our moment so badly. I was falling in love with you by then. I told myself that when we were away that week, I wasn't going to tell you my feelings, but at that moment, I couldn't hold back anymore."

"I wasn't ready then," I tell Ryan before taking another bite.

"I know."

We finish our conversation, and it feels good knowing we have both finally opened up about our feelings and moments when this whole time, it was those things that we held in. Ryan switches our plates again, and he is right. The pasta carbonara was better. Just the fact he knew which one I would like makes me smile.

After dinner, we both decided to head back home, saving our movie tickets for another time. We couldn't be more alike now when it comes to going out. Once upon a time, we were night owls, and now we can barely make it to nine o'clock. When we return to the apartment, it takes only two minutes before we are in bed.

A Love That Blooms

I look forward to the day Tuck returns, and we can all be together again.

We have reached Monday and are both at work for the day. The plan for the week is we both work regular hours today and after the flowers arrive Wednesday. Ryan will help the delivery drivers get them to the Hamptons, where they need to go. I will go down Thursday to start working on the tables and aisle arrangements. We have the rest of the Employees coming Friday to help with flowers. Emma and Baker should already be in the Hamptons. Which means they will never find out about the flowers. The only thing I need to worry about is the flowers showing up.

I have checked the flower order a gazillion times on the computer, and it says they will be here. I need to be patient, but I can't stop pacing the room two days early. I feel like this was the one job I had, considering Ryan helped me take care of everything else in the Hamptons. I have made calls to check on the cake, tables, and anything else needed this weekend that we ordered.

I want to make sure their wedding day is better than they anticipated.

Ryan walks through the front door of the flower shop, carrying a bag of food. He comes to me from around the front counter, kissing me on the cheek.

"Brought you lunch,"

"Thank you, you're amazing."

I pick up the food bag and walk to the back office together.

"Did you know Baker and Emma haven't left town yet"? Ryan says, taking a seat.

"Do what? They were supposed to be there yesterday,"

I sit in the desk chair and take the food out of the bag.

"Yeah, he wants me to meet him in his office in a minute. He said he wants to talk about something before he leaves."

"He probably wants to check in on the schedule for the week."

"I bet you are right."

Ryan gets up and gives me a forehead kiss.

"I'll let you know what he says."

"Thanks. I will talk to you later."

He leaves the office, and I devour the sandwich he brought me.

I wonder why they haven't left yet. Emma and Baker are the two people to be on top of things when needed, so I don't understand why they are still in town.

I finish eating, then throw away my trash when the shop's back door opens.

"Claire, we have a shipment of flowers for you." Aaron, our delivery driver, says.

"Ummm… thank you, but I don't have any shipments today. Can I see what you have in the truck"? I asked him, confused.

I walk out the back door and climb into the back of the delivery truck. I see thousands of flowers, not white or light pink. The flowers are all blue, yellow, dark pink, purple, baby breath, and greenery. The truck is full of buckets of flowers. The most oversized load I have ever seen.

"Uh, Aaron… Where did these come from"?

He looks down at his chart and then back at me.

"Says here, you ordered them,"

Did I order the flowers I imagined instead of what Emma asked for? I did, didn't I?

"Shoot, Shoot, Shoot. Can you take these back? I think I ordered them by accident,"

"Claire, these can't go back. You have to take them."

I start pacing the back of the truck with my hands behind my head.

"Give me a second," I tell him jumping down from the truck.

Walking back inside, I go to the office to get my phone. I immediately dial Ryan.

"Ryan, I screwed up, like badly,"

"What, what did you do? I just saw you like five minutes ago."

"Well, a truckload just showed up with thousands of flowers in the back, and not one of them is white and light pink. They are every color but that. Ryan, I ordered what I imagined instead of what Emma wanted."

"Claire, there is no way. Have them take them back and see if they can get the right ones,"

"He said he can't. I already tried."

"Babe, I hate to do this, but Baker is staring at me. I need to go. I will call you right back."

I can hear Aaron coming through the back door. I hang up the phone, setting it down.

"Claire, I called, and they said they can't take them back, so I am sorry, but you have to keep them," he says, peaking through the office doorway.

"Thanks, Aaron, for trying."

He gets help from some of our employees. They start bringing in the buckets of flowers and placing them at the front of the store. Surely Emma will understand the mishap. She is my best friend, and I hope she understands.

While I wait for Ryan to call me back, I get to work on some of the arrangements for the shop orders. I hope it'll help take my mind off the mistake I made, but with flowers everywhere, it is hard. I would also like to know why Baker needed to talk to Ryan.

It has been at least an hour. I have put together three arrangements and cleaned up around the place. I am sitting in the office desk chair, trying to figure out a plan for all these flowers here since they are days early. Ryan could take them tomorrow and store them in the guest house. Emma and Baker are staying with their parents, so there will be room in the guest house until Ryan and I arrive to sleep there.

I have my head down on the desk when I hear a knock on the door. When I look up, there stands Emma.

"Emma, what are you doing here"? I sound surprised.

"We need to talk," she says before shutting the office door.

I sit back in the chair and take a deep breath.

"If this is about the flowers, I can explain,"

She takes a seat across from me and smiles. Now I have no idea what is going on.

"Claire, I ordered those flowers."

"Whew… I was beginning to think I made a mistake."

I feel like I can finally relax. If Emma ordered them, hers would be here on Wednesday like they are supposed to be.

"I ordered them for the wedding,"

"Do what now"?

Chapter Twenty-one

Emma

Months earlier

I sit on my closet floor, waiting. When I woke up this morning, I knew something wasn't right. My feelings and emotions have been off lately. I blamed wedding planning, but Baker knew it was something else. So now we are here. We are waiting to see if the results are positive. This moment could be life-changing for both of us. We didn't plan for something like this to happen now, but we won't be sad if it is positive. It is just unexpected.

Baker comes around the corner, and I stand up.

"It's positive." He says, holding up the pregnancy test.

I put my hands over my mouth, surprised.

"We're going to be parents,"

He wraps his arms around me, kissing me on the cheek.

"We're going to be parents."

"Baker, we should get married today. We shouldn't have to wait till September. If we want to do this, today will be no different than a couple of months. We can call your parents, go to the courthouse, and make this official. When the wedding date comes, we can have a party with everyone to celebrate this. We can keep it a secret."

"Is that what you want to do? You know I want to be married to you more than anything. I don't want this pregnancy to take away from what you wanted. We could always move the date up, and you still get everything the way you want."

He is correct, and we could move the day up, but I don't need a big wedding. I would be just as happy as eloping today.

I put my hands on both sides of Baker's face, looking him in the eyes.

"I love you, and I want to marry you today. Call your parents and have them meet us at the courthouse. I will tell Claire I am leaving work early for some wedding planning. We can decide later what we want to do about the wedding day."

While Baker makes the phone call to his parents, I get ready for work. I plan to act as if nothing is different today than any other day. Claire will be on to me if I don't act like myself. As much as I love her, she is my best friend. Today's events would devastate her. Since Baker and I got engaged, she has been through many emotions lately. She has tried dating and failed many times to get a wedding date. Hopefully, my plans of getting her a date with Reid Anderson worked this weekend. She deserves the best when it comes to a man, and I want her to be happy like I am.

When Baker and I show up at his office before I head to work, it is no surprise that Ryan is waiting in his office with coffee in hand for Claire. He is always looking for ways to put a smile on Claire's face lately, and it is starting to look like he has a thing for her.

"What's going on with your brother? First, he throws a fit about Claire seeing someone this weekend at your parents, and now he is bringing her coffee."

Baker looks through the glass wall at Ryan, who seems to be waiting for us to head to the flower shop. He is pacing the room, reciting words with the coffee.

"Oh yeah, I forgot to tell you. Ryan has a crush on Claire. My mom told me this weekend."

"WHAT! How could you forget to tell me that"? I asked, slamming my hand down on the desk, getting Ryan's attention.

"Now he is coming over here," Baker whispers.

Ryan walks into Baker's office. He is staring at both of us.

"Are you going to work yet"? He asked me.

I look at Baker, who shrugs his shoulders, sitting in his desk chair.

"Sure," I say, walking out the door. Baker and Ryan follow behind me.

When we walk into the shop, Claire sets up for the day. I walk to the back office, Baker following me. I want to listen to what they are talking about without them noticing, so I stand by the door while Baker sits at the desk chair watching me.

I turn to Baker and whisper, "He is upset she saw someone else this weekend,"

I continue to listen to their conversation when I hear them getting closer. I grab Baker and plant a giant kiss on his lips. I wanted it to look like we were doing something and not listening. Claire then walks in.

"Do you not get enough of that at home… Baker, your brother is trying to get into my business this morning. I would like it if you would take him back with you."

"He's been worried about you all weekend since he seems to be upset you didn't call him," Baker says, walking out of the office.

"It was not a big deal. It was an easy fix." Claire says.

"How did that go, Claire? You never text me about it. Did he ask you out on a date"? I ask her to make sure she doesn't suspect anything.

"Maybe," Claire says.

Ryan looks angry with her answer.

"Claire… really," I tell her, trying to act cool.

"We went out Saturday night and had a fun time. He wants to get together sometime this week." Claire says, which makes Ryan even angrier. He does have a crush on her.

"We are going to head over to the office. We will see you two later," Baker says

I nod to Baker before the guys leave.

"What is Ryans deal"? Claire asked me.

"He just had a bad weekend. Lena was giving him a tough time about who knows what this weekend. They hardly spoke, and when he heard me talking to Baker about you, he even got madder that you did not call him. I did not ask questions, so I do not know what his real deal is"

Claire sits there for a moment thinking, then leaves the office.

This morning might have been a big surprise to Baker and me, but I think I have an even bigger one planned for Claire and Ryan. I need to get Baker on board with my idea.

"I now pronounce you husband and wife. You may kiss your bride."

Baker smiles before taking my face in his hands and kissing me. We are officially married. It is all I have ever wanted since Baker proposed.

Baker and I embrace Catherine and Jack before we all leave the room. They weren't thrilled when we asked them to come today. Catherine wanted us to marry in their backyard, and we still can. Today is just our official day of marriage.

Claire let me out of work earlier than I expected, which gave me time to try on many dresses from my closet to wear for our little ceremony. I chose a white sundress, and Baker wore what he had on for work this morning. It wasn't fancy, and I didn't even mind.

We all walk out to the sidewalk outside the courthouse.

"We are so happy for the two of you, even if this isn't what we wanted," Catherine says.

Baker takes my hand and brings me closer to him.

"I know, mom, but we could still have the wedding in the Hamptons."

"You will, and it'll be a beautiful day for the two of you."

I smiled at Catherine. If she only knew what I had on my mind.

A Love That Blooms

We hug them before saying our goodbyes and thanking them for coming today. I know it took a lot for them to want to be here for our unexpected wedding day.

We get into the car to leave the courthouse to head home. Most people celebrate their wedding day in other ways, but I told Baker we could do something special together at home. Since we have our monthly meeting at our house tonight with Claire and Ryan, we do not have much time to celebrate.

Baker takes my hand while driving.

"Wife. I like the sound of that." He says, smiling.

"Husband," I say, squeezing his hand.

He looks over at me, grinning. Then turns his eyes back on the road.

We pull up outside of our apartment, and he opens my door for me to let me out. We hold hands while walking inside and into the elevator. I stay quiet, still trying to process this day. It is not that I am not excited about being married and having a baby. I am ecstatic. I have had Claire on my mind all morning. She is my best friend; I should have told her about everything today, but she isn't emotionally ready. I miss cheerful Claire. It has been a long time since I have seen her at her best.

Baker and I walk into our apartment, and that is when the idea comes to mind.

"I think we should set Ryan and Claire up. Think about it; Claire has been depressed lately, trying to find a wedding date and then being dumped date after date. Since he has changed, Ryan has been going out with ridiculous women who are not even his type anymore."

"Emma, we just got married. Also found out we are going to be parents, and you are worried about Ryan and Claire," Baker says, taking a seat next to me on the sofa.

"Yes. We are happy. Ryan and Claire deserve to be happy too. Remember when Claire called me last month crying while watching a depressing romance and told me she made a Pinterest board for her dream wedding?"

"That night was horrible. You were so worried about her that you almost thought you needed to move in with her."

It is then that an even better idea comes to me.

"Baker! We should have them go to the Hamptons and finish planning the wedding together. They will have a whole week together in the guest house since your parents are hosting friends next week. We can use Claire's wedding inspiration for some things since we don't even know what we want anyways. It will bring them closer together. I can put a schedule together for them, and we can tell them tonight the plan."

"This isn't a bad idea. I have seen a good change in Ryan; if he likes Claire, this could work. You need to make sure to put some things in there that won't work so they can have some disagreements. You know how well something wrong happening worked out for us." Baker says, winking at me.

I roll my eyes. Baker isn't wrong. If they want a solid relationship, then they will need some disagreements.

I make phone calls to the Hamptons while filling out their schedule for next week and looking over the Pinterest board Claire made. She has a beautiful wedding planned. I won't be able to use every idea she has because then she will be on to us. This will give Ryan and Claire something to throw them off from Baker and me hiding a secret. Baker suggested doing white and pink flowers instead of the colorful ones Claire wants. I will add a pink bridesmaid dress, knowing Claire hates the color pink. It is enough to change that she won't say these are her wedding plans.

I toss the schedule folder on the coffee table in front of Baker.

"Alright. There it is—the plan to hopefully get them to fall in love with each other."

"The Flower shop can't order the flowers, and Dan can't make the arch?" Baker asked, looking up at me.

"Yep. That should be enough disagreements. I also scheduled them for a dance class. That should be another disagreement." I say, laughing.

"This plan will either work or turn out terribly for us."

"Now we just wait."

Chapter Twenty-two

Claire

Emma is sitting in front of me in the office, clearly nervous. I don't know what she is about to say, but I feel it isn't good. She is supposed to be in the Hamptons getting ready for her wedding this weekend and is still here. And why did she order all these flowers?

"Claire, I have so much I need to tell you," Emma says.

"Do you want to go somewhere else to talk"? I asked her since we are in the flower shop office, and it isn't very private here.

She looks around the room and then back at me.

"Here is good with me,"

"Okay then, what is going on"?

"First, I have wanted to tell you this for a while. I am pregnant."

I can't contain my excitement and jump up from the chair to hug her.

"What! Emma that is fantastic news. I am so excited for you and Baker. How far are you? Do you know what you are having? Oh my gosh, I am going to be an aunt." I blab on.

Emma smiles at me, and I take the seat next to her.

"Well, we are almost halfway there. We found out last week about gender and will tell everyone this weekend. I am sorry to keep this from you for so long. That brings me to what I have to tell you. It is important."

I sit back, and my smile turns into a frown.

"Claire, Baker, and I got married already,"

I shake my head. I don't understand.

"What"?

Emma turns to me and takes my hand.

"The day we found out we were expecting. It was the Monday after coming back from the Hamptons. The weekend you stayed here. You were not in a good place then, so we chose to get married and keep the baby a secret until the wedding day. Baker called Catherine and Jack to come, and we married at the courthouse. That night you and Ryan came over for the meeting at our apartment. I am sorry I haven't told you this before, but that week you and Ryan went to the Hamptons for the wedding planning. Baker and I did it for you and Ryan."

"I don't understand. What do you mean for Ryan and me"?

Emma stands up and starts walking back and forth in front of me.

"It was a setup to get you two to fall for each other."

She stops in front of me and bends down to my eye level.

"Baker and I did it for you two to finally become happy. We knew Ryan wanted to be with you. We just needed you two to spend a week together to see if there was anything there. We didn't realize how much you two were made for each other. Claire, I am telling you this because you and Ryan are wonderful. Two perfect people who love each other so deeply. We want to give the wedding to you two."

She has to be kidding. I stand straight up from my seat.

"Emma! Have you lost it? For one, Ryan and I fell in love like three weeks ago. Two, there is no way. I mean, no way, Ryan and I can get married this weekend. This wedding is yours, and we did everything for you. The flowers out there," I point my hand to the door.

"They are yours. Claire, I found the note you wrote down for the wedding flowers. We knew the flower shop couldn't order them, and you were the one that would. On the side of the note were other types of flowers I knew you wanted, so I canceled your order and ordered the right ones."

I shake my head no and then go to find my phone. I need to talk to Ryan. It must be why Baker wanted to speak.

"Emma, I'm so sorry, but we can't take the wedding. I love the sweet thought you and Baker had, but there is no way Ryan and I are ready to get married. This relationship is so new for the both of us."

Emma takes my phone from my hand before I can dial Ryan's number.

"Will you at least talk to Ryan tonight and think about it"?

"I will, but Emma, if I know we aren't ready, he is going to say the same thing,"

Emma walks to the door and opens it. She turns to me, "I love you, Claire."

"Love you too, Emma. Thank you for thinking about me. I know you wouldn't have gone through all this trouble if you knew I wouldn't be happy at the end of it. It worked." I tell her before she leaves the room.

I try to call Ryan as soon as she leaves, and it goes to voicemail. I feel like this is all so much to take in right now, and I need to leave. Get some fresh air. I am in no way angry with them for all of this. It is their best-kept secret. They thought about Ryan and me while getting married and finding out they would be parents. Two giant life steps, and at that moment knew that Ryan and I needed to be together. We should be thankful for them, but I know Ryan fell for me before then, and well, I didn't admit it to Emma, but the trip made me realize it was Ryan for me.

I grab my bag, turning off the office light on my way out. I tell the rest of the employees that I am leaving. I try to dial Ryan one more time and get nothing. When I walk out the front door of the flower shop, his jeep is already gone. He said he would call me when they got done, but he must have known Emma was coming to talk to me.

The walk to his apartment is longer than the walk to mine. I need the extra walk to process everything. I love Ryan with everything I have, but that doesn't mean we jump into marrying each other. I need to know that Ryan thinks the same thing, or maybe that isn't why they talked. Baker had told Ryan not long ago that he needed to make sure he wanted to be with me. Is that because he knew they would say to us all this soon?

I see the jeep parked out front of the apartment, and I know that means Ryan is home. I take the elevator up and walk down the hall to the apartment. When I open the door, Ryan isn't in the living room, so I walk to the bedroom.

Ryan is sitting on the bed with a box on his lap. He is looking through it when I come through the doorway. When he hears me, he looks up at me.

"What is that"? I asked him, standing in the doorway.

"Come here. We need to talk," Ryan puts his hand on the bed beside him.

257

I take a seat and instantly realize the box is one made by Dan.

Ryan proceeds to tell me all about his conversation with Baker. He said Baker told him about the wedding and the pregnancy. Then Baker said it was Emma's idea to set us up with the week away in the Hamptons wedding planning. Emma used my Pinterest board to make the wedding plans because they never knew what they wanted. It was then that I remembered the night I made the board. They changed a few things, like the flowers and colors, to throw me off. They knew that Dan wouldn't be able to make the arch for us, and the flower shop wouldn't be able to order the flowers for us. They thought it would be a reasonable disagreement for us to get through. The funny thing is those moments made us more substantial, and we never fought about them. Then he tells me that Baker, the talk they had during golfing wasn't because of him thinking Ryan would go his old ways. It was because he wanted him to think about me being the one for him. Prepare Ryan before their talk today.

While Ryan is talking to me, he is holding the box. I saw a glimpse of letters carved into the lid, but I wanted to wait till Ryan finished talking before asking about the box. He continued talking about their conversation, and I listened the whole time without saying anything. Baker told him more about everything than Emma told me, and I know it was because Emma wanted to get right to the point of the conversation, the wedding. The thing is, Ryan never mentions it.

Ryan then stops talking and turns towards me.

"How did it go with Emma"? He asked me.

"I guess it went about the same as your conversation with Baker," I say.

He then hands me the box.

"I made this for you the night of the volleyball tournament. After I hit you in the face, I went to Dan's. He showed me how to make one of these. I did all the work on this one myself."

I run my fingers across the top. It has RH&CC carved into the lid. I take the cover off, setting it to the side.

"There are things in there that I kept that have to do with us."

I pulled a picture of us from the Gala, the one we took out front. Then a photo of Tuck and me sleeping on the couch together from the night I watched him while Ryan had a meeting. The next thing makes me smile, big. The receipt from the night we went to the ice cream parlor. The total was a sign to me that maybe we were meant to be together. Some of the rose petals from the night he told me he loved me and gave me the moment I have always wanted. Then at the very bottom of the wood box, a ring. I gasp when I see it. Then I pick it up to look at it.

"Don't be scared. It was the first thing in the box. The night we had our first kiss in the ocean. I went to my parents to talk about what had happened that night. Like I told you, I have always been honest with them. My mom gave me this. I didn't ask for it, but she always told me when I found the one that she would give me her original wedding ring to give to someone special. That night she said she knew you were the one for me and to hold on to it in case the day came. I have never looked at it until today. When Baker said, the wedding should be for us. I came here, turned my phone off, and wanted a moment to think about everything."

"Ryan, I told Emma we can't do it," I say, setting the ring back into the box.

"It's crazy, right." He says, looking at the box.

"It is very much crazy. Ryan, I love you, but we can't get married now. We barely have each other figured out." I set the box beside me and took Ryan's hand.

"I told Baker, thank you for the offer, but the wedding is for them."

I feel a sense of relief after he says that. Not only because he feels the same way about this as I do but because looking at the ring had me thinking he was going to propose.

"It was nice of them to think of us. Baker and Emma got married and found out they were expecting on the same day and still wanted us to be happy too."

"Claire, it was sweet of them to set that week up for us in the Hamptons to grow our relationship, but I know I would still be with you today without their help. I have loved you for a long time, and I was at a point where I knew I wanted to be with you. So, it would be best if you didn't think we were together because it was something they wanted. I've wanted this long before that trip."

He uses his hand to move my chin up to look at him. Then rubs his thumb across my bottom lip before kissing me.

Ryan

When Baker wanted to talk, I never expected what he would say. The wedding and pregnancy were a bit of a shock for me. They have done a fantastic job at hiding those from everyone. Claire and I have been so into each other lately. We overlooked all the signs that that was something they had been hiding. I am excited for them, but trying to throw Claire and me off by getting us together is not something I appreciate. The last thing I would want Claire to consider is that we are together because of them. Yes, that week together was a turning point for us, but I wanted her long before that week. Then when Baker tried to give us the wedding, I couldn't help but get confused. I know Claire is the one for me, but maybe she doesn't feel the same just yet. I was faced with a choice when I left the conversation with Baker. I could have asked Claire to marry me, but that would have been selfish, considering we have never once talked about it. Secondly, I could have just spoken to Claire about the whole thing and asked her what she thought. I needed time to think about everything alone. I didn't want to make a rash decision that could potentially hurt us. I didn't have much alone time before Claire arrived at the apartment.

When I gave Claire the box, I never expected her to be so calm when she saw the ring. I thought it would either scare her away or excite her. She looked at it as if she was considering it. Then, I realized I shouldn't say anything about the situation and listened to Claire. She means so much to me; I should hear what she wants. So she decided for us, which meant we weren't doing it. Do I feel pressured by them asking us to get married? A little bit. Have I known that Claire is the one for me? Yes, and I have told her before that she is the one. When Claire wants that for us, it will be the time for us to take that step. I would never make Claire do something she doesn't want to. Did I tell Baker that the wedding was for them, and we didn't want to do it? Nope, I sure didn't. I told Baker I would think about it, but I couldn't guarantee him that we would do it. So last night, when Claire gave me the confirmation that she wasn't ready by telling Emma no. I called Baker to tell him no, also.

Emma and Baker should be on their way to the Hamptons today. I will try to forget this whole ordeal and treat this weekend as what it has been all along—their wedding. I know that Claire and I's day will come sometime soon. Until then, I will continue showing her the love she deserves and taking steps to get us there.

I park outside the flower shop. I am here to help load the flowers into the delivery trucks, and then I will be on my way to the Hamptons without Claire. She will be staying here taking care of work stuff and will meet me there later this week with some of the shop employees to prepare for the wedding.

I walk through the front door to see Claire working at her workstation. She doesn't notice me, so I come up behind her wrapping my arms around her and then placing a kiss on her cheek.

She turns her face to me. "There you are."

"Sorry, I had to pack my bag. It took me a minute to find my clothes between your clothes and mess."

She spins around in my arms and looks at me. "Sorry, I am a mess. I'll clean that up while you're gone."

"Don't worry about it. I am starting to get used to the mess."

Claire kisses me before slipping out of my arms. She starts walking towards the back office, and I follow her. Then, I notice all the buckets of flowers are missing from around the store.

"Where are the flowers"?

"We loaded them this morning, and they are already on their way. Emma gave them the directions, and we could fit them all in the same load. They will store them in the guest house when they get there. So there is no need for you to worry about them now."

I guess since they know about the flowers now. It wasn't something we needed to take care of ourselves anymore. I don't mind marking one less thing to worry about off my list.

When we get into the office, I close the door behind us. Claire sits at the desk, and I walk up to her, giving her another kiss on the lips. Then put a small piece of hair from her face behind her ear while my other hand rests on her leg.

"Wanted a little more privacy, Claire"?

She smiles at me, "Well, you are leaving me for a couple of days,"

"It will go by quickly."

I tell her that because it will. It feels like forever without each other when we are not together, but it will be quick this week since we have things to get done.

"I know"

Claire is giving me sad eyes, and I know she doesn't want me to leave yet, but I have to. I need to check on Dan, bring the arch to my parents, set up for the wedding, and spend some time with Baker before the wedding. I know he is technically already married, but we made plans to have some time together before the big day—a low-key bachelor party. The girls have planned to have a sleepover the night before the wedding. Emma is expecting, so I don't see that night getting wild.

I wrap my arms around Claire, pulling her into me and then kissing her forehead.

"I love you," I tell her.

"I love you too,"

No matter how many times she tells me, it always makes me smile when she says it.

I let her out of my hold, and she jumps down from the desk. We walk out of the office to the front. It is time for me to leave. Claire gives me one more kiss at the door before I go.

Chapter Twenty-Three

Ryan

When I pull up outside my parent's house, the truck full of flowers is at the guest house unloading. I get out to help and walk up to the guest house. Baker is unloading buckets, and Emma is standing off to the side, watching. When I get closer, I notice all the buckets of colorful flowers sitting by the guest house. I didn't get the chance to see them after they arrived at the shop yesterday. Claire was worried about all the white, so this was a good change for the wedding. When I get closer to the guest house, Emma spots me coming.

"Hey, you showed up just in time. We aren't sure if these will all fit in here."

I walk closer to inspect the number of buckets they have. There are still some in the back of the truck. They have some sitting outside and surrounding the living room. I walk in the door to get a closer look and then walk back out.

"We are going to have to use the bathroom and bedroom. So let's fill the whole guest house with all the flowers, and we can turn the temps down for them. I will sleep in my old room instead."

Emma nods to Baker in agreement, and we start loading the whole guest house with buckets of flowers.

I had plans to sleep here for the week, so Claire and I could stay together when she got here. My old room has a small bed so we wouldn't be able to stay there together. So now, when Claire comes, it looks like she will share a room with Emma in Baker's old room. Baker will probably stay in Audrey's old room, and Audrey will need a hotel room with her husband and kids. It was not the plan, but it is what it is. I knew this week wouldn't go according to schedule.

Once we finish unloading all the flowers, I take my bag to my old room. Then check on my mother, who is taking a nap with Tuck. So, I decided now would be a great time to slip out of the house to check on Dan. I haven't heard from him since I was here last week to make the arch.

When I pull up outside Dan's house, he isn't rocking on the front porch in his chair, so I know he is either in the shop or inside. I get out of my jeep, walk towards the shop around back, and sure enough, Dan sits on his woodworking stool.

"What are you making"? I ask him.

He turns his head towards me, pushes up his glasses, and then looks back to what he was doing.

"What are you doing here? I wasn't expecting you till later this week,"

I take a seat on the stool next to him.

"Well, since I got in town today, I thought I would come to check on you. I wanted to ask you something."

He continues working on what he is making, and I take that as a sign to continue talking to him.

"I know you don't get out much, but I thought it would be good for you to come to the wedding this weekend."

He turns his head back towards me, stopping what he is doing.

"I don't go to weddings but thank you."

"I don't like weddings either. Put on your best dress on Saturday, and I will come to get you. I know Claire would love a dance with you. There will be a nice dinner, and I will ensure you will have a fun time."

Dan doesn't answer me then, so I will take that as his answer. I pat him on the back.

"I will be here around four to pick you up."

I get up from the stool and walk over to the arch I made at the back of the shop. I look it over to check my work and see if anything is wrong with it. I notice screws in places where I didn't put any and turn my eyes back to Dan. Before I can even ask, he already knows what I am about to say.

"I wanted to make sure it wasn't going to fall apart when you move it,"

I smile, "Thank you, Dan."

I walk back to where Dan is sitting and see that what he is making is a frame.

"How have you been feeling lately"?

"I am fine. There is no reason for you to check on me," Dan says sternly.

He has been alone for a long time, and I know he doesn't like having me around for too long, but I feel like I need to be the one to check on him and know he is good. He has no one else, so

267

it is the least I can do for someone who has helped me through some things this summer. I am thankful for him. He probably couldn't say the same, but I want to feel at least like he could be grateful for me too.

"Well, Dan, I am going to go. It looks like you are busy, and since you say you are fine, I will get out of your way. I'll be back to pick up that arch. Don't forget about four o'clock on Saturday."

As I walk away, he waves his hand in the air, which is his way of saying goodbye. I head back to the jeep, knowing I will be back soon.

Everyone is on the back deck when I get back to my parent's house. Audrey has arrived, and her kids are swimming in the pool with Emma. I sit by Baker on one of the lounge chairs by the pool. Claire is the only person missing from this moment, and I wish she could have been here with us. She needed to stay in the city to run the shop before they closed it for the wedding this weekend. When she arrives here, she will be so busy between making the arrangements and helping Emma that I won't be able to spend time with her.

Emma gets out of the water to sit poolside, and you can tell she is expecting. I don't know how Claire and I managed to miss all the signs of them having a baby. It has been a while since I have been around a baby. Audrey's kids Cooper and Kate, are school-age kids now. When they were babies, I wasn't around much. I was either in college or going through my bad phase, and I regret that. So, being around Emma and Baker's baby will be good. I know Claire is going to go nuts whenever it arrives.

I turn to Baker, who is checking out his pregnant wife.

"So, you're going to be a dad soon. How are you holding up"? I asked him.

Baker lets out a small laugh. "Honestly. I am terrified and excited at the same time."

When Baker and I discussed everything at the office, we never discussed the pregnancy. I think I was just in shock, so I didn't exactly know what to say.

"You'll be a great dad, just as Emma will be a great mom."

"Well, thank you, Ryan."

"No problem."

"Since Claire isn't here yet. Do you think you would want to go out for drinks tonight?"

"Are you insinuating that I can drink because Claire isn't here? She doesn't care if I drink. It is me that doesn't like doing it anymore. Is that what you want to do for your bachelor party"?

Before coming here, Baker said he wanted something low-key for his party but didn't mention anything. He knows it has been a while since I have had an alcoholic beverage, but I don't need him thinking I don't drink anymore because of Claire. I don't mind breaking my streak of not drinking for his night, but I will only have one.

"I know you haven't had a drink since you wanted a change for yourself, and I know you changed for her, so I was asking. And yes, this is what I want to do. It could be a long time before I get a chance to have drinks with you for a night." He says, laughing, and I know he said it because he will be a dad soon.

It wouldn't hurt to have drinks with him for one night, and probably the last time we get to do it.

Claire

Exhausted doesn't even begin to describe the day I have had. When I decided it would be better to finish up all shop orders today and close down a day early, I wasn't aware of the amount of work it would entitle. So, now that I finished an hour after closing time, I want nothing more than to lay across the couch and not move until bedtime.

I haven't told anyone in the Hamptons that I will be coming down tomorrow, and I don't plan on telling Ryan either when he calls me tonight before bed. I want to surprise them. I felt left out today while everyone was there, and I am here. I knew it wouldn't hurt us to close down one day early; that way, I could get more things done for the wedding earlier than expected. Emma left me her car to get down there, and I plan to go first thing in the morning.

I am just getting up from the couch to change out of my work clothes when my phone rings. I pick it up to see it is Ryan, so I put it on speaker while I change.

"Hello," I say, taking my shirt off and throwing it on the ground.

"Hey, I just wanted to see how today went. Also, I am going out for drinks with Baker,"

He says it quickly. Like I might have a problem with it.

"Fun," I say, slipping a shirt over my head. "Today was good,"

The background on the phone sounds loud, like he just walked into a bar.

"I can let you go so you can have a fun guys' night," I take a seat on the bed.

"Don't go yet. I haven't talked to you since this morning," Ryan says.

I hear a waitress asking them what they want, and he orders a beer. Then I hear Baker say two shots of something. The word "shots" reminds me of the night Emma and I met them at The Bar in the city.

"Shots, huh"? I asked him.

He laughs, knowing what I meant when I said it.

"Baker and I were talking about that night on the way over here. A lot has changed since that night." Ryan says.

"I would say for the better for all of us," I smile into the phone.

I can hear the waitress set down the drinks and ask them if they want anything else.

"I love you," He says.

Before I tell him I love him back so I can let him go, I hear him say. "Lena!"

"Lena"? I asked him.

"Claire, I have to go. I will call you right back. Promise."

271

Then he hangs up the phone.

I have no idea why Lena would be in a bar in the Hamptons. I trust Ryan, so I am not worried about him. I am concerned about her. She could try all kinds of things with him. It is then that I realize that this is the first time I have been in this situation with Ryan. I lay back on the bed, biting my lip, nervous, just waiting for him to call me back.

Chapter Twenty-four

Ryan

"What are you doing here"? I ask Lena as she takes it upon herself to slide into the booth next to me. I slide over as far as I can, not touching her.

"Some friends and I are staying here for the week. I was going to surprise you at the wedding on Saturday. I am your plus one, remember."

Sadly, I remember joking with her that she was my plus one for the wedding, but I never really meant it. She cannot come to the wedding. Claire would be devastated if she showed up there.

"Lena, you can't come to the wedding. I haven't seen you in a while. Why would you think I would still want you to be there"? I ask her angrily.

She flips her hair back behind her shoulder and gives me a frown. I don't know what she tries to do, but it isn't working for me. I need to get her away from this table, knowing she won't be showing up at the wedding.

"Don't you miss me, Ryan?" She asked me.

Baker sits across the table, sitting back with his arms across his chest. I need him to help me out, so I give him a stern look.

"Lena look, Ryan has moved on and is seeing someone else. You won't be showing up to the wedding. It would just make you look bad." Baker says.

"Yes, I have moved on. I am the happiest I have ever been."

Lena pretends to work up some tears, and I am not falling for it. She needs to leave this booth, and I need to call Claire back to let her know what happened here. I pick up the shot Baker ordered us and tip it back. We just got here, and this is already turning into a mess. Baker throws his hands up to the waitress, ordering two more shots. Lena finally quits her act and gets up from the booth.

"Ryan, can we go outside and talk about this? Who could be better than me"?

"Claire," I tell her.

Her jaw drops, and she starts shaking her head no.

"Her! She is nothing but a poor, lonely florist who can't get a guy,"

Now I am ticked. I get up from the booth, take Lena by the arm, and walk out the bar's front door. Once outside, I stand in front of her as she looks at me.

"Do not go back in there. Do not show up at the wedding. And do not ever come around me ever again. WE ARE DONE HERE."

I let go of her arm and then walked back into the bar. I take my seat right back at the booth. I didn't tell her to never speak of Claire again because it doesn't matter if she does. Claire will and always be better than her.

"We good now," Baker ask me.

I nod and then tip back, taking the second shot he ordered.

"Glad I will never have to deal with a situation like that again," I say to Baker as he is laughing.

"So, Claire is the one"? He asked me.

"I sure hope so," I say as I remember I need to call her back.

I pick up my phone from the table and text her for now. I think I have done enough talking for the night. I texted her that it was nothing and that I would call her about it in the morning. She texts me back, "Goodnight, I love you," and those are words I never get tired of hearing her say.

Now that all that is over. Baker and I can get back to having what will probably be our last night out at a bar. We cheered for our future before discussing how crazy our life was before meeting the girls. We ended the night after a few more drinks and shots. Then everything starts to become a blur. Emma comes to pick us up sometime after one am and takes us back to the house. When I get into my bed, I open my phone to send a few more text messages to Claire before falling asleep with my phone in my hand.

I wake up to the sound of the curtains opening and the bright sunlight shining. I moan before rolling over, snuggling with the sheets. The headache starts appearing, and I remember this is why I don't drink and go out anymore. I need a glass of water with some Tylenol, stat.

"Wake up. Ryan" I hear and immediately think I am in trouble.

I open my eyes to a glass of water on my nightstand with water. Claire is here. Wait, what? I sit up from the bed quickly.

Claire is standing at the end of my bed, looking at me with her hands on her hips.

"What are you doing here? Is this because of last night? I am so sorry," I tell her, wincing from the headache and sunlight.

"Nice to see you too." She says before coming to sit on the side of the bed beside me.

"Sorry. I am so happy to see you. I wasn't expecting you to be here today,"

She smiles at me and immediately realizes I am not in trouble.

"Here," she says, handing me the Tylenol and water. "You will need this,"

I take them from her. I took a sip of water before putting the medicine in my mouth. I am thankful she is here today. It will be better to tell her about last night in person. It will also be extra time to get with her before she divides all her attention between Emma and the wedding.

"Okay, lovesick puppy, tell me all about last night,"

I tilt my head, giving her a confused look before she laughs.

"Ummm…" I rub my temple. The medicine hasn't kicked in yet, and last night is still a blur.

"You know what, we can talk about this later," she says before getting up from the bed. she leans over to me, placing a sweet kiss on my lips.

"Get up and dressed. Let's spend some time together today," Claire tells me while walking towards to bedroom door.

"Come here," I say. Claire stops and turns to me. "I want some more of that," I get up from the bed. When she gets close to me, I grab her hand. I pull her into my chest, wrapping my arms around her. She looks up at me, and I place a soft kiss on her lips. "I missed you last night,"

"I know. All the text messages I had this morning told me so." She smiles.

I remember texting her last night after I sobered up a little before falling asleep. I know it was words expressing my love for her, but I do not remember the exact words I texted. I remind myself to check those messages later. Right now, my phone is dead from falling asleep with it.

I kiss Claire's forehead before she pulls out of our embrace to leave the room. After finding it hiding under my pillow, I plug my phone into the charger. Then I jump into the shower. And when I get out, I throw on some gym shorts and a T-shirt. Then head down the stairs to find Claire in the kitchen with everyone else. It finally feels complete here now that she has arrived. Everyone is gathered around the kitchen island, laughing at Emma telling the story of having to pick us up last at the bar. I don't know everything everyone knows, so I grab Claire by the hand. "I'm sorry, everyone, but I need to steal her for a minute,"

Claire doesn't hesitate when I pull her away from everyone, and we walk out the back door. Once outside, I take her to the lounge chairs by the pool. I want to be far away from everyone but not too far. She sits, and I sit on the chair across from her.

"About last night. You know that Lena showed up. I didn't tell you last night that she is staying in town with friends this week. Lena was going to show up at the wedding to surprise me. I jokingly said a long time ago when I got the invitation that she would be my plus one, and she thought she would still be my date." I tell Claire, taking her hand in mine.

"I feel like there is more to this story," Claire says, frowning.

"I think she was going to try to get me back, but you know there is nothing there. I am also glad I saw her out, or she was going to show up if I didn't. Claire, that would have devastated you. She knows about you and me now. I had some words with her, and you won't have to worry about her coming around again."

I will never tell Claire the words Lena said about her because they will never matter.

Claire is quiet for a moment before saying. "Well, thank you for telling me everything. I admit I was worried when you said her name, but Ryan, I trust you. I know what we have is good, and something like that shouldn't get between us," Claire says, and I sigh with relief.

"I want to know how I got so lucky to score you," I tug her hand and pull her onto my lap. She places her legs over one side of me and lays her head against mine. I rest my hand on her thigh and the other rubbing her back. "So, why didn't you tell me you were coming today"?

"I wanted to surprise you. Also, your phone was dead when I called this morning. I called Emma to check in on you, and she told me when you got back from the bar. I was happy that I could be the one to wake you this morning, I mean afternoon," she lets out a small laugh.

It reminds me that I needed to see those messages. I pull my phone from my back pocket and open my text thread from Claire, only to see the last message I sent her was the one from the bar. I remember that after I sent them, I instantly regretted them. I thought there was a chance she wouldn't believe what they said because I was drunk.

"Claire, babe. You want to show me those messages I sent last night,"

"You don't remember them?"

"I think I deleted them,"

She stands up from my lap, putting her phone to her chest to secure it.

"Ryan did you think if you deleted them, they wouldn't send,"

"Yes, my drunk self thought that," I laugh, then reach up to grab her phone.

She starts running towards the house, giggling, "You are not getting my phone,"

I get up to run after her and grab her before she opens the back door. I pick her up, throw her over my shoulder and start walking towards the guest house. She is smacking my back on the way. "Ryan, let me down,"

"No, not until to tell me every word I said in those messages,"

"Fine. Okay, I will tell you,"

I open the guest house door, and all the flowers greet us. I forgot we were storing them here. I set Claire down, and she turns around to walk in.

"Woah, it doesn't look like we are staying here tonight," she says.

"This is when I tell you you're sleeping with Emma in Baker's old room this week."

She fakes, whines, and then turns to me with a frown. "But I don't wanna,"

"Sorry, there wasn't anything else we could do with all these flowers,"

She turns around again to scan the number of flowers inside the guest house and then walks in. She didn't think this through as she struggled to get around the buckets of flowers. Most have bloomed since yesterday, but most are still buds.

"What are you doing"? I throw my arms out, laughing at her.

She makes it to the dining room and then turns to me.

"I am going to make room for us,"

Claire starts taking flowers from buckets and adding them to other buckets with flowers in them. Smart. Fewer buckets mean more room for the two of us. I walk into the guest house and follow what she is doing. I take some of the buckets with just water and pour them out the front door, then stack them outside. The girl knows what she wants this week: sharing a bed with me. It takes us half an hour before we condense the flower buckets in half. There is now lots of room for Claire and me to sleep here. The buckets are only in the living room and dining room.

"There we go, done." She brushes her hands together to dust them off.

"Great thinking, babe."

We walk out of the guest house to Emma's Car. Claire drove it here since she refused to get herself a car. She and Emma once shared a car, but Claire sold it after she got her new apartment. Claire prefers to walk everywhere or get a ride from me. I grab Claire's bag from the back, and she follows me back into the guest house. I walk into the bedroom to set her bag in the closet, and Claire comes in behind me, plopping down on the bed. I join her on the bed, and she snuggles up to me. Her head is lying on my shoulder, her hand on my chest. I place my hand on the small of her back, bringing her closer to me.

"So, spill the details. The messages didn't scare you away, obviously,"

"No, they were sweet, kind, and everything a girl wants to hear. You probably regretted them because you were drunk, but I think they came from the heart."

"Claire, I feel like there couldn't be more than what I have already told you."

There are some things I haven't told her yet, because I don't want her to feel like I am rushing us. So I haven't said much more than "I love you" or "let's move in together." Sure we talked about feelings, and we wanted to be together when we knew. Indeed, I didn't say the things I hadn't told her yet.

"Yeah. No need to worry. It was just the same stuff you told me already. You just added you missed me so much and couldn't wait to kiss my face,"

"Cute. That's why you called me a lovesick puppy. I am never drinking again," I put my hand on my forehead, giving myself an unnoticeable forehead slap.

We finish up dinner with everyone on the back patio of my parents. Emma, Baker, Claire, and I are the only ones left outside at the patio table. I have Claire positioned on my lap because I haven't been able to take my hands off of her since she arrived here today. I want to be around her every second of this day, knowing she will only be mine until tomorrow. Then she will be Emma's.

"Remember the night here a year ago? We had our short business meeting about buying the new flower shop," I asked them.

Claire laughs, "Oh, I remember. Whose idea was that anyway? Whoever it was, they are brilliant,"

Baker laughs, pointing his finger at me.

Emma leans forward, "It was you, Ryan,"

"You got me. It was all my idea. However, look at how far Blooms has come since we did it. You two have your billboards now. The shop has more employees than you ever imagined, and we are all here. Happier than we ever been." I squeeze my arms around Claire.

"I have to tell you, Ryan, it was a great move for us. We might have turned down Dave Riley million dollar deal, but I think our lives turned out for the better since we turned it down," Baker says, kissing Emma, then rubbing her belly.

"Not to brag, but wasn't it me who picked the girls at the bar that night? I feel like everyone should give me a huge thank you. You're welcome," I say, throwing my hands up.

Everyone starts laughing, and Claire turns to me. "I hated you that night. I wasn't falling for your silly game,"

"It didn't look like you weren't falling for it. I mean, you're here now, right,"?

Emma and Baker say "owwww" in unison.

I lean in, giving Claire a soft kiss on the lips. "Sorry,"

"I guess it didn't take long after that for us to connect," she nods to Baker, "Thank you, by the way, for always making him do things for me," he bounces back. "There were times I didn't like either of you, but I honestly wouldn't trade the road that got us here with anyone else. Emma would agree. We have all had our ups and downs, but the contentment that I feel now made it worth it," Claire says, and it almost makes me tear up just thinking of how we got here.

"Alright, bedtime. It is not the time to get all sentimental," Baker says, getting up from his chair. I couldn't agree more. I want to return to the guest house for some time with Claire to myself.

Claire and I head inside to say our goodnights to everyone else before heading over to the guest house. We could call this place our second home with how much we stay here.

Chapter Twenty-five

Claire

Emma and I have the guest house a mess today. I got up early to have coffee and breakfast with Ryan this morning before we went our separate ways. He is out with Baker running last-minute errands for the wedding and then picking up the arch. Emma and I are making the tables' centerpieces and arrangements for the aisle. We have flowers, stems, and vases scattered throughout the guest house. Once we finish up here, leaving some of the flowers in the buckets for the arch.

Catherine has one of those companies coming out to set up a fancy boho-style picnic on the beach for tonight. It will be for Emma, Catherine, me, and Audrey while Jack has something planned for the guys, and let's hope it doesn't have to do with a bar. I don't think Ryan would want another night of drinking. Even though I think I wouldn't mind some more drunk sweet messages from him.

"How does this look"? I hold up an arrangement for Emma.

"Great," she looks over at me on the floor while sitting on the couch.

A Love That Blooms

We were supposed to wait till the remaining Bloom's employees showed up for help, but we couldn't help but want to get a head start on the wedding prep. The wedding is in just two days, and we want to be ahead of time. I want to enjoy every second of this experience with my best friend. Savory, every moment like this could be the last time we get together before she becomes a mom because it probably will be. Baker and Emma have plans for a two-week honeymoon/babymoon in Bora Bora. Between our business and them prepping to become parents, our time with just the two of us will be rare when they return.

"So, I can tell things with Ryan are going well. Can we talk about how cute the two of you have been lately?" Emma says, leaning back on the couch, taking a break from working.

I blush, "You know he compared our relationship to a flower last night. He said we started as a bud. A flower with potential, but it wasn't ready yet. Then it opened up just a little. Not quite ready to show its promise, but close. Then it bloomed into the most beautiful flower. He said we knew something was between us but needed time, and now we are the most beautiful flower he has ever seen bloom."

"Claire, that has to be the sweetest thing I have ever heard Ryan say. Wow."

"I melted when he told me. I might have also shed a few tears, and then I snuggled up to him and fell asleep in his arms. It was a sweet moment."

"I should use that in my vows," Emma says jokingly.

"Are you telling me that you haven't written your vows yet"?

Emma bites her lip nervously before saying, "Not exactly. Words just don't come easy for me. You had to help me with the letter for Baker the night I met him in the park."

The night Emma was ready to express her feelings for Baker, I wrote most of the letter for him. They were all words she meant, but she has never been good with putting feelings down on paper. I know Emma could probably use my help expressing her love for Baker in her vows. Since feelings of love lately have come naturally to me, I know just the words she could say.

So, Emma and I take a break from floral arrangements for an hour and work on her vows. Instead of doing most of the work for her this time, I just helped her with making it sound just right. When we finished, we decided to get ready for the picnic. This day has gone by quickly, and I look forward to reuniting with Ryan so we can talk about our day.

I dressed for the night alone, wearing a long tan skirt and an off-white cropped sweater. The nights here are starting to get chilly, and I knew I would get cold with the ocean breeze. When I walk out of the guest house to meet the girls down the beach, I am surprised to see the arch already placed down by the ocean. It looks amazing. I walk over to it to look at it before walking to the picnic.

Running my hand down one of the sides, I whisper, "Absolutely incredible,"

"Looks good, doesn't it?" Ryan says from behind me, which then makes me turn around.

He walks up to me, wrapping his arm around my waist and placing a kiss on my forehead. I lean into him and wrap my arms around him in an embrace.

"It is stunning…." I look up at him. "What are you doing here? I thought you guys were out."

"You think I will go out for a night without telling my girl goodbye?" He gives me a sweet kiss on the lips.

"Where are you guys off to"? I ask him.

"Dad has us reservations at the nicest restaurant. We are going to drink wine and talk sports, I assume. That picnic looks pretty legit. Sure, I can't just join you?"

I giggle, "Go have fun with the guys. We will probably talk about girly things that don't pertain to you."

"Well, have fun talking about me," he says, giving me one last kiss before he lets me out of his hold.

He starts walking towards the guys waiting by the car, so I yell out. "I love you,"

He turns to me, walking backward, "I love you more,"

I look at Ryan's work on the arch once more, then walk down to the beach.

When I arrive, all the girls are chatting around the small table. There are different colored earth-toned pillows around the table for seats. The wood table is just a foot off the ground and covered with earth-toned plates, cups, and napkins. There are mauve vases in the center filled with pampas grass. The girls are still talking when I sit by Emma, viewing the sunset on the ocean.

"Sorry I was late. I was looking at the arch Ryan made," I say before taking a drink.

"Isn't it wonderful? I am very proud of him," Catherine says.

Emma answers Catherine before me, "I think it looks identical to the one Claire had on her wedding board,"

I almost spit out my water, "Do what"?

"It was on your wedding board. Baker and I were so overwhelmed by all the wedding things, so we used some of the ideas Claire had." Emma says, and I hide my face in embarrassment. I hoped we could slip by without letting Catherine know about my not-so-great moment.

"Is the correct Claire"? Catherine says. I take my hands away from my face to look at her. This I not going to look good for me.

"I had a terrible night not long ago. I may have watched too many romance movies and drank some wine. I made a wedding board on that ridiculous website and sent it to Emma." I wince, knowing Catherine is going to be disappointed.

Catherine then starts laughing, "Oh Claire, that is nothing to be ashamed of. I think we can all agree that we planned out what we wanted our wedding day to look like before we were even engaged."

We all join Catherine in laughing about how I was embarrassed and then toast to new beginnings for Emma and Baker. Even though they have already been living the married life, they are at least going to get their wedding finally. Then will come, baby.

Speaking of baby, I can't wait any longer to find out.

"So, Emma, what are we having"? I ask her rubbing her belly.

She gets a big grin on her face and then announces.

"It's a girl,"

I can't help but scream in excitement. A girl. A little Emma, who can one day take over the flower shop. Catherine smiles when she sees my reaction; I feel she already knows. Catherine and Jack know everything. They knew me and Ryan would end up together before we did. They knew that Emma and Baker would get through all the things that they went through. They have welcomed us with open arms and are our family.

This morning I woke up in Ryan's arms. A feeling I never get tired of when he sleeps in with me. Most mornings, he has coffee and breakfast in hand, just waiting for me to wake.

After enjoying dinner with the girls, I returned to the guest house to prepare for bed. Ryan showed up just before I fell asleep, telling me how boring their dinner was. Sipping water while everyone else drinks wine while talking about football and business is not fun to Ryan. I told him how the girl's dinner went and let him know Emma and Baker were having a girl. His reaction was the same as mine. Yes, he screamed just a little bit.

After whining not to get out of bed, Ryan finally pulled the sheet off me, picked me up, then dropped me to my feet in front of the shower. "Shower now. You have a big day,"

He isn't wrong. It is the day before the wedding. I have flowers to arrange and assist the people delivering the chairs, tent, and tables coming that will need help setting up. Then most of all, I need to be there for Emma to ensure this is what she envisioned. Then tonight, I will stay with Emma to keep her from Baker. The rules say you sleep in separate rooms the night before your wedding. They may be married already, but I still follow the rules.

While I get to assist in the hard work, Ryan will take Tuck on a walk, then do manly things like golfing. Why do women have to do the hard work today?

Ryan leaves the bathroom for me to get ready. I take my time while showering, knowing this may be my only peaceful moment for today. Ryan left a coffee and a note on the bathroom counter. He is already taking Tuck on his walk. After fixing my hair, throwing it up in a ponytail. I get dressed in black leggings with an oversized white shirt. I need to be comfortable today.

After getting dressed, I walked to the back patio of Ryan's parents with my coffee. I was expecting everyone to be out here ready to go, but there was not a single person in sight. I enter the back door to find all the women in the kitchen.

"Claire, Good Morning. Want some breakfast"? Catherine asked me while holding up a plate of eggs with bacon.

"I am fine, thank you," I say, taking a seat at the kitchen island. "Where are the trucks full of wedding things and the men ?"

Catherine smiles, "Oh honey, did Ryan not tell you? You aren't going to be doing anything today. You and Emma have appointments at the spa. You are both scheduled for blowouts, facials, nails, massages, and anything else to prepare you for tomorrow."

I jump out of my seat, "You're kidding! We are getting a girl's day. That boy of yours didn't tell me anything about this. Should I go change?"

"No, dear, you look perfect for this occasion. You will wear a robe most of the time, so there is no need to worry." Catherine leans against the counter, drinking her coffee.

She looks phenomenal, by the way. She has come back to herself this week. I haven't seen a single sign of someone who had a heart attack over a month ago, which makes me so happy to see.

"Catherine, you should come with us. I think you deserve a girl's day more than any of us," I tell her this because it is true. She needs to get out of the house.

"Are you sure? I would hate to intrude."

I look to Emma, sitting at the dining table eating, and then at Catherine.

"We would love for you to join us. Audrey can too,"

Catherine gasped and then smiled at me. "Well, it looks like we are all going. The men can take care of everything here while we are gone. Ryan might have a bigger bill than he expected from the spa."

My jaw drops. Ryan set this up.

Ryan

"Alright, we can head back now. The women have left," I tell Baker and my dad. We all turn around to start the walk back to the house.

I wanted to be there to see the priceless look on Claire's face when my mother told her she was not only not helping with wedding things today but going to the spa. She deserves it. She has spent countless hours lately working on the wedding and the shop. She needed a day to wind down and relax. I didn't want to be the one to tell her because she probably would have told me no. So I scheduled the appointment for them and let mom be the one to say to her. My mother didn't know she would be the one to spill the news.

The girls think we have a golf day planned. In actuality, we are the ones that will be setting up all things weddings today. Liv and Lexi from the flower shop are coming into town to finish the flower arrangements. The women should be at the spa for hours. We even have lunch and dinner served for them in case it takes us a while to get stuff done here. Emma and Claire are staying with each other tonight, and I have plans for Claire in the morning before she gets ready for the wedding. It is all going to come together nicely. Then after this weekend, I will have Claire all to myself. We can go back to the city, our apartment, and finish the process of getting her moved in with me. Tuck can finally come back home since mom is doing better. Life feels right lately.

"So, mom and Audrey went too," Baker asked me.

"Looks like Claire invited them too from what mom texted me," I say.

Dad smiles, and I know it is because Claire invited mom too. I know my mother deserved to go too, but I wasn't sure if she would be up for it. Claire is always thinking of others before herself.

When we return to the house, the truck pulls in with the tent, tables, and chairs to set up in the back. I let Tuck go inside for some rest before helping them unload the truck.

The plan is to set the tent up on the small grass area mom and dad have in the back. The reception will take place under the tent. The tables will also be there for dinner. There are white chairs that we will set up on both sides of the aisle for the ceremony. The arch will face the ocean and be the ceremony's backdrop. Honestly, this wedding is a dream. Some of it just happened to be Claire's dream.

After hours of unloading the equipment, the truck leaves, leaving me, Baker, Dad, and Clark (Audrey's husband) to set everything up. They did help us get the tent set up before leaving. I start setting up tables under the tent while Dad and Baker set up chairs for the aisle. Clark left us quickly for a work call. I want to get this finished before the sun sets. The women should be back then, and I want to hear all about how it went from Claire before she leaves me for the night.

"So what is the plan for us tomorrow"? I ask Baker. I know everything the women have planned, but Baker and I haven't discussed it.

"There isn't a plan besides getting ready, and the photographer will take photos of us before the wedding. The groom always has the easiest day."

There is the reason we haven't discussed anything because there wasn't anything to discuss. Since Claire isn't the bride, I know there can be moments that I can see her throughout the day.

Chapter Twenty-six

Claire

"Claire, wake up," I hear Ryan's voice say in my dream. That is until I feel something brush across my face. I slap whatever it is away.

"Get up, sleepyhead," Ryan's voice again.

I moan because this isn't a dream. It's real.

"What," I say, knowing it is still dark outside.

"You are the best morning person. I have a surprise for you," Ryan places a kiss on my forehead. Good choice, considering I have terrible morning breath.

I lift from the bed. It is dark.

"Don't wake up, Emma," I whisper. Knowing it is her wedding day today, and she needs sleep.

"Hate to break it to you, but she is in Baker's bed. You are a terrible babysitter," he laughs.

I rub my eyes and then look to where Emma should be sleeping. She isn't there. I knew she would sneak away.

I move the sheets off me and then stand from the bed. Ryan takes my head, and we head down the stairs and out the back door. It is the middle of the night, and I have no idea why Ryan would want to surprise me with something at this hour.

"Where are you taking me"? I whisper to him.

"We are going to watch the sunrise on the balcony,"

Sweet, it was what I wanted to do on Emma's wedding day. Not. It's early; as Ryan knows, I am not a morning person.

We walk into the guest house, where the smell of coffee greets me. Thank goodness. I am going to need a lot of it today. Still holding my hand, Ryan pours coffee into two coffee mugs, and then we head out on the balcony. It isn't as dark as it was a minute ago, and now I realize this is sweet of Ryan to think of this.

He sits in one of the chairs and pulls me onto his lap. We both manage not to spill a single drop of coffee while doing it. I lay my head against his. I am enjoying this moment. At the same time, I am still not fully awake.

"How was last night with Emma"? Ryan asks me.

Emma seemed quiet yesterday at the spa, and she shed a few tears last night before bed. She blames pregnancy hormones, but I think it is something else. Maybe she is worried about the wedding, but why would she be if they were already married?

"It was okay. I wish I knew what was wrong, but Emma won't say,"

"The wedding, the pregnancy, and that her life will change soon. She has a lot on her mind, I would say." Ryan says, and he is right. Their life is going to be changing soon in a big way.

He runs his fingers down my arm to my hand and intertwines our fingers together. "Claire, I can't wait to return to the city after this. I want to get you moved into the apartment. Then start the next step of our relationship."

"What step is next"?

He pulls my face towards his with his hand on my chin. "I would like for this is the next step for us. I want to get married. Then move back here, open my own real estate office, and you open a flower shop here. I am ready for that, and I will be waiting for the day you are ready,"

I smile at him, giving him a soft kiss.

"Look, the sun is rising," he says, and I turn my head to watch the sunrise with him.

Ryan's words don't surprise me. I know he feels that way. This week with him and his family has felt like home to me, and I know I never want this feeling to go away. I want to bottle it up, keeping it forever.

Ryan and I head inside the guest house to prepare for today when the sun is just above the ocean. I notice a small gift bag on the table and a card in front of it with my name.

"This is for you. I wanted to give you a gift for the wedding. You have worked so hard on all this and everything else you have done lately. You deserve something more than a spa day. You do not have to open it now. You can wait," He says, handing me the bag and sliding the card inside.

"Ryan, you didn't have to do that. I didn't get you anything,"

"I have you, and that is all I need," his words send goosebumps up my arms.

I take the bag from Ryan and know I will open it while getting ready with Emma.

After giving each other our goodbyes until later today, I take the bag from Ryan along with the things I need for today. I head to the house to Jack and Catherine's room, where all the women will be getting ready for the day. I sit the bag down on their bed, nervous about opening it.

Emma is already getting her makeup started when I walk in the door. There is a makeup artist here. The hairstylist should be here soon.

"Claire, where did you go so early this morning"? Emma ask me

"More like, where did you go this morning? You were supposed to be sleeping in the bed with me, not sneaking away to Baker's bed. Also, I was watching the sunrise with Ryan."

"Awe, that is so sweet."

She has her eyes closed, getting her eyeshadow done when Catherine walks in with an armful of dress bags.

"I have all the dresses here. I will hang them up," Catherine says, walking over to her closet.

I sit in the chair next to Emma, so I can be next to get my makeup done. I want to check in on her to guarantee she is better today than yesterday.

"How are you holding up so far today"?

Emma peeks out of one eye to look at me. "I am fine,"

She is good at holding in her feelings, so I know if something is bothering her, she will likely not talk about it. So I decide to leave it alone for now unless she starts crying again.

Catherine is talking to the makeup lady about how amazing her family is, so I figured now would be a good time to open the gift Ryan gave me. I get down from the chair, pick up the bag, and then walk down to Ryan's old room, where I know no one will be.

I pull out the tissue paper to see a small blue Tiffany box at the bottom of the bag. I take it out first, opening it to reveal a necklace. It's a silver chain with a dark blue diamond charm surrounded by tiny diamonds. I put the necklace down on my lap and then pulled the card. I open the envelope to a blank white card, so I open it.

Claire,

For the first time in my life, everything feels right. Like I am where exactly where I need to be

I can't imagine my life without you or remember what it was before you.

I love your heart for others. I love that you are messy.

I love that I get to cook for you because you can't.

I want everything with you one day.

You're it for me. You are my "Happing ending," and I hope I am yours.

I love you forever.

P.S. Blue is your color, babe.

I wipe the tears from my face and close the necklace box. I set it back in the bag along with the card. I chose Ryan, and that means I won. I chose forever.

The words he sent in the text the other night weren't drunk text. They came from his heart just like I thought because he wrote them on paper this time, the very same words. It was also this same room I sit in now that he once said to me, "I don't want you to be the one who got away. I want you to be the one."

Hours later, we are all finally done getting our hair and makeup. I have a button-up shirt with leggings, so I don't mess my hair and makeup up when getting dressed. I take a minute to walk down the stairs outside. I want to see the progress on the decorations.

When I walk through the back door, I instantly notice the arch. I walk down the path to the beach to take a closer look. The colorful arrangements are all placed in their places along the aisle. Liv and Lexi decorated the arch with the remaining flowers, most draping down off the angles. They hung the white cloths over the top, draping down the sides and blowing in the breeze. I walk back to the tent. All the tables have white tablecloths with colorful flower centerpieces. The string lights hung across the top, with flowers draping off them. The wedding decorations look better than I imagined. I head back inside before Ryan catches me. I would love to see Ryan and thank him for the lovely gift, but I don't want to cry my makeup off my face before the ceremony.

When I return to the room, Emma is waiting for me.

"I want to show you something," she takes my hand, and I follow her to the closet.

She opens the closet door and pulls out the dress bag with my name. She unzips it and pulls out the most beautiful baby blue dress.

299

"I know how much you always wear blue, so I picked this one for you instead of the pink dress."

"Emma," I hug her. "You didn't need to do that. The pink was okay,"

"Claire, you hate pink. It was not okay," she laughs, and she isn't wrong.

The ceremony starts in an hour. So, I take the dress from Emma and put it on. We need to get Emma dressed so she will be more than ready to walk down the aisle. I look at myself in the mirror in Catherine's bathroom before stepping into the room again. The dress Emma picked for me is identical to the pink one I tried. It is silk, dips at the top, and is loose on me.

When I enter the room, Catherine is already taking Emma's dress out of the bag. Emma is pacing the space in the white silk robe Catherine had made for us. She looks nervous. So I go up to her to give her another hug. She stops in place when I hug her, telling her it will be okay. She is going to be the most beautiful bride.

"Alright, Emma, let's get this dress on you," Catherine says to her.

Catherine holds the dress out to Emma, and while she looks like she is going to throw up, she walks over to put the dress on. She slides it up her legs, still wearing the robe. Once we get it up on her, she slips the robe off, and I take it from her throwing it on the bed. Emma holds the dress in place while I try to zip up the back. The zipper is tight around the bottom of her back, but I manage to get it zipped up. Once on, I walk around to the front of her to look at her.

"Emma, you look amazing," I say to her. The dress fits her like a glove. She is perfect in all areas, and her baby bump is fully displayed. She walks to the grand mirror in the room and looks at herself. At first, she smiles, turning from side to side.

Then after a minute, she starts crying. I don't need her messing up her makeup, so I walk over to her and start fanning her face with my hand.

"Emma, please don't cry until the ceremony. You look amazing," I tell her, and she nods her head to me while looking in the mirror. She pauses her crying for a second.

"Honey, do you love this one, or do you want to try on the other dress," Catherine asks her. I am confused. I only know about the only dress Emma has on.

"This one is fine, thank you, Catherine,"

"What is the other dress"? I ask them.

"Oh, Claire dear. When Emma got into town, she was worried her dress might not fit, so we went into town to try on a few more, and she found this beautiful long sleeve lace fitted dress with a train. It has a little more room around the waist. We figured if anything, she could wear it for just the reception. She could have a dress change,"

"That is a great idea. A dressing change, everyone is doing those these days." I look at Emma in the mirror, and she still looks on her face that something is off.

"Emma, if you want to wear the other dress, it won't hurt my feelings. I know we picked this one together, but this is your day, so wear the dress you want to wear," I hug her again, letting her know that what I said, I mean it.

"That's not it," Emma says before full-blown bawling.

I start to worry that we may not have enough time to calm her down to get her down the aisle. "Catherine, what time do we need to get Emma downstairs"?

"We need to have her downstairs no later than five-fifty-five. The ceremony is at six,"

I look over to the clock on the nightstand, and we have twenty minutes till go time.

"Let me see this other dress," I look at Catherine.

Chapter Twenty-seven

Ryan

I look down at my watch, and it is five-fifty-five. Baker and I patiently wait for the women to walk down the aisle. I can't wait to see Claire in her bridesmaid dress. I haven't seen her since this morning, and she never said anything after opening her gift. I expected her to at least come to find me and thank me for it. The women have been upstairs all day getting ready. While Baker and I took time, I went to pick up Dan just before needing to get dressed for the ceremony. After getting Dan his seat, I changed, and now we are just standing here in front of the arch, waiting. The guest here at the wedding are family, along with the socialites of my parents. My dad is already seated in the front row, and my mother should be coming when Claire comes out.

"How much longer"? I whisper into Baker's ear as I am getting impatient, waiting for this to start.

He clears his throat before saying, "It is almost time,"

He looks just as impatient as me. He is standing there, holding his hands out in front of him.

I turn my head, taking a look at the ocean. The sun is starting to set, and it reminds me of watching the sunrise this morning with Claire.

The navy blue tux Baker got me to wear is starting to sweat me. There is a breeze tonight, but this night's nervousness is beginning to get to me. Baker is wearing the same blue tux but doesn't seem to sweat as much as I am. I adjusted myself just when I thought this would never start. The music starts playing.

In the distance, I see movement at the back door of my parent's house. A group of people is walking out, and I can't determine who is who from this far away. They start making their way down the path, and that is when I notice Emma wearing the blue dress she bought for Claire. It only takes a second for me to see Claire, wearing a long sleeve lace wedding dress, holding a bouquet of colorful flowers, and my mom walking her down, hand in hand.

I lose it.

The tears start running down my face while I ugly cry.

This moment is more than I dreamed.

It's what I wanted but couldn't say.

Everything makes sense right now.

When Claire gets closer, I see tears falling down her and my mother's faces. She looks gorgeous. Her hair is halfway down in wavy curls, and she is wearing the necklace I gave her. If only I could take her into my arms and kiss her right now.

I get myself together for a second and realize I now stand where Baker was. He somehow switched us while I was watching Claire come down the aisle.

I walk over to Claire and my mother, where my mother then hands her off to me. I take her hand, and she says, "Hi."

"So, we're doing this," I whisper in her ear while walking back to the officiant.

"Is that okay?"

When we get in front of the officiant, I hold up one finger to him, "Give us just a second," I say. I look over to my mom and dad sitting in the front row, holding hands and smiling. Dan is next to them, looking like he is witnessing a miracle. Then I look over at Emma, who is standing behind Claire. Her face tells me this is what she wants, and she gives me a nod. Baker comes up behind me and puts his hands on my shoulders before whispering, "The bride is waiting,"

I look at Claire, who looks so breathtaking and perfect. I put my hand up to her face, using my thumb to rub away a tear on her cheek. "This is more than okay. This is what I wanted." I drop my hand to hers. "I want to kiss you so bad right now,"

"You have to wait," she says, smiling.

The officiant begins the ceremony, and I keep my eyes on Claire the whole time. Today is my life's best day, and I want to savor every moment of this. While I don't know yet what got Claire down this aisle, I can only hope it was because she felt the same when she read my words earlier today. Why wait when our forever can start today?

After saying her vows, I pull out the ring my mother gave me from my pocket. Claire gasped, not knowing I had been carrying it in my pocket all this time. I have been waiting for the perfect moment to give it to her. What better moment than to give it to her as my wife? We had to borrow Baker's wedding band for her to provide me. We can worry about getting myself one later.

When he finally says, "You may kiss the bride," I take Claire's face into my hands and lay the best kiss she has ever gotten from me on her lips. All I want right now is to whisk her away and have her all to myself, but now we celebrate.

The photographer pulls us to the side, asking for pictures. At the same time, all the guest make their way to the tent for dinner. We start with some of just Claire and me and then add Baker and Emma. It is the perfect time for everyone to spill their secrets. So I begin by asking, "Does anyone have anything they want to say"?

Baker stands beside me, and after the photographer takes the picture, he finally says. "There is nothing to say. It was supposed to be you and Claire's day all along."

Claire turns to me and says, "It's true. After reading your words this morning, I realized why to wait another day. This wedding couldn't have been more ours. We planned it all, we both worked so hard to make it perfect for them, but it didn't feel like theirs since they had their wedding. Emma had a dress waiting for me, and that is when I knew I wanted nothing more than to be yours forever. No one talked me into this, Ryan. I wanted this just as much as I knew you did."

I spin Claire around to look at me, "Babe, I would have never once thought someone talked you into this. When I saw you walking down that aisle, I knew you wanted this." I kiss her, "You know what this means, though,"

The photographer sets us up for one more photo with all of us, including my parents. When she gets it, the shot is wanted. Claires says, "What,"

"Sorry, Baker, but I am putting in my two weeks' notice right now," I say.

"Do what now"? Baker says.

Everyone else looks at me, wondering what I mean. Claire knows, though. She smiles at me while taking my hand. "Claire and I are moving here. We will travel to all the places we have always wanted to go. Then when we get back, I will open Hayes Realty in the Hamptons."

Baker is speechless. Emma starts crying, knowing that means Claire will be leaving her. Claire is consoling her. At the same time, Mom comes over to hug me. My dad stands back, giving me a look that says, "I am proud of you." We disagreed about this months ago, so it feels good to know he is happy with my decision.

I watch Claire as she talks to Emma across the table, feeling so lucky. We are all seated at the main table under the tent, enjoying the meal the chefs prepared for the wedding. My parents had a four-course dinner planned for the wedding. We had our first dance together as a married couple. Claire got her one slow dance in with Dan before joining me at the table. Dan is now enjoying dinner at the same table as my parents. I haven't been able to take my eyes off Claire all night. She looks so beautiful in her dress. It fits her tiny frame perfectly, as if the dress was only hers all along. I believe it was because this day couldn't have been more ours.

While Claire was dancing with Dan, I asked Baker if the way this turned out was alright with him. He said he couldn't be happier with how it all came together for us. Emma had second thoughts about the whole thing since they told us, but she didn't want to push it on Claire. I am thankful for that. If not today, I know Claire and I's day would have been soon. There was the ring in my pocket for a reason.

I wrap my arm around Claire, getting her attention. She stops her conversation with Emma and turns her head my way. "What's next? I am ready to get out of here."

She giggles, "We still have to cut the cake,"

How could I forget that delicious cake Claire and I picked out months ago?

"Right, cake, and then we are leaving,"

"What's the rush"?

"Well, Mrs. Hayes. By the way, that name sounds good to you. This day has been perfect, as much as I have enjoyed this. Now that I officially have you forever. We have something we need to do when all this is over."

"Oh really now, what's that"?

I smirk, "You'll just have to wait and see,"

At that time, my mother comes over to the table to get us. It is time to cut the cake, and I won't be going easy on Claire. She will take some of this to the face for making me cry today. I take Claire's hand, help her from her chair, and head over to the cake table. Someone added flowers to the all-white cake Claire and I ordered when they decorated today. It looks exactly like we both envisioned.

The photographer comes over to snap some shots. Claire and I are standing next to each other, and I feel we should make this a little more intimate. So I get behind her to help her cut the cake. Once she has a slice, I grab it and instantly go to smash it in her face, but she ducks down, knowing what I had planned. I instead take a nice slice of cake to the front. Claire stands back up, laughing so hard. I take some cake left on my face and smash it on hers. Everyone then starts gasping that

I wipe away as much cake as possible and help Claire clean herself up. Then plant a kiss on her lips. "Now we have somewhere to be," I take her hand and walk away from everyone and out of the tent towards the guest house. I don't want that traditional everyone to throw the rice, or everyone holding a sparkler, whatever is the thing right now while leaving as husband and wife. I want something between the two of us.

When we leave the tent, Claire doesn't ask questions and follows behind me while holding my hand. It is until we get to the jeep that she starts wondering what is going on.

"What exactly are we doing again"?

"It's a surprise,"

She gets in and buckles up as I do the same. Then I back out of my driveway. I take Claire's hand and kiss her softly on the knuckles. She smiles at me, and it brings me such a warm feeling knowing I get this forever.

I have never been one to be around a crowd of people or have attention drawn to me, and I can say the same for Claire. So this way of ending our wedding fits us. I turn to drive down the road just outside of town and look at Claire's face light up. She knows what we are going to do.

I stop the jeep just when we get to the ocean.

"Ready," I ask her.

"Ready? Of course, I am."

She leans into me and kisses me before standing in her seat.

"I am serious. Be careful. You are precious cargo,"

She laughs and then grips the top of the jeep tightly.

I begin driving slowly because I mean it, this is fun for her, but I need to be careful. She throws her arms out, smiling, and her hair blows through the wind. I look at her and see a happy, free-spirited woman I love. The woman I get for the rest of my life. I can't wait to see what forever brings us.

When I get to the end of the ocean, she takes her seat next to me. I take her hand, kiss her cheek, and then tell her. "I love you,"

"I love you more,"

Chapter Twenty-eight

Claire

Four years later

I hear my phone ring on the bench beside me. I stop reading my book and then place it down. It is Emma.

"Hey," I say.

"Where are you guys? We are at Mom and Dad's waiting on you,"

I look at my watch and notice time must have gotten away from me while reading.

"Be there shortly. I will see you soon." I tell her before hanging up the phone.

I get up from the backyard bench and walk to the shop. Ryan has been working here for hours now and must have also lost track of time. I walk into the shop to see Ryan working on his secret project and Tuck lying beside him. I have no idea what it could be since, right now, it is just a bunch of different-sized pieces of wood.

I walk over and take a seat on his stool. "They are waiting for us,"

He turns around and then starts walking towards me. Once in front of me, he places a kiss on my forehead. Then asks, "Learn anything new from your book,"

"Just a few things. Are you ready to go"?

"Let me clean up. Then we can go over there,"

He takes my hand, helping me up from the stool, and then we walk over to the house, Tuck following us, so we can get ready to leave. Mom and Dad are hosting another beach volleyball tournament, and as you know, Ryan and I don't miss these. We have been the winners of almost every game in the last four years.

Once inside the house, Ryan quickly heads to the bathroom to shower while I change into my jersey and shorts. After Ryan and I married, Catherine gifted us red jerseys with our names on the back. We no longer wear those fabulous shirts she had made for us those years ago. Ryan changes into his matching jersey when he gets out of the shower, and we get into the jeep, Tuck included, to leave. Since we live down the road from them, it only takes a few minutes to get there.

When there, we walk through the house to see everyone already eating lunch out back before the big game takes place. Audrey, her husband Clark, Cooper, Kate, Catherine, and Jack, sit at one table on the patio. Emma, Baker, and their three-year-old daughter, Adler, at the other. Ryan and I quickly make plates inside before taking them outside to join Emma and Baker at their table.

"Finally. I was beginning to think you two weren't coming," Emma says.

We sit down across from them before Ryan says. "Come on, have we ever missed a tournament?"

Baker laughs before asking Ryan, "How's the secret project coming"?

Ryan has been working on something that is a surprise for me. We took a month-honeymoon exploring all the places we ever wanted to go. When we returned, we moved into the guest house while opening Ryan's real estate office. Ryan learned more woodworking from Dan before we lost him to cancer, just before our first anniversary. He had been living with that secret for over a year before telling us, only giving us a week to say our goodbyes to him.

Shortly after Dan passed, Ryan and I bought his property, knowing that was where we belonged. After tearing down Dan's house, we built our dream home. I wanted to remodel his home, but it just wasn't possible. It was in bad shape. Dan had made several picture frames over the year before he passed, and they now hold photos of Ryan and me in our home. We have one special one that holds a photo of Dan and Susie hanging by the front door. It may be a new home on the land, but I still wanted to remember it was Dan and Susie's home before ours.

"I should be finished with it soon," Ryan smirks, putting his arm around me.

"So, Adler, you want to tell Auntie Claire where you are going when you return to the city"?

Adler frowns, and Emma giggles.

Emma rubs her belly before brushing away some baby hairs from Adler's face while she returns to eating her food. Adler starts her first year of preschool soon, and Emma has told me she is not excited about it.

"She will get used to it. We don't have a choice. The flower shop has been the busiest it has ever been, and I know I will need to get back to working full-time sometime soon."

"Well, Adler, I am very excited for you. You will make lots of new friends wearing all those cute dresses. Maybe you will make a best friend and be friends forever. Just like your mommy and me,"

Emma and Baker bought a summer house in the Hamptons a couple of places down from Catherine and Jack's, the year they had Adler. They spend their summers with everyone before returning to the city. I have thoroughly enjoyed it every summer since. I make up for lost time with Emma and Adler since I don't get to see them every day. Ryan and I still visit the city some weekends, and as much as that was where

A Love That Blooms

Emma and I started our business and I met Ryan, I don't miss the place. Baker and Emma are doing a great job running their companies and are very successful.

If you are wondering, Ryan and I gave over our parts of the Blooms and Hayes Realty to them. Only so we could have our own here. Ryan has been successfully running Ryan Hayes Realty as I have been running Blooms for You. It has honestly been hard choosing to open a flower shop without Emma by my side. It is why I do it all independently. Ryan and I bought the tiniest shop next to his business, and my primary customer is Catherine Hayes. I never get busy, and I am okay with that. Ryan Hayes's Realty is booming, but at a slower pace than Ryan once was, so Ryan and I get to spend much more time together than if we still lived in the city.

Everyone finishes their lunch, and it is time to start this tournament. Since Cooper and Kate are older now, they get to participate. Audrey is paired with Cooper first since Clark hates volleyball and works instead. Emma and I sit next to each other in the lounge chairs to watch them. Baker and Ryan are off in the distance practicing with Kate. She will be taking Emma's spot as Baker's partner.

"So, how's the reading coming? Learning all kinds of things you didn't know"? Emma asked me.

"Honestly, so many things, and I am nervous,"

"Claire, you are going to do great. You have waited so long for this." She says to me as she rubs her belly.

I sit up from my chair to join her in rubbing her belly and feel a kick. Which then makes me tear up. This baby in her stomach growing so remarkable is not Emma and Baker's. It is ours.

Ryan and I started trying to grow our family right after losing Dan. We knew we would have a baby just when our dream house was ready. We had a perfect plan, except it wasn't so perfect. Months of trying turned into a year. Then we saw double lines on a test not once but twice, only to be heartbroken to hear the words miscarriage just weeks later. We tried everything until those weren't options anymore. We gave up hope on our dream of having a family. That was until Emma and Baker showed up on our doorstep just a year ago, willing to help any way they could. So, we went through the process of Emma being our surrogate, and she got pregnant with our miracle on the first try. I cried for days after finding out we were finally getting our dream. Then I lived with worry for months. This summer, I spent most of my time with Emma, trying to enjoy these last few months being around her ever-growing belly. Not one person in the family knows the gender. All Ryan and I want is a healthy baby.

"Emma, Thank you... For doing this for us."

"Claire, I love you. I know how much you and Ryan wanted a family. I am thankful that you let me be the one to help you get that." she leans in, hugging me. "Now quit reading that baby book and worrying. I promise you that becoming a mother comes naturally. You and Ryan are going to be amazing parents."

A lonely tear runs down my cheek. I cry a little bit every time I am around Emma and thank her almost daily. She is blessing us with the greatest gift, and I wouldn't have it any other way with my best friend.

Baker and Ryan start walking in our direction. I know it is because Ryan and I turn for the tournament. Catherine and Jack lost against Aubrey and Cooper. Not intentionally or anything. Catherine has taken life easy since her heart attack years ago. She has been doing great and plans to be a stay-at-home grandma once the baby comes. Catherine is only giving up lunch dates with her girlfriends. She couldn't be more excited to be getting another grandchild, one she can spend time with most days. And while I know Catherine wants to help us. If this baby is a girl, she will spend most days with me at the flower shop, learning the basics of flowers.

When the guys get to us, Baker sits by Emma while Ryan holds his hand out for me to get up. "It's our turn. Think we can beat Audrey and Coop?"

I get up from the chair. "Do you not have faith in us today?" I turn to Emma before walking away. "We'll be back, right back,"

Ryan and I walk down the path to the volleyball net, holding hands. Ryan has never grown out of the honeymoon phase. He is always attentive and treats me like our relationship is the greatest thing to happen to us because it is. Who knows where we would be if we never gave each other a chance? Even through all those days and months of sadness we endured. He never once left my side and held me most days that I couldn't even get out of bed.

"Alright, here is the plan. We are losing this one," Ryan whispers in my ear.

I whisper back, "Is there a reason behind this,"

"Yes. The prize is dinner and a movie. Cooper has this huge crush on this girl and could use the prize."

"Copper is nine, and you're already trying to get him a date," I say, shaking my head at Ryan.

Ryan shrugs his shoulder at me, smiling.

When the game starts, I look terrible at looking like we are trying to win this. Cooper is on to me and yells, "Come on, aunt Claire, I know you're better than that." I am Coop, but your uncle Ryan here is trying to win you a girlfriend. Ryan laughs back, and I see him using me as our excuse for losing this.

We are just one point away from losing this when I hear some commotion on the patio. I turn my head to see what it is, and the ball flies past my face and hits the ground. We lost. Ryan also stops playing to see what is going on. Catherine is running over to Emma and Baker.

"I think it is the time!" She yells out to us, "Emma's water broke,"

Ryan turns to me, and I am in shock. He puts his hands on my arms and leans down to my face.

"Claire, it's time. We need to go to the hospital now,"

"Now, like right now," I say. The only words I can comprehend to say this minute.

Ryan takes my hand, and we head up the path.

When I see Emma, she looks normal and happy. I am not the one giving birth and am a ball of nerves right now. Baker helps Emma get through the house and into their car. Catherine and Jack take Adler with them. I stand still outside of the jeep door.

"Claire, get in the car," Ryan says to me.

Right, I need to get into the car to get to the hospital.

I get in the jeep and buckle up. It is then that the nerves get the best of me, and I start crying. I didn't finish reading my book to prepare for this today. Ryan and I have had the nursery done for months. We decided on neutral and warm tones, with a white room. I knew once the baby came, we could change the décor if we wanted to.

Ryan rubs his hand down my arm to my hand to try to calm me down on the way there.

"Claire, this is it. We're going to be parents today,"

I can't wait for this moment. The one we have so longed for, for years.

By the time we reach the hospital, my nerves have completely calmed down and have turned into excitement.

We walk in, not far behind Baker and Emma. They get her into a wheelchair, and the nurse starts walking her to the back. We all walk to the door behind her. The nurse stops us before we can all even walk through the doors.

"Listen, only one person can be in the room,"

We didn't talk about this part. Emma is going to need a c-section. She had one with Adler, and we knew she would need one this time, but not one of us has talked about who will be in the room with her. Baker and Ryan both turn to me. "Claire is going," Baker says first.

"Obviously, right," Ryan says.

I nervously pulled on my neck. Ryan again puts his hands on my arms and gets to my level. "Listen here. You are going into the room. I want you to remember every minute in that room so you can tell me about it later. You hear me?"

I nod, and then he says, "I love you so much. Now go get our baby," He then kisses my forehead before turning me around to walk with Emma.

"I love you," I tell him.

The nurse wheels Emma into a room, and I help them change her. Then they take her away to begin the process. I stay in a room to change into a gown and cap. I take a seat on the chairs and tap my foot, waiting. When the nurse walks in, "We're ready,"

This is it. I am minutes away from finally becoming a mom.

317

Emma is lying on the table when I walk in, and she looks up at me, smiling. I take a seat next to her. I can't see anything on the other side of the table, but I can hear them getting ready to work on her. She pulls her hand up to mine, and I hold her hand.

"How are you feeling?" I ask her.

Don't worry about me. I will be just fine." She tells me, squeezing my hand.

I hear the doctor talking to the nurses, and I know we are getting close. Emma is relaxed and doesn't seem bothered by anything they do to her. She is just holding my hand and smiling at me. I start getting nervous waiting when I hear the doctor say, "Here we go,"

Then I hear crying. I let go of Emma's hand and throw my hands over my mouth. My tears start falling down my face. I am a mom.

"It's a boy," the doctor yells out.

Emma's face is shocked, and I look at her, "A boy,"

She says back, "It's a boy. Congratulations, Claire." Then she starts crying and reaches for my hand again.

Not only am I crying because I am a mom to a baby boy, but also because of Emma. My best friend gave him to me; I am forever grateful to her.

They bring him wrapped in a blanket and put him in my arms. He is the most adorable little chubby-cheeked baby. I cry more tears before kissing him on the cheek. I get closer to Emma so she can get a better look at him and then push back his baby hat to see he has a head of blonde hair, just like Ryan.

"Claire, he is perfect," Emma tells me.

"Isn't he... Thank you, Emma," I tell her while looking at my precious gift.

They work on Emma, and the nurse comes over to take him from me. They want to check on him to make sure everything is good with him.

Emma looks over to me as I watch them take him away. "You need to go tell everybody. He will be just fine while you go. "

I get up and leave the room, taking everything off me once I get into the next room. Then I rush down the hall and out the double doors. Everyone is standing around, and they run over to me when they see me.

I throw my hands in the air, "It's a boy," I yell out.

They all celebrate, and Ryan picks me up, throwing his arms around my waist, and spins me around. Then brings me down, placing a soft kiss on my lips.

"He looks just like you, blonde hair and all," I tell Ryan.

He wraps his arms around me in a tight embrace.

"When can we see him"?

Everyone hears Ryan ask me that question and looks to me for the answer. I pull out of Ryan's embrace and hold his hand.

"They are fixing Emma up and doing one last check on him. They both should be in a room very soon, and we can all go see them." they all give a sign of relief. "Baker?" he looks over to me, "Emma did a great job. Thank you,"

He nods to me, "Anything for you guys."

Ryan kisses me on the forehead before we all walk to the waiting area to sit and wait. It shouldn't be long before we can hold him. Ryan looks over to me and whispers in my ear, "Does the name fit him"?

I look at him and smile. "Yes, very much so."

He smiles back at me, and we continue waiting.

It didn't take long for Ryan and me to agree on one boy and girl name. We had backups just in case the name didn't fit them.

We wait an hour when a nurse comes out to tell us we can see them now. When we all get up, I take it upon myself to walk behind everyone else. I have already seen him and Emma, and I know how much everyone else can't wait to see them.

We walk down the hallway, all of us staying quiet. Baker is the first to walk into the room with Adler in his arms. Catherine and Jack are behind them, and then Ryan turns to take my hand before he walks in. Audrey, Clark, Cooper, and Kate are in front of us.

Emma is holding him when we walk in, and everyone is gasping at him. Emma holds him out for everyone to see before placing him over to Ryan, and that is when I see the best sight I have ever seen. Ryan with his son for the first time. I cry first, then Ryan, and then turn to see everyone in the room in tears.

I wrap my arms around Ryan, holding him, and he pulls me closer to him.

Then Ryan announces, "Everyone, meet Henry Ryan Hayes,"

I look up at him and smile.

We pull up to the house for the first time with Henry in the backseat with me. Ryan announces for me to close my eyes. He was ready to surprise me. He left the hospital yesterday with Baker, saying he had something important to work on at home. So I stayed at the hospital with Emma and Henry, soaking up his newborn smell before coming home.

"I will get Henry, and then I will help you out. Don't peek," He says to me before getting out of the car. I can't help but giggle with anticipation, wondering what his surprise could be.

I hear the door open, and he takes Henry in his seat out of the backseat.

Then he grabs my hand to help me out.

We walk towards the house. I have one hand in Ryans and the other over my eyes, so I can't see anything.

He stops walking and says, "Okay, open your eyes,"

I open my eyes to see an oversized wooden rocking chair on the house's front porch.

"Wow, you made that. Ryan, that is amazing," I walk over to it and take a seat,"

"Isn't it great?" He says, sitting Henry's car seat on the porch, and starts taking him out.

"Yes, but why is there only one," I ask him.

He picks Henry up, holding him in his arms. Then he walks over to me and helps me up. Ryan sits in the rocking chair with Henry and pulls me onto his lap. It is all we have ever wanted at this moment.

"For this reason, right here,"

The End

If you loved this book, check out The Deal-Breaker to read Emma and Baker's love story. You will also see how Claire and Ryan's friendship started.

A Love That Blooms

Made in the USA
Coppell, TX
10 January 2023

10909871R00184